"The Middle Ages, with their overtones of darkness and evil, are a particularly appropriate setting for a mystery.... The dramatic denouement, in a torchlit courtyard, is an eminently logical surprise."

Detroit Free Press

"That delightful medieval Benedictine monk, Brother Cadfael, of the monastery at Shrewsbury, returns in another engaging blend of youthful romance and shrewd detection."

Publishers Weekly

"Another Peters delight, featuring vital characters, a beautifully organized puzzle, and history made real."

The Kirkus Reviews

Also by Ellis Peters:

The Brother Cadfael Chronicles

A MORBID TASTE FOR BONES*

ONE CORPSE TOO MANY*

MONK'S HOOD*

ST. PETER'S FAIR*

THE VIRGIN IN THE ICE*

THE SANCTUARY SPARROW*

THE DEVIL'S NOVICE*

DEAD MAN'S RANSOM*

THE PILGRIM OF HATE*

AN EXCELLENT MYSTERY*

THE RAVEN IN THE FOREGATE*

THE ROSE RENT

THE HERMIT OF EYTON FOREST

*Published by Fawcett Books

The LEPER of ST. GILES

The Fifth Chronicle
of Brother Cadfael

ELLIS PETERS

FAWCETT CREST • NEW YORK

A Fawcett Crest Book
Published by Ballantine Books
Copyright © 1981 by Ellis Peters

All rights reserved under International and Pan-American Copyright Conventions. Published in the United States by Ballantine Books, a division of Random House, Inc., New York.

Library of Congress Catalog Card Number: 82-2101

ISBN 0-449-20541-x

This edition published by arrangement with William Morrow and Company, Inc.

Manufactured in the United States of America

First Ballantine Books Edition: April 1985
Sixth Printing: February 1988

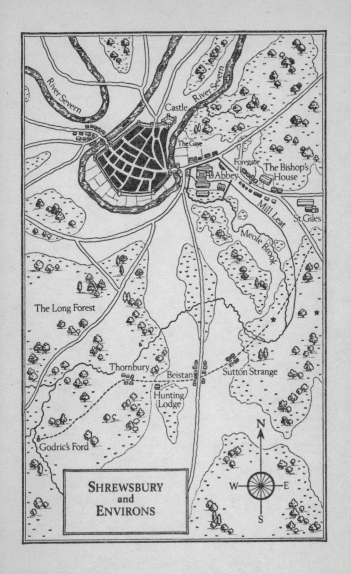

River Severn
River Severn
Castle
The Gaye
Foregate
Abbey
The Bishop's House
Mill Leat
St. Giles
Meole Brook
The Long Forest
Thornbury
Beistan
Sutton Strange
Hunting Lodge
Godric's Ford
N
W · E
S
SHREWSBURY
and
ENVIRONS

1 &

BROTHER CADFAEL SET OUT FROM THE GATEHOUSE, THAT Monday afternoon of October, in the year 1139, darkly convinced that something ominous would have happened before he re-entered the great court, though he had no reason to suppose that he would be absent more than an hour or so. He was bound only to the hospital of Saint Giles, at the far end of the Monks' Foregate, barely half a mile from Shrewsbury abbey, and his errand was merely to replenish with oils, lotions and ointments the medicine cupboard of the hospital.

They were heavy on such remedies at Saint Giles. Even when there were few lepers, for whose control and assistance the hospice existed, there were always some indigent and ailing souls in care there, and the application of Cadfael's herbal remedies soothed and placated the mind as well as the skin. He made this pilgrimage on an average every third week, to replace what had been used. These days he made it with all the better will because Brother Mark, his much-prized and dearly-missed assistant in the herbarium, had felt it to be his destiny to go and serve with the unfortunate for a year, and a visit to Saint Giles was now a blessed reminder of peaceful days departed.

For to make all plain, Cadfael's forebodings had nothing whatever to do with the momentous events soon to be visited upon the abbey of Saint Peter and Saint Paul of Shrewsbury, no reference to marrying and giving in marriage, no omens of sudden and violent death. He was expecting, rather, that in his absence some vessel full of precious liquid would be broken, some syrup left to boil over, some pan to burn dry, in his workshop in the herb-gardens, or else that his brazier would be fed too generously, and set light to the parcels of dried herbs rustling overhead and, in the worst case, to the whole workshop.

Mark had been gentle, dutiful and neat-handed. In his place Cadfael had been given, for his sins, the most cheerful, guileless, heedless and handless of cherubs, eternally hopeful, never chastened, a raw novice of nineteen fixed for ever at the age of a happy child of twelve. His fingers were all thumbs, but his zest and confidence were absolute. He knew he could do all, his will being so beneficent, and fumbled at the first baulk, for ever astonished and aghast at the results he produced. To complete the problem he presented, he was the most good-humoured and affectionate soul in the world. Also, less fortunately, the most impervious, since hope was eternal for him. Under reproof, having broken, wrecked, mismanaged and burned, he rode the tide serenely, penitent, assured of grace, confident of avoiding all repetition of failure. Cadfael liked him, as he was infuriated by him, out of all measure, and gloomily made large allowance for the damage the lad was almost certain to do whenever left to follow instructions unsupervised. Still, he had virtues, besides his sweetness of nature. For rough digging, the chief challenge of autumn, he had no peer, he plunged into it with the vigour others devoted to prayer, and turned the loam with a love and fellow-feeling Cadfael could not but welcome. Only keep him from planting what he dug! Brother Oswin had black fingers!

So Brother Cadfael had no thought to spare for the grand

wedding which was to take place in the abbey church in two days' time. He had forgotten all about it until he noted, along the Foregate, how people were gathering in voluble groups outside their houses, and casting expectant looks away from town, along the London road. The day was cloudy and chill, a faint mist of rain just perceptible in the air, but the matrons of Shrewsbury were not going to be done out of a spectacle on that account. By this road both wedding parties would enter, and word had evidently gone before them that they were already approaching the town. Since they would not actually enter the walls, a good number of the burgesses had come forth to join the people of the Foregate parish. The stir and hum were almost worthy of a minor fair-day. Even the beggars gathered about the gatehouse had an air of holiday excitement about them. When the baron of an honour scattered over four counties arrived to marry the heiress to lands as great as his own, there must be lavish largesse to be hoped for in celebration.

Cadfael rounded the corner of the precinct wall, by the open green of the horse-fair, and continued along the highroad, where the houses thinned out, and fields and woods began to reach green fingers to touch the rim of the road in between. Here, too, the women stood before their doors, waiting to glimpse bride and groom when they came, and in front of the large house halfway to Saint Giles a knot of interested gazers had gathered to watch the bustle of activity through the open gates of the courtyard. Servants and grooms flickered to and fro between house and stables, flashes of bright liveries crossed the yard. This was where the bridegroom and his retinue were to lodge, while the bride and her party would lie at the abbey guest-hall. Recalled to mild human curiosity, Cadfael loitered for a moment to stare with the rest.

It was a large house, well walled round, with garden and orchard behind, and it belonged to Roger de Clinton, bishop of Coventry, though he rarely used it himself. The loan of it to Huon de Domville, who held manors in Shropshire, Cheshire, Stafford and Leicester, was partly a friendly gesture towards Abbot Radulfus, and partly a politic compliment to a powerful baron whose favour and protection, in these times of civil war, it would be wise to cultivate. King Stephen might be in firm control of much of the country, but in the west the rival faction was strongly established, and there were plenty of lords ready and willing to change sides if fortune blew the opposite way. The Empress Maud had landed at Arundel barely three weeks previously, with her half-brother Robert, earl of Gloucester, and a hundred and forty knights, and through the misplaced generosity of the king, or the dishonest advice of some of his false friends, had been allowed to reach Bristol, where her cause was impregnably installed already. Here in the mellow autumn countryside everything might seem at peace, but for all that men walked warily and held their breath to listen for news, and even bishops might need powerful friends before all was done.

Beyond the bishop's house the road opened between trees, leaving the town well behind; and at the fork, a bow-shot ahead, the long, low roof of the hospice appeared, the wattled fence of its enclosure, and beyond again, the somewhat higher roof of the church, with a small, squat turret above. A modest enough church, nave and chancel and a north aisle, and a graveyard behind, with a carven stone cross set up in the middle of it. The buildings were set discreetly back from both roads that converged towards the town. Lepers, as they may not go among the populous streets of towns, must also keep their distance even to do their begging in the countryside. Saint Giles, their patron, had deliberately chosen the desert and the solitary place for his habitation, but these had no choice but to remain apart.

It was plain, however, that they had their fair share of human curiosity like their fellows, for they, too, were out watching the road. Why should not the unfortunate at least be free to stare at their luckier brethren, to envy them if they could manage no better than that, to wish them well in marriage if their generosity stretched so far? A shifting line of dark-gowned figures lined the wattle fence, as animated if not as agile as their healthy fellow men. Some of them Cadfael knew, they had settled here for life, and made the best of their cramped lives among familiar helpers. Some were new. There were always new ones, the wanderers who made their way the length of the land from lazarhouse to lazarhouse, or settled for a while in some hermitage on the charity of a patron, before moving on to new solitudes. Some went on crutches or leaned hard on staves, having feet maimed by the rot of disease or painful with ulcers. One or two pushed themselves along on little wheeled carts. One hunched shapeless against the fence, bloated with sores and hiding a disfigured face within his cowl. Several, though active, went with veiled faces, only the eyes uncovered.

Their numbers varied as the restless wandered on, shunning the town as they must shun all towns, to some other hospice looking out over another landscape. By and large, the hospital here sheltered and cared for twenty to thirty inmates at a time. The appointment of the superior rested with the abbey. Brothers and lay brothers served here at their own request. It was not unknown that attendant should become attended, but there was never want of another volunteer to replace and nurse him.

Cadfael had done his year or more in this labour, and felt no recoil, and only measured pity, respect being so much greater an encouragement and support. Moreover, he came and went here so regularly that his visits were a part of a patient and permanent routine like the services in the church. He had dressed more and viler sores than he troubled to remember, and discovered live hearts and vigorous minds within the mottled shells he tended. He has seen battles, too, in his time in the world, as far afield as Acre and Ascalon and Jerusalem in the first Crusade, and witnessed deaths crueller than disease, and heathen kinder than Christians, and he knew of leprosies of the heart and ulcers of the soul worse than any of these he poulticed and lanced with his herbal medicines. Nor had he been greatly surprised when Brother Mark elected to follow in his steps. He was well aware that there was one step beyond, which Mark was predestined to take without his example. Brother Cadfael knew himself too well ever to aim at the priesthood, but he recognised a priest when he saw one.

Brother Mark had seen him approaching, and came trotting to meet him, his plain face bright, his spiky, straw-coloured hair erected round his tonsure. He had a scrofulous child by the hand, a skinny little boy with old, drying sores in his thin fair hair. Mark teased aside the hairs that clung to the one remaining raw spot, and beamed down fondly at his handiwork.

'I'm glad you're come, Cadfael. I was running out of the lotion of pellitory, and see how much good it's done for him! The last sore almost healed. And the swellings in his neck are better, too. There, Bran, good boy, show Brother Cadfael! He makes the medicines for us, he's our physician. There, now, run to your mother and keep by her, or you'll miss all the show. They'll be coming soon.'

The child drew his hand free, and trotted away to join the sad little group that yet would not be sad. There was chattering there, a morsel of song, even some laughter. Mark looked after his youngest charge, watched the ungainly, knock-kneed gait that stemmed from undernourishment, and visibly grieved. He had been here only a month, his skin was still tissue-thin.

'And yet he is not unhappy,' he said, marvelling. 'When no one is by, and he follows me about, his tongue never stops wagging.'

'Welsh?' asked Cadfael, eyeing the child thoughtfully. He must surely have been named for Bran the Blessed, who first brought the gospel to Wales.

'The father was.' Mark turned to look his friend earnestly and hopefully in the face. 'Do you think he can be cured? Fully cured? At least he's fed, now. The woman will die here. In any case—she has grown indifferent, kind enough, but glad to have him off her hands. But I do believe he may yet go back whole into the world.'

Or out of it, thought Cadfael; for if he follows you so assiduously he cannot but get the savour of church or cloister, and the abbey is close at hand. 'A bright child?' he asked.

'Brighter than many that are brought up to the Latin, and can reckon and read. Brighter than many a one who goes in fine linen, and with a nurse coddling him. I shall try to teach him somewhat, as I can.'

They walked back together to the doorway of the hospital. The hum of expectant voices had risen, and along the highroad other sounds were gradually drawing near, compounded of the jingling of harness, the calls of falconers, conversation, laughter, the muffled beat of hooves using the grassy verge in preference to the naked road. One of the bridal processions was approaching.

'They say the bridegroom will be the first to come,' said Mark, stepping from the open porch into the dimness of the hall, and leading the way through to the corner where the medicine cupboard was kept. Fulke Reynald, a steward of the abbey and superior of the hospital, had one key; Brother Cadfael held the other. He opened his scrip, and began to stow away the preparations he had brought. 'Do you know anything about them?' asked Mark, succumbing to curiosity.

'Them?' murmured Cadfael, preoccupied with his review of the gaps in the shelves.

'These gentlefolk who are coming to marry here. All I know is their names. I should not have paid so much heed,' said Mark, shame-faced, 'except that our people here, who have nothing but their sores and maimings, have learned more of it than I have, only God knows how, and it is like a spark warming them. As though anything bright that shines on them is more aid than I can give. Yet all it is, is a wedding!'

'A wedding,' said Cadfael seriously, stacking away jars of salves and bottles of lotion made from alkanet, anemone, mint, figwort, and the grains of oats and barley, most of them herbs of Venus and the moon, 'a wedding is the crux of two lives, and therefore no mean matter.' He added the fruits of mustard, which belongs rather to Mars, but provides formidable pastes and poultices to fight malignant ulcers. 'Every man and woman who has faced the ordeal,' he said thoughtfully, 'must feel concern for those about to face it. Even those who have not, may speculate with sympathy.'

Matrimony was one joust he had never attempted, wide as his experience had been before he entered the cloister; but he had brushed fingertips with it once, and circumvented it more than once. He felt some astonishment, once he began remembering.

'This baron has a famous name, but I know no more of him, except that he's in good odour, they say, with the king. I think I may once have known an old kinsman of the lady. But whether she's from the same line is more than I know.'

'I hope she may be beautiful,' said Mark.

'Prior Robert would be interested to hear you say so,' said Cadfael drily, and closed the cupboard door.

'Beauty is a very healing thing,' said Brother Mark, earnest and unabashed. 'If she is young and lovely, if she smiles on them and inclines her head as she rides by, if she does not shrink at seeing them, she will do more for those people of mine out there than I can do with probing and poulticing. Here I begin to know that blessedness is what can be snatched out of the passing day, and put away to think of afterwards.' He added, recoiling into deprecation: 'Of course it need not be someone else's wedding feast. But how can we waste that, when it offers?'

Cadfael flung an arm about Mark's still thin and waiflike shoulders, and hauled him away, out of the dimness within, to the gathering excitement and brightening light without. 'Let's hope and pray,' he said heartily, 'that it may be the source of blessedness even to the pair caught up in it. By the sound of it, one of them is due here this moment. Come and let's see!'

The noble bridegroom and his retinue approached in a shimmer of bright colours, with horn-calls and soft, continuous clamour of harness bells, a cortège stretching fifty paces, and fringed with running servants leading the pack ponies, and two couples of tall deerhounds on leashes. The sorry little straggle of out-casts shuffled forward eagerly the few paces they dared, to see the better those fine fabrics and splendid dyes they could never possess, and set up a muted, awed murmur of admiration as the procession drew level with their wattle fence.

In front, on a tall black horse, his own accoutrements and his mount's very splendid in scarlet and gold, rode a broad-built, gross, fleshy man, inelegant but assured in the saddle, and accorded a station well ahead of all his train, so that his preeminence should be seen to be absolute. Behind him came three young squires abreast, keeping a close and wary watch on their lord, as though he might at any moment turn and subject them to some hazardous test. The same tension, just short of fear, passed down the hierarchies that followed, through valet, chamberlain, groom, falconer, down to the boys who were towed along by the hounds. Only the beasts, horse and hound alike, and the hawks on the falconer's frame, went sleek and complacent, in no awe of their lord.

Brother Cadfael stood with Mark at the gate in the wattle fence, and gazed with sharpening attention. For though any one of the three young squires would have done very well for a bridegroom, it was only too plain that none of them was Huon de Domville. It had not entered Cadfael's head until now that this baron might be already well past the prime, no young lover embarking on marriage in the proper years for that undertaking, but with more grey than black in his short, full beard, and only a curled fringe of grey hair and the glisten of a bald crown showing at the temple, where his elaborately twisted capuchon was tilted rakishly aside. A squat, muscular, powerful body still, but well past fifty if he was a day, and more likely nearing sixty. Cadfael hazarded that by now this one must already have used up at least one wife, and probably two. The bride, rumour said, was barely eighteen, fresh from her nurse. Well, these things happen. These things are done.

Then, as the rider drew close, Cadfael could not take his eyes from the face. A wide, flat forehead, rendered tall by the receding hair, cast almost no shadow over the shallow settings of small, black, shrewd eyes, as poorly endowed with lashes as with sockets, but malevolently intelligent. The trimmed beard left uncovered a narrow, implacable mouth. A massive, brutal face, muscled like a wrestler's arm, unsculpted, unfinished. A face that should not have had a subtle mind behind it, to make the man even more formidable, but undoubtedly had. And that was Huon de Domville.

He had drawn close enough now to observe what manner of creatures they were who bobbed and peered and pointed excitedly about the little church, and along the churchyard wall. It did not please him. The black eyes, like small plums embedded in the hard dough of his face, turned dusky red, like smouldering coals. Deliberately he wheeled his horse to their side of the road, leaving the opposite verge, which was wider, and mounting the grass on the near side, and that solely in order to wave the miserable rabble back to their kennels. And his manner of waving was with the full lash of the riding-whip he carried. Doubtful if he ever used it on his horse, blood-stock of this quality being valuable and appreciated, but for clearing his path of lepers it would serve. The tight mouth opened wide to order imperiously: 'Out of my way, vermin! Take your contagion out of sight!'

They shrank and drew back in humble haste out of reach, if not out of sight. All but one. Half a head taller than his fellows, one lean, cloaked figure stood his ground, whether out of inability to move quickly, or want of understanding, or in mute defiance. He remained erect, intently gazing through the eye-slot in the veil that covered his face. When he did take a pace back, without turning his head, he went heavily upon one foot, and was too slow to avoid the lash of the whip, if indeed he had intended to avoid it. The blow took him on shoulder and breast. His maimed foot turned under him, and he fell heavily in the grass.

Cadfael had started forward, but Mark was before him, darting down with an indignant cry to drop to his knees and spread an arm over the gaunt figure, putting his own braced body between the fallen man and the next blow. But Domville was already past, disdainful of further noticing the dregs of the world. He neither hastened nor slowed his pace, but rode on without a glance aside, and all his train after him, though holding rather to the roadway, and some with averted faces. The three young squires passed, embarrassed and uneasy. The big, tow-headed youngster in the middle actually turned full-face to the two on the ground, flashed them a dismayed stare from eyes as blue as cornflowers, and rode with his chin on his shoulder until both his fellows elbowed him back to caution and his duty.

The whole cortège passed while Mark was helping the gaunt old man to his feet. The servants followed woodenly, armoured against the world by their servitude. Certain more lordly figures, guests or minor relatives, passed blandly, as though nothing whatever had occurred. In their midst a demure cleric fingered his beads, faintly smiling, and ignored all. Rumour said that one Eudo de Domville, a canon of Salisbury, was to perform the marriage ceremony; a man in good odour with the church and the papal legate, and in line for advancement, and probably eager to remain so blessed. He passed with the rest. The grooms, the pages, the deerhounds followed, and all the little bells on bridles and jesses tinkled their way past, and dwindled slowly along the first reach of the Foregate.

Brother Mark came up the incline of grass with his arm about the old leper. Cadfael had drawn back and left them to each other. Mark had no fear of contagion, since he never gave a thought to the peril, all his energy being absorbed into the need. Nor would he ever be surprised, or complain, if at last contagion did seize upon him and draw him even closer to the people he served. He was talking to his companion as they came, mildly and cheerfully, for they were both used to spurning, they did not pay it overmuch notice. Cadfael watched them come, marked the one-sided but steady and forceful gait of the old man, and the breadth of the gesture with which his left hand, emerging momentarily from the shrouding sleeve, put off Mark's embracing arm, and set a space between them. Mark accepted the dismissal with simplicity and respect, and turned to leave him. Cadfael had seen, moreover, that the left hand, once long and shapely, lacked both index and middle fingers, and had but two joints of the third, and the texture of the maimed parts was whitish, wrinkled and dry.

'No very noble proceeding,' said Mark with rueful resignation, shaking the debris of grass from his skirts. 'But fear makes men cruel.'

Brother Cadfael doubted whether fear had played any part. Huon de Domville did not look the man to be afraid of anything short of hellfire, though it was true that the outcasts' disease did not fall far short of hellfire.

'You have a new man there?' he asked, gazing after the tall leper, who had moved along the bank to regain a good view of the road. 'I do not think I have seen him before.'

'No, he came in a week or more ago. He is a wanderer, he goes on perpetual pilgrimage, from shrine to shrine as close as in his condition he may. Seventy years old, he says he is, and I believe him. He will not stay long, I think. He makes a stay here because Saint Winifred's bones rested here in the church before being received into the abbey. There, so close to the town, he may not go. Here he may.'

Cadfael, who had knowledge of that renowned virgin's whereabouts which he could never confide to his innocent friend, scrubbed thoughtfully at his blunt brown nose, and reflected tranquilly that even from her far-distant grave in Gwytherin, Saint Winifred would bestir herself to hear the prayers of a poor, afflicted man.

His eyes followed the tall, erect figure. In the shrouded anonymity of dark cloak and hood, and the cloth veil that hid even the faces of those worst disfigured, men and women, old and young, seemed to go secretly and alone through the remnant of life left to them. No gender, no age, no colouring, no country, no creed: all living ghosts, known only to their maker. But no, it was not so. By gait, by voice, by stature, by a thousand infinitesimal foibles of character and kind that pierced through the disguise, they emerged every one unique. This one in his silence had a dominating presence, and in his stillness even under threat a rare and daunting dignity.

'You have talked with him?'

'Yes, but he says little. From his manner of speaking,' said Mark, 'I think lips or tongue must be corrupted. Words come slowly, a little mangled, and he tires soon. But his voice is quiet and deep.'

'What remedies are you using on him?'

'None, for he says he needs none, he carries his own balm. No one here has seen his face. That is why I think he must be sadly maimed. You'll have noticed one foot is crippled? He has lost all toes on that one, but for the stump of the great toe. He has a special shoe built to give him support, a stable sole to walk on. I think the other foot may also be affected, but not so badly.'

'I saw his left hand,' said Cadfael. Such hands he had seen before, the fingers rotted away until they fell like dead leaves, the corrosion of the flesh gnawing slowly until even the wrist shed its bones. Yet it seemed to him that this devouring demon had died of its own greed. There was no ulcerous crust remaining; the seamed white flesh where the lost fingers had once been was dry and healed, however ugly to the view. Firm muscles had moved in the back of the hand when he gestured.

'Has he given you a name?'

'He says his name is Lazarus.' Brother Mark smiled. 'I think it is a name he gave himself at a late christening—perhaps when he cut himself off from family and home, according to law. It is a second birth, lamentable though it may be. He was godfather at his own second baptism. I don't enquire. But I wish he would use our help, and not rely only on his own tending. He must surely have some sores or ulcers that could benefit by your ointments, before he leaves us as he came.'

Cadfael mused, watching the withdrawn figure, motionless at the head of the slope of grass. 'Yet he is not numbed! He has his powers of body still, in all such members as are left to him? He feels heat and cold? And pain? If he strikes his hand against a nail, or a splinter in the fence, he knows it?'

Mark was at a loss; he knew the disease only as he had encountered it, unsightly, ulcerated, full of sores. 'He felt the sting of the whip, I know, even through the armour of his cloak. Yes, surely he feels, like other men.'

But those who have the true leprosy, thought Cadfael, recalling many he had seen in his crusading days, very long ago, those who whiten like ash, those whose skin powders away in grey patches, in the extreme of their disease do not feel, like other men. They injure themselves, bleed, and are unaware of the injury. They let a foot stray into the fire, sleeping, and only awake to the stench of their own flesh burning. They touch and cannot be sure they touch, hold and cannot lift what they would take up. Without sensation, without purpose, fingers, toes, hands, feet, drop away and rot. As Lazarus had lost fingers and toes. But such victims do not walk, however lamely, as Lazarus walked, do not prise themselves up from the ground with active, effective energy, or grasp a support as Lazarus had grasped the arm Mark offered in his aid, and that with the maimed hand. Not unless, not until, the devil that devoured them has died of his own corruption.

'Are you thinking,' asked Mark hopefully, 'that this may not be leprosy, after all?'

'Oh, yes!' Cadfael shook his head at once. 'Yes, no question of it, this was certainly leprosy.'

He did not add that in his opinion many of the ills they treated here, though they carried the same banishment and were called by the same name, were not true leprosy. Any man who broke out in nodes that turned to ulcers, or pallid, scaly eruptions of the skin, or running sores, was set down as a leper, though Cadfael had his suspicions that many such cases arose from uncleanliness, and many others from too little and too wretched food. He was sorry to see Brother Mark's hopeful face fall. No doubt he dreamed of curing all who came.

Along the road came the first distant murmur of another company approaching the town. The whisperings of the watchers, subdued since Domville's inauspicious passing, took on the cheerful chirping of sparrows again, and they crept a little way down the slope of grass, peering and craning for the first glimpse of the bride. The bridegroom had brought little but dismay with him. The lady might do better.

Brother Mark shook off his small disappointment, and took Cadfael by the sleeve. 'Come, you may as well wait and see the rest of it now. I know you have everything in order there in the herbarium, even without me. Why should you hurry back?'

Remembering the particular gifts of Brother Oswin, Cadfael could think of many reasons why he should not leave his workshop for too long, but also of at least one good reason for remaining. 'I daresay another half-hour will do no harm,' he agreed. 'Let us go and take our stand by this Lazarus of yours, where I may observe him without offending.'

The old man did not stir as he heard them approaching, and they halted somewhat aside, not to disturb his remote contemplation. He had, thought Cadfael, the self-sufficient tranquillity of a desert hermit; as those early fathers had sought out their austere solitudes, so he created his about him, even among men. He towered over both of them by a head, and stood straight as a lance, and almost as meagre, but for the lean, wide shoulders under the shrouding cloak. Only when the sound of the approaching company blew suddenly closer on a stirring wind, and he turned his head to look intently towards the sound, did Cadfael glimpse the face beneath the hood. The hood itself covered the brow, which by the form of the head should be lofty and broad, and the coarse blue cloth of the veil was drawn up to the cheekbones. In the slit between, only the eyes showed, but they were arresting enough, large, unblemished, of a clear, pale but brilliant blue-grey. Whatever deformities he hid, his eyes saw clearly and far, and were accustomed to looking on distances. He paid no heed to the two who stood near to him. His gaze swept beyond them, to where the approaching party showed as a shimmer of colours and a shifting of light.

There was less ceremony here than with Huon de Domville's retinue, and the numbers were smaller. Nor was there a single dominant figure in the lead, but a flurry of mounted grooms as outriders, and within their circle, as though within an armed guard, three came riding abreast. On one side a dark, sinewy, olive-faced man perhaps five and forty years old, very splendidly dressed in sombre, glowing colours, and well mounted on a light, fast grey, surely part Arab, thought Cadfael. The man had plenteous black hair coiling under a plumed cap, and a clipped black beard framing a long-lipped mouth. It was a narrow, closed face, subtle and suspicious. On the other side rode a lady of about the same years, thin and neat and sharply handsome, dark like her lord, and mounted on a roan mare. She had a pursed, calculating mouth and shrewd eyes, beneath brows tending to a frown even when the mouth smiled. Her headdress was of the most fashionable, her riding habit had the London cut, and she rode with grace and style, but the very look of her struck with a coldness.

And in between these two, dwarfed and overshadowed, there paced a tiny, childlike creature on a palfrey too large for her. Her touch on the rein was light, her seat in the saddle listless but graceful. She was sumptuously arrayed in cloth of gold and dark blue silks, and within the burden of her finery her slight form seemed cramped and straitened, like a body coffined. Her face gazed ahead, beneath a gilded net heavy with dark-gold hair, into emptiness. A softly rounded face, with delicate features and great iris-grey eyes, but so pale and subdued that she might have been a pretty doll rather than a living woman. Cadfael heard Mark draw in startled breath. It was a shame to see youth and freshness so muted and bereft of joy.

This lord, too, had noted the nature of this place, and of those who had come out from it to see his niece go by. He did not, like Domville, spur deliberately at the offence, but swung his mount the other way, to give the infected a wider berth, and turned his head away to avoid even seeing them. The girl might have passed by without so much as noticing them, so deep was she drowned in her submissive sadness, if the child Bran, all shining eyes, had not so far forgotten himself as to run halfway down the hillock for a nearer view. The flash of movement in the corner of her eye caused her to start and look round, and

seeing him, she came suddenly to life in the piteous contemplation of an innocent even more wretched than herself. For an instant she stared at him with nothing but horrified compassion,
and then, seeing that she mistook him, seeing that he looked up
at her smiling, she smiled too. It lasted only the twinkling of an
eye, but for that while she shone with a warm, bright, grieving
kindness; and before the clear sky clouded again she had leaned
across her aunt's saddle-bow, and tossed a handful of small
coins into the grass at the child's feet. Bran was so enchanted
that he could not even stoop to pick them up, but followed her
progress wide-eyed and open-mouthed as she passed by.

No one else in the company offered largesse here. No doubt
it was being reserved to make a greater impression at the abbey
gatehouse, where there would certainly be a crowd of hopeful
beggars waiting.

For no very sound reason, Cadfael turned from the child to
look at the old man Lazarus. Bran could afford to take candid delight in the bright colours and pretty clothes of those more for-
tunate than himself, without envy or greed, but the old in
experience might well find a bitter flavour in viewing impossible
fruit. The old man had not moved, except that as the riders
passed by his head turned to hold those three in sight, with never
a glance to spare for the gentlewomen and servants who followed. The eyes staring between hood and veil glittered pale,
brilliant and blue as ice, unblinking, as long as the bride remained in sight. When even the last pack-pony had vanished
round the curve of the Foregate, he still stood motionless, as
though the intentness of his stare could follow them as far as the
gatehouse, and pierce the walls to keep unbroken watch on them
within.

Brother Mark drew long and rueful breath, and turned to gaze
wonderingly at Cadfael. 'And that is she? And they mean to marry
her to that man? He could be her grandsire—and no gentle or
kindly one, either. How can such things be?' He stared along the
road as the old man was staring. 'So small, and so young! And did
you see her face—how sad! This is not with her will!'

Cadfael said nothing; there was nothing reassuring or consoling to be said. Such things were the commonplace of marriage where there were lands and wealth and powerful alliances to be gained, and small say the brides—or often enough the young bridegrooms—had in the disposal of their persons. There might even be brides who could see shrewdly enough the advantages of marrying men old enough to be their grandsires, where there was material good to be gained, since death might very soon relieve them of their husbands but leave them their dower and the status of their widowhood, and with some luck and a deal of cleverness they might manage to make a second match more to their liking. But by her face, Iveta de Massard saw the fate that awaited her rather as her own death than her bridegroom's.

'I pray God help her!' said Mark fervently.

'It may be,' said Brother Cadfael, rather to himself than to his friend, 'that he intends to. But it may also be that he has a right to expect a little support from men in setting about it.'

In the courtyard of the bishop's house in the Foregate, Huon de Domville's servants were unloading the packhorses, and running about with bedding and hangings, and the finery that would grace the marriage service and the bridal bed. Domville's butler already had wine decanted for his master and Canon Eudo, who was a distant cousin, and the chamberlain had seen to it that there was firing and comfort waiting in the best chamber, a loose, warm gown after the rigour of riding clothes, furred slippers after the long, elegant boots had been drawn off. The baron sprawled in his cushioned chair, spread his thick legs, and nursed his mulled wine, well content. It was nothing to him that his bride's procession was drawing near from Saint Giles. He had no need and no desire to waste his time standing to watch his purchase go by; he was already sure of her, and he would be seeing enough of her after the marriage. He was here to conclude a bargain highly satisfactory to himself and to the girl's uncle and guardian, and though it was an agreeable bonus that the child happened to be young, beautiful and appetising, it was of no very great importance.

Joscelin Lucy turned over his horse to a groom, kicked a bale of napery out of his way, and was making off back to the gate and the road when his fellow Simon Aguilon, the oldest of the three squires in Domville's service, caught him by the arm.

'Where are you off to so fast? He'll be bawling for you the minute he's emptied his first cup, you know that. It's your turn to wait on their nobilities!'

Joscelin tugged at his flaxen thatch, and loosed a sharp bay of laughter. 'What nobility? You saw as well as I did. Strike a poor devil who daren't strike back, and as near as death ride him down, for no offence in the world. Devil take such nobility! And devil take him and his thirst, too, until I've seen Iveta go by.'

'Joss, you fool,' cautioned Simon urgently, 'you'll let that tongue of yours wag too loud and once too often. Cross him now, and he'll toss you out naked to go home to your father and explain yourself, and how will that help Iveta? Or you, either?' He shook his head over his friend, though good-humouredly, and kept his hold on him. 'Better go to him. He'll have your hide, else!'

The youngest of the three turned from unsaddling his mount, and grinned at the pair of them. 'Oh, let him have his glimpse, who knows how many more there'll be?' He clouted Joscelin amiably on the shoulder. 'I'll go and run his errands for you this time. I'll tell him you're busy making sure all the butts of wine are handled gently, that'll please him. Go and gaze—though what good it will do either of you. . . .'

'Will you, though, Guy? You're a good fellow! I'll take your turn of duty when you ask it!' And he was off again gatewards, but Simon flung an arm about his shoulders and bounded into step beside him.

'I'll come with you. He won't need me for a while. But hear me, Joss,' he went on seriously, 'you take too many risks with him. You know he can advance you if you please him, it's what your father wants and expects, you're a fool to put your future in peril. And you can please him, if you give your mind to it, he's none so hard on us.'

They passed through the gate and stood in the angle of the wall, leaning shoulder to shoulder against the stone gate-pillar and gazing along the Foregate, two tall, strong young men, Simon the elder by three years, and the shorter by the width of a hand. The sullen, tow-headed lad beside him gnawed a considering lip, and scowled at the ground.

'My future! What can he do to my future, more than toss me back to my father in disgrace, and what the devil need I care about that? There are two good manors will be mine, that he can't take from me, and there are other lords I could serve. I'm a man of my hands, I can hold my own with most . . .'

Simon laughed, shaking him rallyingly in the arm that circled his shoulders. 'You can indeed! I've suffered from it, I know!'

'There are lords enough wanting good men of their hands, now the empress is back in England, and the fight's on in earnest for the crown. I could fend! You could as well be thinking of your own case, lad, you've as much to lose as I have. You may be his sister's son, and his heir now, but how if—' He set his teeth; it was hard to utter it, but he was perversely determined to drive the knife deep into his own flesh, and twist it to double the pain. '—how if things change? A young wife . . . How if he gets a son of this marriage? Your nose will be out of joint.'

Simon leaned his curly brown head back against the stones of the wall, and laughed aloud. 'What, after thirty years of marriage to my Aunt Isabel, and God knows how many passages with how many ladies outside the pale, and never a brat to show for it all? Lad, if he has a seed in him, for all his appetites, I'll eat the fruit myself! My inheritance is safe enough. I'm in no danger. I'm twenty-five, and he's nearing sixty. I can wait!' He straightened alertly. 'Look, they're coming!'

But Joscelin had already caught the first glimmer of colour and movement along the road, and stiffened to gaze. They came on briskly, Godfrid Picard and his party, in haste to gain the hospitable shelter of the abbey. Simon loosed his clasp, feeling Joscelin draw away.

'For God's sake, boy, what's the use? She's not for you!' But he said it in a despairing sigh, and Joscelin did not even hear it.

They came, and they passed. The ogres on either side of her loomed lean and subtle and greedy, heads arrogantly high, but brows knotted and faces pinched, as though there had already been some happening that had displeased them. And there between them was she, a pale desperation in a golden shell of display, her small face all eyes, but blind eyes, gazing at nothing, seeing nothing. Until she drew close, and something—he wanted to believe his nearness and need—disquieted her, caused her to shiver, and turn her great eyes where she hardly dared turn her whole head, towards the place where he stood. He was not certain that she saw him, but he was certain that she knew he was there, that she had felt, scented, breathed him as she passed between her guards. She did not make the mistake of looking round, or in any way changing the fixed, submissive stillness of her face; but as she passed she lifted her right hand to her cheek, held it so a moment, and again let it fall.

'I do believe,' sighed Simon Aguilon, bringing his friend back in his arm to the courtyard, 'that you haven't given up, even now. For God's sake, what have you to hope for? Two days more, and she's my lady Domville.'

Joscelin held his peace, and thought of the uplifted hand, and knew in his heart that her fingers had touched her lips; and that was more than had been agreed.

The entire guest-hall of the abbey, apart from the common quarters, had been given over to Sir Godfrid Picard and his wedding party. In the privacy of their own chamber, within, Agnes Picard turned to her husband with an anxious face. 'I still do not like this quietness of hers. I do not trust her.'

He shrugged it off disdainfully. 'Ah, you fret too much. She has given over the battle. She is altogether submissive. What can she do? Daniel has his orders not to let her out of the gate, and Walter keeps watch on the parish door of the church. There's no other way out, unless she finds a means to fly over the wall, or leap the Meole brook. No harm in keeping a close eye on her, even within, but not so close as to draw too much attention. But I'm sure you mistake her. That timid mouse has not the courage to stand up at the altar and declare herself unwilling.'

'As well!' said the lady grimly. 'I hear this Abbot Radulfus has a fine conceit of his own rights and powers, and is no respecter of barons if he feels his writ infringed. But I wish I could be as sure of her tameness as you.'

'You fret too much, I tell you, woman. Once bring her to the altar, and she'll speak her words as taught, and no bones about it.'

Agnes gnawed a lip, and still was not quite convinced. 'Well, it may be so . . . But for all that, I wish it was done. I shall breathe the easier when these next two days are over.'

In Brother Cadfael's workshop in the herbarium, Brother Oswin shuffled his feet, folded his large, willing but disastrous hands, and looked sheepish. Cadfael looked apprehensively round the hut, aware of ill news to come, though it was an advance if the lad even realised it when he had done something mad, without having it pointed out to him. Most things appeared to be still in their places. The brazier burned low, there were no noticeable evil smells, the wines in their great flasks bubbled gently to themselves as usual.

Brother Oswin rendered account selfconsciously, gleaning what credit he could before the blow fell. 'Brother Infirmarer has fetched the electuaries and the powders. And I have taken Brother Prior the stomachic you made for him. The troches you left drying I think should be ready now, and the dried herbs for the decoction you spoke of, I have ground to fine powder ready for use tomorrow.'

But . . . Now he was coming to the bad news. That look of astonished reproach, that a thing well-meant and confidently undertaken should so betray him.

'But such a strange thing . . . I don't understand how it could happen, the pot must surely have been cracked, though I

22

could see no break in it. The linctus you left boiling . . . I did watch it most carefully, I'm sure I took it from the brazier when it was just the right thickness, and I stirred it as you told me. You know you said it was wanted urgently for old Brother Francis, his chest being so bad . . . I thought I would cool it quickly, to be able to bottle it for you, so I took the pot from the fire and set it in a bowl of cold water . . .'

'And the pot burst,' said Cadfael resignedly.

'Fell apart,' owned Oswin, bewildered and grieved, 'in two great pieces, and shed forth all that honey and the herbs into the water. An extraordinary thing! Did you know the pot was cracked?'

'Son, the pot was sound as a bell, and one of my best, but nor it nor any other here is meant to be taken straight from the fire and plumped into cold water. The clay does not like so sharp a change, it shrinks and shatters. And while we are on that, take heed that glass bottles have the same objection,' added Cadfael hastily. 'If warm things are to be put in them, the bottles must be warmed first. Never thrust any matter straight from heat to cold or cold to heat.'

'I have cleared away all,' said Oswin apologetically, 'and thrown out the pot, too. But all the same, I am sure there must have been a crack somewhere in it . . . But I am sorry the linctus is wasted, and I will come back after supper and make a fresh brew in its place.'

God forbid! thought Cadfael, but managed to refrain from saying it aloud. 'No, son!' he said firmly. 'Your duty is to attend Collations and keep the true round of your order. I will see to the linctus myself.' His supply of pots would have to be defended from Brother Oswin's excellent intentions henceforth. 'Now be off and get ready for Vespers.'

Thus Brother Oswin's latest achievement in the herbarium was the reason for Cadfael returning to his workshop that evening after supper, and for his involvement in all that happened afterwards.

2 ✒

Sir Godfrid Picard and his lady came to Vespers in state, with Iveta de Massard diminutive between them like a lamb led to sacrifice. A hard-faced elderly maid carried Lady Picard's prayer book, and a valet attended Sir Godfrid. The girl had put off her display finery, and came simply dressed in dark colours, with a veil over her great sheaf of gold hair. She stood and knelt throughout with downcast eyes and pale, mute face. Cadfael watched her with curiosity and sympathy from his place among the brethren, and wondered the more, the more he gazed. What kin could she be to the crusader whose name had been a legend among his contemporaries, however this present generation might have forgotten him? Nearly forty years dead, and a man is dead indeed.

At the end of Vespers, as the brothers filed out to supper, Iveta rose, and went swiftly forward, hands clasped, into the Lady Chapel, and there sank to her knees before the altar. It seemed to Cadfael that Agnes Picard would have followed her, but that her husband laid a restraining hand on her arm, for Prior Robert Pennant, ever attentive to Norman nobility of his own kind, was bearing down upon them in all his lofty, silver-haired grandeur, with some civil invitation which could not well be refused. The lady cast one sharp glance at the devout figure of her niece, who seemed to be totally absorbed in fervent prayer, and surrendered gracefully, pacing beside the prior on her husband's arm.

Cadfael made a very hasty supper among his fellows, still disturbed by the events of the day, for which, unhappily, all his herbs had no remedy. As well that he had a specific task to occupy him during the evening, thanks to the inexhaustible optimism of Brother Oswin.

Iveta remained on her knees until all had been silent about her for some minutes, the prior's voice fading away into distance, assiduously attentive. Then she stole up from her place and went to peer cautiously through the south door into the cloister. Robert had drawn the guests into the garth with him to admire the last of the carefully tended roses. Their backs were turned to her, and the western walk of the cloister stood empty before her. Iveta gathered up her skirts and her courage, only she knew with how much heroism and how little hope, and ran like a frightened mouse from cats, out into the great court, and there looked round her desperately.

She knew this enclave not at all, it was the first time she had entered it; but she saw between the buildings of the guest-hall and the abbot's lodging the green of pleached hedges framing a narrow alley, and the heads of trees nodding beyond. There must be the gardens, at this hour surely deserted. Somewhere there he had said he would wait for her, and as she passed him she had given him the signal that she would not fail him. Why had she done so? This could be nothing better than a farewell. Yet she sped towards it with a despairing courage she would have done better to summon up long ago, before it was too late. She was already solemnly affianced, a contract almost as binding as marriage itself. Easier far to slip out of life than out of that bargain.

The thick green walls enclosed her, twilight within twilight. She drew breath and slowed to a walk, uncertain which way to go. The path to the right led between the rear of the guest-hall and the abbey fish-ponds, and beyond the second pool a little footbridge crossed the mill leat near the outflow, and brought her to a gateway in a mellow stone wall. With one more wall between herself and detection she felt unaccountably safer, and there was a curious comfort and calm in the wave of spiced sweetness that rose about her as her skirts brushed the greenery within. Rosemary and lavender, mint and thyme, all manner of herbs filled the walled garden with aromatic odours, grown a little rank now with autumn, ready to sink into their winter sleep very soon. The best of their summer was already harvested.

A hand reached out of an arbour in the wall to take her hand, and a voice whispered in haste: 'This way, quickly! There's a hut here in the corner. . . .an apothecary's shop. Come! No one will look for us in there.'

Every time she had ever been able to draw close to him—the times had been very few and very brief—she had been startled and reassured by the very size of him, head and shoulders above her, wide in breast and shoulder, long in the arm, narrow and fleet in the flank, as though his engulfing shadow could wall her in from all threats, like a tower. But she knew it could not, and he was as unblessed and vulnerable as she. The very thought had made her even more timorous than she was for herself. Great lords, if they once take against, can quite destroy young squires, however tall and strong and well versed in arms.

'Someone may come there,' she whispered, clinging to his hand.

'At this time of the evening? No one will come. They're at supper now, they'll be in the chapterhouse afterwards.' He drew her along with him in his arm, under the eaves rustling with dried herbs, into the wood-warm interior where glass gleamed

26

on the shelves, and the brazier, fed to burn slowly until it was needed, provided a small eye of fire in the dimness. The door he left open, just as it stood. Better move nothing, to betray the visit of unauthorised strangers. 'Iveta! You did come! I was afraid. . . .'

'You knew I'd come!'

'. . . afraid you might be watched too closely, and every moment. Listen, for we may not have long. You shall not, you shall not be delivered over to that gross old man. Tomorrow, if you'll trust me, if you will to go with me, come at this hour again, here. . . .'

'Oh, God!' she said in a soft moan. 'Why do we make believe there can be any escape?'

'But there can, there must!' he insisted furiously. 'If you truly want it . . . if you love me . . .'

'*If* I love you. . . .!'

She was in his arms, her own slight arms embracing with all their might as much of his hard young body as they could span, when Brother Cadfael, in all innocence, his sandals silent on his well-kept grass paths, darkened the doorway and startled them apart. He was a good deal more astonished than they, and to judge by their faces, much less terrible than whatever they had momentarily taken him for. Iveta recoiled until her shoulders were brought up against the wooden wall of the hut. Joscelin stood his ground by the brazier, feet solidly spread. Both of them recovered countenance with a gallantry that was more than half desperation.

'I cry your pardon,' said Cadfael placidly. 'I did not know I had patients waiting. Brother Infirmarer will have recommended you to me, I take it. He knew I should be working here until Compline.'

He might have been speaking Welsh to them, of course, but with luck they might pick up the hints he was hastily offering. Desperation does tend to sharpen the wits at need. And he had heard, as they had not, the brushing of garments along the path outside, the rapid, irate tread of a woman's feet bearing down on them. He was standing by the brazier, striking flint and steel to light his little oil-lamp, when Agnes Picard appeared in the doorway, tall and chill, brows drawn together into a level, unbroken line.

Brother Cadfael, having lit and trimmed the wick, turned to gather up into a box the troches Brother Oswin had left drying, little white cakes of carminative powder bound with gum. The act enabled him to keep his back turned serenely upon the woman in the doorway, though he was very well aware of her. Since it was plain that neither of the young people was yet capable of uttering a sensible word, he went on talking for them all.

'It will be the tiring journey,' he said comfortably, closing the box upon his tablets, 'that has brought on your headache. It was wise of you to consult Brother Edmund, a headache should not be neglected, it may deprive you of the sleep you need, otherwise. I'll make you a draught—the young gentleman will not mind waiting a few moments for his lord's needs . . .'

Joscelin, recovering, and resolutely keeping a shoulder turned on the baleful presence in the doorway, said fervently that he would gladly wait until the Lady Iveta had whatever she required. Cadfael reached for a small cup from a shelf, and selected one from a row of bottles. He was in the act of pouring when a voice cold and piercing as fine steel said behind them, with deliberation: 'Iveta!'

All three of them swung round in a very fair show of being innocently startled. Agnes came forward into the hut, narrowing her eyes suspiciously.

'What are you doing here? I have been looking for you. You are keeping everyone waiting for supper.'

'Your lady niece, madam,' said Cadfael, forestalling whatever the girl might have roused herself to say, 'is suffering from a common distress after the exertion of travel, and Brother Infirmarer rightly recommended her to come to me for a remedy.' He held out the cup to Iveta, who took it like one in a dream. She was white and still, the sum of her frustration and fear showed only in her eyes. 'Drink it off now, at once, before you go to supper. You may safely, it will do you nothing but good.'

And so it would, whether her head ached or no. It was one of his best wines, he kept it for his special favourites, since the amount he made of it each year was small. He had the satisfaction of seeing faint astonishment and pleasure sparkle through the desperation of her eyes, even if it faded soon. She put the empty cup back into his hand, and gave him the palest of smiles. At Joscelin she did not venture to look at all.

In a small voice she said: 'Thank you, brother. You are very good.' And to the presence that loomed darkly watching her: 'I am sorry I have delayed you, aunt. I am ready now.'

Agnes Picard said never a word more, but stood aside in cold invitation to the girl to precede her out of the room, eyed her steadily and glitteringly as she passed, and then, before following her, gave the young man a long, intent look that threatened all possible evil. The civilities might have been preserved, but very certainly Agnes had not been deceived, never for a moment.

They were gone, the bride and her keeper, the last rustle of skirts silenced. There was a long moment of stillness while the two left behind gazed helplessly at each other. Then Joscelin let out his breath in a great groan, and threw himself down on the bench that stood against the wall.

'The hag should fall from the bridge and drown in the fish-pond, now, this moment, while she's crossing! But things never work out as they should. Brother, don't think me ungrateful for the goodwill and the wit you've spent for us, but I doubt it was all thrown away. She's had her suspicions of me some while, I fancy. She'll find some way of making me pay for this.'

'At that, she may be right,' said Cadfael honestly. 'And God forgive me for the lies!'

'You told none. Or if she has not a headache, she has what's worse, an ache of the heart.' He ran angry fingers through his shock of flaxen hair, and leaned his head back against the wall. 'What was it you gave her?'

On impulse Cadfael refilled the cup and held it out to him. 'Here! The like potion might not do you any harm. God he knows whether you deserve it, but we'll scamp the judgement until I know more of you.'

Joscelin's eyebrows, winged and expressive, and darker by many shades than his hair, rose in appreciative surprise at the savour of the wine. His forehead and cheeks had the rich golden tan of an outdoor life, rare enough among those of such fair colouring. The eyes, now conning Cadfael rather warily over the rim of the cup, were as radiantly blue as Cadfael remembered them from Saint Giles, like cornflowers in a wheat-field. He did not look like a deceiver or a seducer, rather like an overgrown schoolboy, honest, impatient, clever after his fashion, and probably unwise. Cleverness and wisdom are not inevitable yoke-fellows.

'This is the best medicine I ever tasted. And you have been uncommonly generous to us, as you were uncommonly quick in the uptake,' said the boy, warmed and disarmed. 'And you know nothing about us, and had never seen either of us before!'

'I had seen you both before,' Cadfael corrected him. He began to measure his various pectoral herbs into a mortar, and took a small bellows to rouse the brazier from its quiescent state. 'I have a linctus to make before Compline. You'll not mind if I start work.'

'And I am in the way. I'm sorry! I've put you out enough already.' But he did not want to go, he was too full of matter he needed to unload from his heart, and could not possibly offer to anyone but just such a courteous chance acquaintance, perhaps never to be seen again. 'Or—may I stay?'

'By all means, if you're at leisure to stay. For you serve Huon de Domville, and I fancy his service might be exigent. I saw you pass by Saint Giles. I saw the lady, too.'

'You were there? The old man—he was not hurt?' Bless the lad, he genuinely wanted to know. In the middle of his own troubles, up to the neck, he could still feel indignation at an affront to another's dignity.

'Neither in body nor mind. Such as he live with a humility that transcends all possibility of humiliation. He was above giving a thought to the baron's blow.'

Joscelin emerged from his own preoccupation sufficiently to feel curiosity. 'And you were there among them—those people? You—Forgive me if I offend, it is not meant!—you are not afraid of going among them? Of their contagion? I have often wondered—*someone* tends them. I know they are forced to live apart, yet they cannot be utterly cut out of humanity.'

'The thing about fear,' said Cadfael, seriously considering, 'is that it is pointless. When need arises, fear is forgotten. Would you recoil from taking a leper's hand, if he needed yours, or you his, to be hauled out of danger? I doubt it. Some men would, perhaps—but of you I doubt it. You would grip first and consider afterwards, and by then fear would be clearly a mere waste of time. You are free of your lord's table tonight, are you? Then stay and give account of yourself, if you're so minded. You owe me at worst an excuse—at best, some amends for breaking in uninvited.'

But he was not displeased with his unruly intruder. Almost absent-mindedly Joscelin had taken the bellows from him, and was encouraging the brazier into reviving life.

'He has three of us,' said the boy thoughtfully. 'Simon waits on him at table tonight—Simon Aguilon, his sister's son—and Guy FitzJohn is the third of us, he's in attendance, too. I need not go back yet. And you know nothing about me, and I think you're in doubt whether you did right to try and help us. I should like you to think well of me. I am sure you cannot but think well of Iveta.' The name clouded his face again, he gazed ruefully into the satisfactory glow he was producing. 'She is . . .' He struggled with adoration, and exploded rebelliously: 'No, she is not perfection, how could she be? Since she was ten years old she had been in wardship to those two! If you were at Saint Giles, you saw them. One on either side, like dragons. Her perfection has been all crushed out of shape, too long. But if she were free, she would grow back into her proper self, she would be brave and noble, like her ancestors. And then I would not care,' he said, turning eyes blindingly blue and bright upon Cadfael, 'if she gave it all to someone else, not to me. No, I lie—I should care infinitely, but I would bear it, and still be glad. Only this—this wicked market-bargaining, this defilement, this I will not endure!'

'Mind the bellows! There, draw it out, you've given me all the fire I want. Lay it by on the stone there. Good lad! A name for a name is fair exchange. My name is Cadfael, a Welsh brother of this house, born at Trefriw.' Cadfael was pounding honey and a morsel of vinegar into his powdered herbs, and warming his pot by the fire. 'Now who may you be?'

'My name is Joscelin Lucy. My father is Sir Alan Lucy, and has two manors in the Hereford borders. He sent me as page to Domville when I was fourteen, as the custom is, to learn my squire-craft in a greater household. And I won't say my lord has been so hard a man to serve. I could not complain for myself. But for his tenants and villeins, and such as fall under his justice. . .' He hesitated. 'I have my letters, I can read Latin hand. I was at school with monks, it stays with a man. I don't say my lord's worse than his kind, but God knows he's no better. I should have asked my father to take me away to another lord, if . . .'

If this courtship, to dignify it by that name, had not begun to be mooted between Domville and the Massard heiress. If the boy had not seen, marvelled at, been captivated by, that tiny, fragile, virginal creature between her two dragons. His lord's entry where she was had been entry also, at whatever hopeless distance, for his esquires.

'By staying with him,' said the youth, wrenching at the insoluble complications of his predicament, 'I could at least see her. If I left him, how could I ever get near? So I stayed. And I do try to serve honestly, since I so promised. But oh, Brother Cadfael, is this just? Is it right? For the love of God, she is eighteen

32

years old, and she shrinks from him, and yet, for all I can see, he is better than what she now has. She has no happiness now, and can look for none in her marriage. And I love her! But that's by the way. Of small account, if *she* could be happy.'

'Hmmm!' said Cadfael with mild scepticism, and stirred his gently bubbling pot, which began to fill the hut with a heady aromatic sweetness as it simmered. 'So many a lover has probably vowed, but with one eye on his own advantage, all the same. I suppose you'll tell me you're willing to die for her.'

Joscelin melted suddenly into a boy's grin. 'Well, not with any great eagerness! I'd liefer live for her, if it can be arranged. But if you mean, would I do all in my power to set her free to take another of her own choice, yes, I would. For this match is *not* of her choice, she dreads and loathes it, she is being forced into it utterly against her will.'

There was no need to labour it; the first glimpse of her face and bearing had said it all for him.

'And those who should most guard her and work for her good are using her for their own ends, and nothing more. Her mother—she was Picard's sister—died when Iveta was born, and her father when she was ten years old, and she was given over into her uncle's ward as her nearest kin, which is natural enough, if her kin had proved natural to her! Oh, I am not so blind as not to know there's nothing new in a guardian making the best profit for himself out of his ward, instead of using his own substance on her behalf, and plundering her lands instead of nourishing them for her future good. I tell you, Brother Cadfael, Iveta is being sold to my lord for his voice and countenance with the king, and advancement under his shadow—but for more than that. She has great lands. She is the only Massard left, all that great honour goes with her hand. And I suspect that the bargain they've struck over her means the carving up of what was once a hero's portion. A great swathe out of those lands of hers will surely stay with Picard, and some of what goes with her to Domville will have been milked hard for years before it passes. A very fine arrangement for both of them, but crying wrong to Iveta.'

And every word could all too well be true. Such things happen where a child is left orphan and heiress to great estates. Even if the child be a boy, and young enough, thought Cadfael, and with no one to protect him, he can be married off to make a profitable alliance for his guardian, to join up lands convenient for exploitation, to spite a rival, just as nimbly and irresistibly as can a girl; but with a girl the thing is more usual, and less to be questioned. No, no one in authority between baron and king will lift a finger to interfere with Iveta's destiny. Only, perhaps, some rash young hothead like this one, at his own risk and hers.

He did not ask what they had been whispering together about, when he stumbled in upon their embrace. However fretted and angry, young Lucy had still something, some faint, hoarded hope in his sleeve, so much was clear. Better not to ask, not to let him utter it, even if he offered. But there was one thing Cadfael needed to know. The only Massard left, he had said.

'What was the name of her father?' he asked, stirring his thickening brew. Before Compline he would be able to set it aside to cool gradually.

'Hamon FitzGuimar de Massard.'

He stressed the patronymic with ceremony and pride. There were still some among the young, it seemed, who had been taught a proper regard for the great names of the dead.

'Her grandsire was that Guimar de Massard who was at the taking of Jerusalem, and was captured afterwards at the battle of Ascalon, and died of his wounds. She has his helm and his sword. She treasures them. The Fatimids sent them back after his death.'

Yes, so they had, in courtesy to a brave enemy. They had been asked also to return his body from its temporary burial, and had received the request graciously, but then the intermittent squabbling among the Crusader leaders had cost them the chance of securing the port of Ascalon, and the negotiations for the return of the paladin's body had been neglected and forgotten. Chivalrous enemies had buried him with honour, and there he rested. It was all very long ago, years before these young people were ever born.

'I remember,' said Cadfael.

'And now it's great shame that the last heiress of such a house should be so misused and defrauded of her happiness.'

'So it is,' said Cadfael, lifting his pot from the fire and standing it aside on the beaten earth of the floor.

'And it must not continue,' said Joscelin emphatically. 'It shall not continue.' He rose, with a vast sigh. 'I must go back, no help for it.' He eyed the array of bottles and jars, and the dangling bunches of herbs that furnished the workshop with infinite possibilities. 'Have you not something among all these wonders that I could slip into his cup? His or Picard's, what does it matter which? Either removed from this world would set Iveta free. And leave the world the sweeter!'

'If that is seriously meant,' said Cadfael firmly, 'you are in peril of your soul, boy. And if it is mere levity, you deserve a great clout on the ear for it. If you were not so big, I might attempt it.'

The flashing smile came and went in an instant, warmly if ruefully. 'I could stoop,' he offered.

'You know as well as I do, child, that you would not touch such foul methods as murder, and you do yourself great wrong to misuse words.'

'Would I not?' said Joscelin softly, the smile clean gone. 'You do not know, brother, how far I would put my soul in peril to make all safe for Iveta.'

Cadfael fretted about it all through Compline, and into the warming-room for the last quiet half-hour before bed. Of course there had been nothing for it but to take the boy sternly to task, tell him firmly and truly that he must abjure all such black thoughts, out of which nothing good could come. None but knightly measures were open to him, since he was destined for knighthood, and he should, he must, forswear all others. The trouble was that the boy had shown very sound sense in retorting that he would be a great fool to challenge his lord to honest combat, after the manner of knighthood, since Domville would not even take such an impertinence seriously, but simply throw him out of his household and be done with him. And how would Iveta be helped then?

But need that mean that he was really capable of contemplating the use of murder? Remembering the open brown face, very poorly provided for dissembling, and the headlong manner, surely not adapted to going roundabout, Cadfael could hardly believe it. And yet there was that fragile golden miniature of a girl with her sad, resigned face and empty eyes, two days from her hated marriage, and her fate was a weighty enough matter to demand, if it could not justify, a death or two.

The urgency touched Cadfael, no less than Joscelin Lucy. For here was Guimar de Massard's granddaughter, stripped of all her kin but these two who hedged her in like guardian dragons. And how could the last of the Massards be left to her fate, without a finger raised from all those who had known her grandfather, and reverenced his memory? As well abandon a comrade wounded and surrounded in battle.

Brother Oswin crept diffidently to Cadfael's side in the warming-room. 'Is the linctus already prepared, brother? The fault was mine, let me do something to make amends. I will rise early and bottle it for you. I have caused you such extra travail, I should make some repayment.'

He had caused more travail than he knew, and more perplexity of mind, but at least he had recalled Cadfael to the remembrance of his first duty here; after, of course, the observance of the rule.

'No, no,' said Cadfael hastily. 'The boiling is very well, and it will cool overnight and thicken, after Prime is time enough before bottling. You are reader tomorrow, you must keep the offices strictly, and think only of your reading.'

And leave my brew alone, he thought, as he went to his cell

and his prayers. It came clear to him suddenly how like were Brother Oswin's large hands to those of Joscelin Lucy, and yet how the one pair made havoc of whatever they touched, and the other pair, for all their size, moved with delicate dexterity, whether on the reins of a speckled grey horse, or sword and lance, or circling the tender body of a heart-heavy girl.

And with equal adroitness, thus driven, on the means of murder?

Cadfael arose well before Prime next morning, and went to bottle his overnight brew, and take a measure of it to Brother Edmund at the infirmary. The day had dawned misty and mild, without wind. In the still air sounds were muted and movements softened, and the great court presented an ordinary picture of routine activities from Prime to breakfast, through the first Mass for the lay servants and workmen, the second Mass and the chapter that followed, on this occasion cut short and briskly conducted, there being so much following business to be seen to for the next day's marriage. There was therefore a rather longer interval left for relaxation before High Mass at ten, and Cadfael took the opportunity of returning to the herb-gardens, and earmarking for Brother Oswin's afternoon duty those tasks which seemed best proofed against his knack of well-intentioned devastation. Autumn was a good time, since there was digging to be done, to make the cleared ground ready for the operation of the frosts to come.

Cadfael returned to the great court before ten o'clock, when brothers, pupils, guests and townsmen were beginning to gather for High Mass. The Picards were just issuing forth from the guest-hall, Iveta forlornly small and mute between uncle and aunt, but looking, or so Cadfael thought, resolutely composed, as though a faint, reviving wind had blown through the heavy stillness of her despair, and given her heart at least to hope for a miracle. The elderly maidservant, as forbidding of visage as Agnes herself, walked close behind. The child was hemmed in securely every way.

They were moving at leisure towards the cloister and the south door, with Brother Denis the hospitaller in attendance, when the decorous quiet was rudely broken by a furious clatter of hooves at the gatehouse, and into the court galloped a rider on a speckled grey horse, at such headlong speed that he almost rode down the porter, and scattered the servants like hens before the fox. Reining round abruptly with great slithering of hooves on the moist cobbles, he flung the bridle on his horse's neck, and leaped down with flaxen hair erected and blue eyes blazing, to plant himself squarely in Godfrid Picard's path, feet spread and jaw jutting, a young man in a formidable rage.

'My lord, it's *you* have done this thing to me! I am cast off from my service, thrown out without reason, without fault, with nothing but horse and saddle-bags, and ordered to quit this town before night. This in a moment, and no word of mine will be heard in excuse! And well I know to whom I owe the favour! You, you have complained of me to my lord, and got me turned off like a dog, and I will have satisfaction from you for the favour, man to man, before ever I turn my back on Shrewsbury!'

3

LIKE A FLUNG STONE IN A PLACID POOL, THIS VIOLENT INVASION cast out flurries of ripples in all directions, to beat against gatehouse and guest-hall and cloister. Brother Denis fluttered uncertainly at gaze, unaware even of the identity of this large and very angry youth, and desirous only of restoring peace in the court, but without the least notion of how to set about it. Picard, brought up almost breast to breast with the solid young body and grim face, flamed red to the cheekbones, and then blanched white with answering fury. He could not go forward, he would not go aside, and even if the startled cluster of servants had not been pressing close behind, he would not have given back by an inch. Agnes glared outrage, and quickly reached to grip Iveta by the arm, for the girl had started forward with a faint, desolate cry, the subdued stillness of her face broken, and for one moment sparkling with frantic emotion, as shattered ice takes the light and dazzles. Just for that instant she would have forgotten everything but the boy, sprung to his side without conceal, flung her arms round him, if her aunt's grasp had not plucked her back without gentleness, drawn her close to a rigid, sombrely gowned side, and held her there with steely fingers. Whether from long submission or from newly alerted wit, she shrank and was still, and the light, but not the pain, ebbed out of her face. Cadfael saw it, and was inextricably caught. No young thing hardly out of her nurse's care should so suffer.

He remembered that look later. At this moment he was held by the impact of Joscelin Lucy's wildly unwise youth and God-frid Picard's subtle, experienced maturity. It was not so un-equal a combat as might have been expected. The boy was above himself, and unquestionably a man of his hands, and a son of confident, if minor, privilege.

'I may not ask you to draw, here,' he said high and clearly. Anger raised his voice, as though to reach a marshal in the lists. 'I challenge you to name the place and time where we may draw, to good effect. You have done me an offence, I am cast off by reason of your persuasion, do me right, and stand to what you have urged against me.'

'Insolent rogue!' Picard spat back at him disdainfully. 'I am more likely to set my hounds on you than dignify you by cross-ing swords with you. If you are dismissed for a profitless, treacherous, meddling, ill-conditioned wretch, you are rightly served, be thankful your lord did not have you whipped from his door. You have got off lightly. Take care you don't provoke worse usage than you already have. Now stand out of my way, and get you gone homewards, as you were ordered.'

'Not I!' vowed Joscelin through his teeth. 'Not until I have said all that I have to say, here before all these witnesses. Nor will I go for being ordered. Does Huon de Domville own the ground I stand on and the air I breathe? His service he can keep, there are other households at least as honourable as his. But to run with mean tales to him, and blacken my name, was that fair dealing?'

Picard gave vent to a wordless bellow of impatient rage, and turned to snap imperious fingers at his menservants, half a dozen of whom, solid men-at-arms of an age to be experienced in rough play, came forth blithely enough, three on either side, closing in a half-circle.

'Take this wastrel out of my sight. The river is handy. Put him to cool in the mud!'

The women drew back in a flurry of skirts, Agnes and the maid dragging Iveta away by both wrists. The men-at-arms advanced, grinning but wary, and Joscelin was obliged to take some paces back, to avoid being encircled.

'Stand clear!' he warned, glaring. 'Let the coward do his own work, for if you lay hand on me there'll be blood let.'

He had so far forgotten himself as to lay hand to hilt, and draw the blade some inches from the scabbard. Cadfael judged that it was high time to intervene, before the young man put himself hopelessly in the wrong, and both he and Brother Denis were starting forward to thrust between the antagonists, when from the cloister surged the tall presence of Prior Robert, monumentally displeased, and from the direction of the abbot's lodging, swift and silent and thus far unnoticed, the equally tall and far more daunting figure of Abbot Radulfus himself, hawk-faced, shrewd-eyed, and coldly but composedly angry.

'Gentlemen, gentlemen!' Robert spread long, elegant hands between. 'You do yourselves and our house great dishonour. Think shame to touch weapon or threaten violence within these walls!'

The men-at-arms recoiled thankfully into the crowd. Picard stood smouldering but controlled. Joscelin shot his sword very hastily back into the sheath, but stood breathing heavily and cherishing his fury. He was not an easy young man to abash, and harder still to silence. He made a half-turn that brought him eye to eye with the abbot, who had reached the borders of the dispute, and stood lofty, dark and calm, considering all the offenders at leisure. There fell a silence.

'Within the bounds of this abbey,' said Radulfus at last, without raising his voice, 'men do not brawl. I will not say we never hear an angry word. We are also men. Sir Godfrid, keep your men at heel on these premises. And you, young man, so much as touch your hilt again, and you shall lie in a penitent's cell overnight.'

Joscelin bent head and knee, though the abbot might well have thought the gesture somewhat perfunctory. 'My lord abbot, I ask your pardon! Threatened or no, I was at fault.' But owning his fault, he kept his rage. A close observer might even have wondered if he was not contemplating the possible advantages of offending again, and being cast as promised into a cell within these walls. Locks may be picked, lay brothers suborned or tricked—yes, there were possibilities! He was disadvantaged, however, by a fair-minded disposition not to offend those who had committed no offence against him. 'I stand in your mercy,' he said.

'Good, we understand each other. Now, what is this dispute that troubles the peace here?'

Both Joscelin and Picard began to talk at once, but Joscelin, for once wise, drew back and left the field to his elder. He stood biting a resolute lip and regarding the abbot's face, as Picard brushed him contemptuously aside in the terms he had expected.

'Father, this impertinent squire has been turned off by his lord for a negligent, ill-conditioned fellow, and he credits me with so advising my lord Domville, as indeed I felt it my duty to do. For I have found him presumptuous, pressing his company upon my niece, and in all ways a troubler of the peace. He came here to brawl with me, resenting his well-deserved dismissal. He has no more than his due, but he will not be schooled. And that is all the matter,' he said scornfully.

Brother Cadfael marvelled how Joscelin kept his mouth shut on the flood of his grievance, and his eyes fixed respectfully upon Radulfus, until he was invited to speak. He must surely have acquired in these few moments a healthy respect for the abbot's fairness and shrewd sense, so to contain himself. He had confidence that he would not be judged unheard, and it was worth an effort at self-control to manage his defence aright.

'Well, young sir?' said Radulfus. It could not be asserted that he smiled, his countenance remained judicially remote and calm; but there might have been the suggestion of indulgence in his voice.

'Father Abbot,' said Joscelin, 'all of us of these two houses came here to see a marriage performed. The bride you have seen.' She had been hustled away out of sight, into the guest-hall, long before this. 'She is eighteen years old. My lord—he that *was* my lord!—is nearing sixty. She has been these last eight years orphaned and in her uncle's care, and she has great lands, long in her uncle's administration.' Some indication of his unexpected drift had penetrated by then, Picard was boiling and voluble. But Radulfus dipped a frowning brow, and raised a silencing hand, and they gave way perforce.

'Father Abbot, I pray your help for Iveta de Massard!' Joscelin had gained his moment, and could not hold back. 'Father, the honour of which she is lady spans four counties and fifty manors, it is an earl's portion. They have farmed it between them, uncle and bridegroom, they have parcelled it out, she is bought and sold, without her will—Oh, God, she has no will left, she is tamed—*against* her will! My offence is that I love her, and I would have taken her away out of this prison . . .'

The latter half of this, though Cadfael had drawn close enough to hear all, was certainly lost to most others under a shrill clamour of refutation, in which Agnes played the loudest part. She had a voice that rode high over opposition, Joscelin could not cry her down. And in the midst of the hubbub, suddenly there were crisp hoofbeats in the gateway, and horsemen pacing into the court with the authority of office, and in numbers calculated to draw ear and eye. The thread alike of Joscelin's appeal and Picard's refutation was broken abruptly; every eye turned to the gate.

First came Huon de Domville, the muscles of his face set like a wrestler's biceps, his small, black, malevolent eyes alertly bright. Close at his elbow rode Gilbert Prestcote, sheriff of Shropshire under King Stephen, a lean, hard, middle-aged knight browed and nosed like a falcon, his black, forked beard veined with grey. He had a sergeant and seven or eight officers at his back, an impressive array. He halted them within the gate, and dismounted as they did.

'And there he stands!' blared Domville, eyes glittering upon Joscelin, who stood startled and gaping. 'The rascal himself! Did I not say he'd be stirring up trouble everywhere possible before he took himself off? Seize him, sheriff! Lay hold on the rogue and make him fast!'

He had been so intent on his quarry that he had not immediately observed that the abbot himself was among those present. His eye lit on the austere and silent figure belatedly, and he dismounted and doffed in brusque respect. 'By your leave, Father Abbott! We have dire business here, and I am all the sorrier that this young rogue should have brought it within your walls.'

'Such disturbance as he has so far caused us,' said Radulfus coolly, 'does not seem of a sort to require the attendance of sheriff and sergeant. I gather that if he has offended, he has also been brought to book for it. To dismiss him your service is your right. To pursue him further seems somewhat excessive. Unless you have further complaint to make against him?' He looked to Prestcote for his answer.

'There is indeed more,' said the sheriff. 'I am instructed by my lord Domville that since this squire was ordered to pack and go, a thing of great value has been missed, and looked for in vain within the household. There is ground for suspicion that this man may have stolen it in despite of his lord, and in revenge for his dismissal. He stands so charged.'

Joscelin was staring in astonished derision, not yet even angry on this count, and certainly not afraid. 'I, steal?' he gasped in huge contempt. 'I would not touch the meanest thing that belonged to him, I would not willingly take away on my shoes the dust of his courtyard. Go, he bade me, and so I did, out of his house, and have not even stopped to gather together everything that was mine there. All that I brought away is here on my body or in the saddle-bags there.'

The abbot raised a restraining hand. 'My lord, what is this valuable thing which is lost? How does it bulk? When was it missed?'

'It is the wedding gift I intended for my bride,' said the baron, 'a collar of gold and pearls. It could lie in the palm of a man's hand, once out of its case. I meant to bring it to the girl today, after Mass, but when I went to take it, and looked within the case, I found it empty. Nigh on an hour ago, I suppose, for we wasted time hunting for it, though the leaving of the empty case should have told us it was not lost, but stolen. And but for this turbulent boy, who was turned off for good reason and took it very defiantly, no one else has left my household. I charge him with the theft, and I will have the remedy of law, to the last particle.'

'But did this young man know of this collar, and where to lay hand on it?' demanded the abbot.

'I did, Father,' Joscelin acknowledged readily. 'So did all three of us who served him as squires.'

Still more horsemen had appeared in the gateway, several of Domville's outridden retinue, and among them Simon and Guy, by the look of their faces by no means eager to be noticed or take any part in this encounter. They looked on from the background, uncertain and unhappy, as well they might.

'But I have not touched it,' Joscelin went on firmly. 'And here am I, just as I left the house, take me away and strip me if you will, you'll find never a thread that is not mine. And there is my horse and my saddle-bags, turn out whatever you find, and let the lord abbot be witness. But no, he added vehemently, seeing Domville himself make a move towards the grey horse, 'not you, my lord! I will not have my accuser's hands pawing my belongings. Let an impartial judge do the searching. Father Abbot, I appeal to your justice!'

'That is but fair,' said the abbot. 'Robert, will you do what is needful?'

Prior Robert received the request with a dignified inclination of the head, and made a solemn procession of his advance upon the duty allotted him. Two of Prestcote's men-at-arms unbuckled the saddle-bags from their place, and when the horse, nervous at the press of people, sidled unhappily, Simon impulsively slipped down from his mount and ran to take the bridle and soothe the fidgety grey. The saddle-bags lay open on the cobbles of the court. Prior Robert plunged his hands into the first, and began to hand out the simple items of clothing and accoutrement their raging owner had stuffed unceremoniously within, barely an hour previously. The sergeant received them solemnly, Prestcote standing close by. Linen shirts, crumpled in a furious fist, chausses, tunics, shoes, a few items of spare harness, gloves . . .

Prior Robert ran his long hand about the interior to show that it was empty. He leaned to the second. Joscelin stood braced on long, shapely legs, barely attentive, his bold brown face arrogantly smiling. Though his mother, Cadfael thought, watching, would have something pithy to say about the way he handled the shirts she made for him, when he got home. *If* he got home . . .

And how if he did? What followed then for the girl who had been hustled away and shut up somewhere with the elderly maidservant for gaoler? In all this she was the absent witness. No one asked her what she knew or what she thought. She was not a person, merely a piece of valuable merchandise.

The second bag yielded a handsome gown for best wear, villainously crumpled, sundry belts and baldrics, a blue capuchon, more shirts, a pair of soft shoes, a best pair of chausses, also blue. The mother who had made all these had had an eye fondly to her offspring's fair colouring and blue eyes. And marvel, there was a bound book in thin, carved wooden covers, the young man's prayer book. He had said that he was lettered.

Lastly, Prior Robert plucked out a small roll of fine linen, and began to unwrap it on his palm. He raised a wondering and approving face.

'It is a silver scallop-shell medal. Whoever owned it made the pilgrimage to Compostella, to the shrine of Saint James.'

'It is my father's,' said Joscelin.

'And that is all. This bag is also empty.'

Domville started forward suddenly with a crow of triumph. 'Ah, but what's here? There's something yet in the linen roll—I caught a glint . . .' He plucked at the dangling end of the cloth, almost wrenching it from the prior's hand. The silver medallion fell to the ground, some inches more of its wrapping unrolled, and something flashed and fell after, uncoiling like a little golden snake, to lie in a pool of fine yellow links and creamy pearls between the cobbles at Joscelin's feet.

He was so dumbfounded that he could not find a word to say, but stood staring at the small, precious thing that damned him. When at last he raised his eyes, and caught the intent gaze of all those other eyes, Domville gleefully content, the sheriff grimly satisfied, the abbot aloof and sad, and everywhere mute accusation, he shook violently, stirring out of his shocked stillness. He cried out passionately that he had not taken it, that it was not he who had put it there. But he uttered his denial only once, recognising at once its inevitability and its uselessness. He had some mad thought of putting up a fight for it, but met the abbot's stern, disillusioned eye, and deliberately put away the thought. Not here! He had pledged himself to forswear offence against this place. So here there was nothing he could do but submit. Once outside the gates it would be another matter, and the surer they were of his submission, the fewer crippling precautions they were likely to take. He stood mute and unresisting as the sergeant and his men closed in upon him.

They stripped him of sword and dagger, and kept close hold of him by both arms, but because they were many and he was but one, and seemed utterly subdued, they did not trouble to bind him. Domville stood by, vengefully grinning, and did not deign to stoop to pick up his property, leaving it for Simon to hurry forward, abandoning the grey horse's bridle, to retrieve the collar and hand it to him. He cast a very doubtful and anxious look at Joscelin as he did so, but said never a word. The Picards looked on with evident and malicious satisfaction. A nuisance out of their way, and if Domville pleased, out of everyone's way, for ever. Such a theft, with the additional odour of petty treason about it, even if he had already been dismissed his lord's service, could cost a man his neck.

'I will have the full penalty of law on him,' said Domville, and fixed a commanding stare upon the sheriff.

'That will be matter for the court,' said Prestcote shortly, and turned to his sergeant. 'Have him away to the castle. I must have some talk with Sir Godfrid Picard and the lord abbot, I'll follow you.'

The prisoner went with lamb-like meekness, his fair head drooping, his arms lax and submissive in the grip of two brawny men-at-arms. Brothers and guests and servants fell away to leave him passage, and a horrified silence closed after his passing.

Brother Cadfael was left gazing as numbly as the rest. It was hard indeed to recognise the belligerent youngster who had galloped into the great court so short a time before, or the audacious lover who had penetrated into the enemy's territory to plot something desperate with a girl too frightened to reach for what her heart desired. Cadfael could not believe in such sudden translations. On impulse he made off towards the gate in haste, to keep the sorry little procession in sight. Behind him as he went he heard Simon Aguilon's voice asking: 'Shall I take his grey back to our stable, sir? We cannot abandon the poor beast, *he's* done no wrong.' It was not quite clear from the tone whether he believed the poor beast's master had done any, but Cadfael doubted it. He could not be the only one who had reservations about that theft.

Joscelin and his guards were reaching the approaches of the bridge when Cadfael emerged into the Foregate and hastened after them. The hill of Shrewsbury, with its towers and houses cresting the long line of the wall, gleamed fitfully in a moist and feeble sunshine beyond the full flow of the Severn, and far to the right the tall bulk of the castle showed, the prison to which prisoner and escort were now bound. Since the height of the summer there had been heavy rains, and the flood coming down from Wales had swelled the flow here into a rapid high water that swallowed the lower reaches of the islands. The nearest section of the bridge, the drawbridge that could cut off approach to the town at need, was down and bearing plenteous traffic, for the last of the harvest was coming in, fruit and roots for fodder, and the provident were looking to their stores for the winter. Three horsemen rode ahead of the prisoner and his escort, three more brought up the rear, but Joscelin and those who held him went on foot, not briskly, for no prisoner in his right mind is in any haste to have a cell door slammed on him, but not slowly, either, for he was sharply prodded when he hung back. Carts and townspeople afoot drew to the side out of their way, and stood to stare, some so interested that they forgot themselves and closed in again at once, staring after, and barred the way for the following horsemen.

There had frequently been high feeling between the town and the king's sheriff of the shire, and Prestcote's sergeant was wary of using whip or threat on burgesses whose retaliatory sting had sometimes proved sharp. Thus it happened that when the prisoner had passed through the narrowing gate of the drawbridge tower, and the starers turned to gape and blocked the way, the following horsemen contented themselves with calling civilly for passage, and an increasing gap opened between them and their charge. Cadfael, slipping nimbly past the horses to join the curious in the gateway, had a partial view of what followed.

Still dejectedly slouching, Joscelin had reached the crown of the bridge's central span, where the parapet was no more than waist-high. It appeared that he stumbled, allowing the three before, who were archers, to move a yard or so ahead before they realised it. There was a cart drawn aside to the left, the entire group therefore moved to the right to pass by. As they drew near to the wall, Joscelin suddenly braced the deceptively limp sinews of his fine large body, swept both the guards who held him round in a dizzying circle to the right, sweeping them off their feet before they knew what was happening, tore his arms free, and leaped one sprawling adversary to reach the wall. One of those following clawed desperately at his foot as he vaulted to the parapet, but he kicked out vigorously and sent the man staggering. Before any other could get a hand to him, he had leaped strongly out over the flood, and plunged feet-first and cleanly into the centre of the river, and there vanished from sight.

It was beautifully done, and Cadfael, who saw it, could not but rejoice. For no good reason, he was suddenly sure in his own mind that Joscelin Lucy had never laid hand on Domville's gold, that Agnes's report to her husband of the meeting in the herb-garden, and Picard's complaint and warning to the imperilled bridegroom, had occasioned the boy's dismissal, and the dismissal had been expressly designed to make it possible to pursue the young man on a false charge of theft, and cast him safely into prison, out of the way of wide-ranging plans. They could not afford to leave him loose. He must go.

And he was gone, but of his own will, magnificently. Cadfael was leaning breathlessly over the downstream parapet like dozens of other eager watchers. Voices clamoured, some impartial, some partisan. There would always be plenty of law-abiding citizens here to cheer on any prisoner who broke free from the sheriff's hold.

The sergeant, who would certainly be held responsible for the loss, had leaped into action with a bellow of rage, and was roaring orders fore and aft at his men. The two horsemen ahead were sent galloping forward, to ride down to the riverside under the town walls, the three behind were turned back to perform the same service upon the abbey bank, to be ready to pick up the fugitive on whichever shore he tried to land. But both parties had to go roundabout, while the Severn, faster than any of them, went surging serenely forward, bearing away the invisible quarry downstream. The foot soldiers who were left had two archers among them, and at the sergeant's order they strung their bows in haste and thrust their way to the parapet, clearing away the gathering crowds that might hamper their drawing arms.

'Fast as he breaks surface,' yelled the sergeant, 'loose at him! Wing him if you can, kill him if you must!'

Minutes slid by, while the riders reached shore and began to wind a reckless way down to the waterside, and still there was no sign of the flaxen crest breaking the smooth-running surface.

'He's gone!' someone lamented, and some of the women drew pitying sighs.

'Not he!' shrilled an urchin flat on his belly across the parapet. 'See there? Nimble as an otter!'

Joscelin's pale head sprang up for a moment, sleek and streaming, far downstream. An arrow struck and drew shivering ripples only a foot or so aside, but by then he was back under the water, and when he again broke clear to draw breath he was almost out of bowshot. A second shaft fell well short of him, and he stayed in mid-stream, in full view, letting the flow take him with it, apparently as much at home in the water as he was on land. The archers got a derisive cheer for their pains from the imps of the town, or such of them as were safely out of reach, while the glimpse of a long arm impudently waving farewell from downstream raised a great ripple of half-suppressed laughter.

On either bank the horsemen coursed, hopelessly outdistanced, two threading their way along the path under the town wall and the abbot's vineyard, three now far along the rich level on the other side, where the abbey's main vegetable gardens and orchards stretched the length of the fields called the Gaye. They had as much hope of overtaking Joscelin Lucy as of holding their own with the floating leaves that surged past on the central current. The Severn ran silently and without fuss, but deadly fast.

They were craning and straining now after a fair head no larger than a little clot of foam spun by an unexpected eddy. Now barely visible, the next moment not visible at all. He had dived again, to make sure, thought Cadfael, watching intently, that no one should see which shore he approached, or where he drew himself out of the water. He was beyond the vineyard, he had the vast bulk of the castle walls on his left hand, bushes and low trees clothing the waste ground below, and on his right, beyond the orchards, woodlands coming down to the waterside. Small doubt which he would choose, but he refrained from showing himself again until he was ashore and into the trees. Cadfael, selecting carefully what seemed the most favourable cover, thought he caught, not so much a glimpse of the man, as a momentary convulsion of the leaning branches, and a brief sparkle in the water, as Joscelin hauled himself up the bank and vanished into the woods.

There was no more to see or to do here. Cadfael recalled himself to his neglected duty, and made off back to the abbey gatehouse, turning his back upon the gratified urchins and cursing guards. Small profit now in wondering how the boy would fare, weaponless, horseless, without money or dry clothing, and with a certain hue and cry out after him from this moment. Better make himself as scarce as ever he could, on foot or however offered, and put all the space possible between himself and Shrewsbury before night. All the same, Cadfael found himself doubting very much whether he would do anything so sensible.

It came as no great surprise to find that the news had gone before him. Just as he was approaching the gatehouse, Gilbert Prestcote came cantering out with a face of thunder, his remaining men-at-arms hard on his heels. He had nothing against Joscelin Lucy, and by his bearing throughout, no particular reverence for Huon de Domville, but the incompetence of his sergeant would stick in his craw like a nutshell, and unless the prisoner was recovered in short order, there was likely to be a stormy time ahead for all the luckless guards.

The porter emerged cautiously as the dust was settling, to gaze after them, and shook a rueful head as Cadfael came up. 'So the thief got away from them, after all! There'll be the devil to pay now, he'll turn out the whole garrison after the lad. And him on foot to outrun their horses! His own's away back to the bishop's house with the other young squire.'

They were gone, Huon de Domville, Simon Aguilon, Guy

FitzJohn, grooms and all, and if the news of the escape had only so far reached the abbey gatehouse, they were gone in the firm belief that the thief was safe in hold.

'Who brought the word?' asked Cadfael. 'He was quick off the mark. He can't have stayed to see the play out.'

'Two lay brothers were just coming up from the Gaye with the last of the late apples. They saw him jump, and came in a hurry to tell. But you're not far behind them.'

So as yet it was cried no furthere than here. There were plenty of people, brothers, servants and guests, stirring about the great court in excitement and speculation, and some sallying forth to see what was toward along the riverbank. Huon de Domville's displeasure, when the word overtook him, would be vented elsewhere. Here Cadfael observed Godfrid and Agnes Picard in the doorway of the guest-hall, absorbed in some low-voiced and intent colloquy of their own, and their faces were taut and wary, and the way they eyed each other was all calculation and alarm. This development would not suit them at all; they wanted the troublesome boy safe behind locked doors in the castle, with a neck-charge hanging over him if Domville chose to press it to extremes.

There was no sign of Iveta. No doubt she was shut away within, with Agnes's dragon to guard her. Nor did she appear for some hours, though her uncle and aunt were seen purposefully crossing and recrossing between the abbot's lodging, the guest-hall and the gatehouse on several occasions, and once Picard rode out for the greater part of an hour, surely to the bishop's house to confer with Domville. Cadfael fretted through the early afternoon over his own responsibility, neglectful of his customary watch on Oswin's activities, and somewhat chastened to discover that, for once unregarded, his assistant had spilled nothing, burned nothing, weeded out no precious plants by mistake, and broken nothing. It might, of course, be a special dispensation of providence, a courtesy to Cadfael's obvious preoccupation, but it might just as well be a reproof to him for keeping too unnerving an eye on his pupil.

His problem was simple to state but hard to solve. Ought he to go to Abbot Radulfus, and tell him just what he had witnessed and taken part in, the previous evening? To interfere in the affairs of complete strangers on such brief and suspect evidence may be a dangerous business, however well-meant. For all he knew, the plausible boy might be a fortune-hunter who had attempted to seduce Iveta into decamping with him for his own ends; and certainly he was quite attractive enough to have won her over. Yet however Cadfael tried to view the people concerned from all angles, without prejudice, he could not discover in the Picards any vestige of warmth or tenderness towards the girl.

The matter was solved for him when Abbot Radulfus sent for him, halfway through the afternoon. He obeyed the summons in mild speculation, and even milder apprehension, reflecting philosophically that lies may not always be so easily forgiven, even when well intended. Besides, it would be unwise to underestimate Agnes Picard, even if he had not so far taken any steps to get in her way, beyond pouring opportunist oil on very stormy waters.

'I have received a complaint about you, Brother Cadfael,' said the abbot, turning with deliberation from his writing-desk. His voice, as always, was cool, incisive and courteous, his face unreadably calm. 'Oh, not by name, but I fancy the brother who was still at work in the herb-garden after supper last night is hardly likely to be any but you.'

'I was there,' said Cadfael readily. There was but one way of dealing with Radulfus, and that was directly and openly.

'In company with the Lady Iveta, and that young man who is now being hunted among the riverside coverts? And conniving with them in so irregular a meeting?'

'Hardly the one or the other,' said Cadfael. 'I walked in upon them in my own workshop, to my discomfort and theirs. So did Lady Picard only a moment later. That I put as soothing a face on it as possible, that I do avow. There was tempest threatening. Let us say I fired an arrow or two to break the clouds.'

'One version,' said the abbot serenely, 'I have heard from Sir Godfrid, who no doubt had it from his lady. Let me hear yours.'

Cadfael told it, as fully as he could recall, though he stopped short of mentioning Joscelin's reckless claim that he would not stop at murder. Hot-headed youngsters say such things, while their faces and their manner belie them. At the end of it Radulfus peered at him long and frowningly, and pondered.

'For your shufflings with truth, Brother Cadfael, I leave that to your confessor. But do you truly believe that this girl is afraid of her kinsman? That she is being enforced to courses hateful to her? I heard for myself what the accused man said. But he stood to gain greatly if he won her away from the marriage planned for her, and his motive may be as rotten as greed always is. A comely person is no warranty of a comely spirit. It may well be that her uncle has planned well for her, and it would be sin to disrupt his plans.'

'There is one particular,' said Cadfael carefully, 'that troubles me most. This girl is never seen alone, but always with uncle and aunt fencing her in on either side. She barely speaks, for someone else always speaks for her. I would be satisfied in my mind if you, Father, could but once speak with her freely alone, without witnesses, and listen to her unprompted.'

The abbot considered, and admitted gravely: 'There is much in what you say. It may be nothing but over-care that hems her so, yet her own voice should also be free to speak. How if I should pay a visit myself to the guest-hall, and see if I cannot make occasion to be alone with her? It would settle my mind, no less than yours. For I tell you frankly, Sir Godfrid assures me this squire has misused the entry he enjoyed as his lord's attendant, to pay furtive court to the girl, who was content enough before, and turn her head with his attentions and compliments. If that is all, this morning's happenings may have opened her eyes, and caused her to reconsider.'

There was no telling from his words or manner whether he accepted unquestioningly the truth of the accusation of theft, or the evidence of his eyes. He was too subtle not to have examined the alternatives.

'I intend,' he said, 'to invite the bridegroom with his nephew, and Sir Godfrid Picard, to sup with me here tonight. It gives me the occasion to carry the invitation myself. Why not now?'

Why not, indeed? Cadfael went out with him into the misty autumn afternoon cautiously pleased with the interview. Radulfus was an aristocrat and the equal of a baron, and entertained austere ideas of the duty of young people to be guided by those set in authority over them; but he was not blind to the frequent failings of elders, thus privileged, to impose benevolent order on the lives of their children. Let him but once gain some moments alone with Iveta, and he could not fail to win her confidence. She would not let slip such a chance. In this household he was master, he could stretch his hand over her and she would be protected even against kings.

They came out through the abbot's garden into the great court, and crossed towards the guest-hall. Cadfael would have taken his leave and returned to the gardens, but instead, they both halted at gaze. For on the stone bench by the wall of the refectory Iveta was sitting, her eyes diligently lowered over the prayer book in her lap, the veiled sunlight a soft sheen over her dark-gold hair. The confutation of everything that had been said of her: she was alone, seated there in the open quietly reading, not another soul of her uncle's household in sight.

Radulfus checked and gazed, and turning, made for the place where she was sitting. She heard, perhaps, the rustle of his habit; his walk was all but silent. She looked up, and her face was almost glacially calm and still. So white was her skin that it was hard to say whether she showed paler than normal, but when she saw the abbot bearing down on her she smiled, at least with her lips, and rose to make him a delicate reverence. Cadfael had drawn close at his back, hardly believing, not at all understanding, what he saw.

'Daughter,' said Radulfus gently, 'I am glad to see you thus at peace. I feared this morning's upsets must have disturbed you sadly, when you are contemplating so solemn a change in your estate, and have need of consideration and calm. You had, I think, a better opinion of that young man than he deserved, and cannot have been prepared for such a discovery. I am sure it distressed you.'

She looked up at him with a clear, still face, and unblinking eyes steady but empty, and said: 'Yes, Father. I never thought any evil of him. But I have put my doubts by me now. I know my duty.' Her voice was very low, but quite firm and deliberate.

'And your mind is at rest about tomorrow's sacrament? I, too, have a duty, my child, towards all who come within my cure here. I am accessible to all. If there is anything you wish to say to me, do so freely, and there shall no one prevent or persuade but I will hear you faithfully. Your peace, your happiness, is my concern while you are within my walls, and shall have my prayers after you leave them.'

'I do believe it,' said Iveta, 'and I thank you. But my mind is settled and content, Father. I see my way clear, I am not to be swayed any more.'

The abbot looked at her long and earnestly, and she met his eyes without a quiver, and maintained her pale, resolute smile. Radulfus chose to have everything plainly stated, for this might be the only opportunity. 'I understand well that this marriage you will be making tomorrow is very much to the mind of your uncle and aunt, and suitable in rank and fortune. But is it also to your mind, daughter? You undertake it of your own will?'

She opened already wide eyes even wider, purple as irises, and parted innocently wondering lips, and said simply: 'Yes, of course, Father. Certainly of my own will. I am doing what I know it is right and good that I should do, and I do it with all my heart.'

4 ♨

SIMON AGUILON TOOK ADVANTAGE OF THE HOUR WHILE HIS
lord was sleeping off his dinner and his rage together, and
slipped away alone and in haste through the bishop's rear garden, down past the barns and orchards, and let himself out
through the wicket in the wall, into the belt of scattered woodland that ran parallel with the Foregate. Somewhere well downstream, so the witnesses had said, Joscelin has vanished from
view, and somewhere quite close to the spot where he was last
seen he must have come ashore. Surely on the right bank, away
from the castle. Why heave oneself ashore in the very nest of
the enemy, even if there was cover to be had? There was better
on the abbey shore, well below the Gaye.

They were hunting him, of course, but methodically, without
haste. The first step had been to plant guards on all the roads
that radiated from the town, and space roaming patrols between, to make a ring through which he could scarcely hope to
break. Once that was done, they could afford to be slow and

thorough in sifting all the cover within the ring. He had neither horse nor weapon, nor any means of getting either. Domville, once apprised of his flight, had had the grey horse removed from the common stable where Simon had taken him, and locked away privately, for fear his owner should venture in during the night to get possession of him and make a bid for escape. It was only a matter of time before he was re-taken.

Simon made his way deep into the woods downstream, until he considered he must have penetrated somewhere near the place where Joscelin had come ashore. Here, well inland, the growth was thick, with plenteous underbrush, and he found two separate small streams making their way towards the river. Wet as he would already be, Joscelin could well afford to use the bed of one of these as his path, in case they brought out dogs to hunt him. Simon followed the second stream inland into deep woodland. When he halted to listen, there was no sound anywhere about him but the occasional note of a bird. He stood with pricked ears, and began to whistle a dance tune they had picked up together from Domville's chaplain, who had a gift for music, and relished secular songs as well as the liturgy.

Simon had made his way gradually a further quarter of a mile away from the river, still whistling his estampie at intervals, before he got a response. The thick bushes on his right rustled, a hand was put out to part them, and he caught the gleam of a wary eye peering out.

'Joss?' he said in a whisper. Even if the hunt had not yet come this way, an inquisitive peasant gathering wood could give the alarm and spoil all. But the woodland silence hung undisturbed.

'Simon?' He was slow to trust. 'Are they making you their decoy? I never touched his damned gold.'

'I never thought you did. Hush, keep in cover!' Simon drew nearer, to hear and be heard in whispers. 'I'm here alone, I came to look for you. You can't lie out tonight, soaked from the river. I can't get your horse out to you yet, he's locked away. And all the roads are barred. You'll have to sit it out in hiding a

59

day or so, until they lose interest and grow slack. *He'll* give over wanting your blood, once tomorrow's over.'

The bushes shook with Joscelin's tremor of protest and detestation, for after tomorrow all would be lost, and all won. 'God witness,' he said through his teeth, 'I'll not give over thirsting for his. If they do marry her, I can still widow her.'

'Hush, you fool, never say such things! Supposing others heard you? You're safe enough with me, I'll help you as best I can, but . . . Be still and let me think!'

'I can shift for myself,' said Joscelin, rising cautiously erect in his covert, soiled and draggled, his fair hair plastered to his head still, but drying in wilful drifts of yellow at his temples. 'You're a good fellow, Simon, but I advise you take no foolish risks for me.'

'What do you want me to do?' Simon sounded exasperated. 'Stand back and let you be taken? See here, the safest place for you now, the one place they'll never think to look, is inside the bishop's grounds. Oh, not in house or stables or court, naturally. But that's the one household and garden this hunt is going to pass by. Everyone else's barns and byres will be ransacked. There's a hut in the corner of the grounds, by the door I came out at, where they store the hay from the back field. You could lie dry enough there, and I could bring you food—and the wicket in the wall we can bar inside, no one can come through from without. Then, if I can get Briar out to you somehow . . . What do you say?'

It was good sense enough, and Joscelin said yes to it with fervour and gratitude. What he did not say was that the want of a horse was nothing to him as yet, for he had no intention of going anywhere until either he had found some way of rescuing Iveta, or lost hope and heart and probably life in the attempt.

'You're a good friend, and I won't forget it. But take care for yourself, one of us in this coil is enough. Listen!' He caught Simon by the wrist, and shook him earnestly. 'If things fall out badly, and I'm ferreted out and taken, you knew nothing of it, I made my own way. Deny me, with all my goodwill. If there's meat or other matter to account for, I'll say I stole, and you'll let it rest at that. Promise! I should be ashamed if I brought you into question.'

'You'll not be taken,' said Simon firmly.

'No, but promise!'

'Oh, very well, since you're so set, I'll let you stew—or at least go roundabout to hook you out of it. I like my skin whole, like most men, I'll take good care of it, one way or another. Come on, then! While things are quiet and I'm not missed.'

The way back was shorter, since they could make directly for the rear wall of the bishop's garden, and there was cover all the way. Once or twice Simon, going before, set up a soft whistling, and Joscelin dropped into the bushes, but each alarm passed in a moment, the small sounds that had set it off traced to birds taking flight, or wild things creeping among the dry brush. The wicket in the wall stood ajar as Simon had left it. He went first to open it cautiously and look round within, and then beckoned, and Joscelin dived through it thankfully, and heard it closed and barred behind him. And there was the low wooden fodder-store close against the wall. Within, it smelled of dry grass, and the fine dust stirred by their feet tickled the nose, and stung.

'No one will come here,' said Simon, low-voiced. 'The stables in the yard are well stocked. And it's snug enough lying. Keep close and quiet. I go with my uncle to sup with the abbot tonight, but I'll bring you meat and drink before then. You'll dry off nicely here in the hay.'

'It's a palace,' said Joscelin heartily, and squeezed his friend's arm with grateful warmth. 'I'll not forget this to you. Whatever happens now, praise God, I shall know there's one person who refuses to believe me a thief, and one friend I can rely on. But bear in mind, if it comes to it, I'd rather sink alone than drag you down into the muck with me.'

'Leave Simon's well-being,' said that young man with a confident grin, 'to one who loves him well. You take care of your own skin, I'll vouch for mine. And now I'm gone! He'll be yelling for me to help him dress for Vespers. That's the price he pays for supping with the abbot!'

Brother Cadfael marked their presence at Vespers, Huon de Domville sombrely splendid for the abbot's table, in rich crimson and black, Canon Eudo imperturbably demure and ascetic, like a much younger Prior Robert studying for sainthood, but keeping a weather eye on the secular prospects around him, all the same. And in attendance, the young squire Simon Aguilon, curly-haired, athletic and discreet, with a brown, open face stricken into unusual gravity by the events of the day.

The Picards also attended, but the bride, Cadfael noted, did not, nor did the elderly maid. He had caught glimpses of Iveta twice during the later afternoon, but once again with a guardian on either side. She maintained her calm and composed bearing, she wore the same pale but proud and confident face, the slight smile was ready to visit her lips at a glance; but only that once, Cadfael reflected thoughtfully, had she been unquestionably alone, unwatched, at liberty to speak her mind without restraint. And so she had, and confounded all expectation. There was no way of getting round it. She had believed the worst of young Joscelin Lucy, and put him out of her grace with a resolution that seemed far beyond her scope. She was reconciled to her marriage and determined to go through with it, in bitter recoil, perhaps, from a far more pleasing dream which had proved disillusionment on waking.

Then she was all too ingenuous, Cadfael decided, and far too easily convinced. Was there not a cup hidden in the sack of the boy Benjamin, in the Bible story, to make it possible to detain him? And had not the same stratagem been used many times since? But she was very young, and had been, perhaps, so artlessly in love that it took little art to overturn her too rash affection. Yet the trouble with things so obviously suspect, after all, is that they may indeed be true.

He watched the guests cross to the abbot's lodging after Vespers, and observed the return of Agnes Picard to the guest-hall.

There was no room for action, nothing to be done about anything. Cadfael went to his own supper in the refectory, and afterwards to the readings in the chapter-house, but had mislaid, for some reason, both his appetite and his concentration.

The abbot's guests, no doubt, supped well, but they did not sit very late afterwards. Cadfael had gone to close his workshop before retiring, well after Compline, and was returning to the dortoir when he saw, by the lantern at the gate, Domville and his squire mounting to return to the bishop's house, and Picard taking his leave of them. Canon Eudo, evidently, was spending the night with the abbot, to see all made ready for the morrow.

They had drunk well enough, by the jovial ring of their voices, but certainly not to excess, since Radulfus was an abstemious man himself, and provided as he thought right and fitting, but not beyond. The sharp yellow light distinguished them scrupulously, showed the baron gross, self-indulgent but powerful still, in purse, possessions, body and mind, in no way a small or inconsiderable man. Picard was slenderer, viewed whichever way, a dark, devious, able man, whose subtlety could well complement Domville's brutal force. Those two together could be formidable to any antagonist. The young man stood patient, assiduous but disinterested, his thoughts probably elsewhere, but his temperament equable. He would not be sorry to heave himself into his bed.

Cadfael watched them ride, saw the youngster hold his lord's stirrup, almost heard his stifled yawn. He mounted after, light and glad, and fell in at Domville's elbow, keeping his station neatly with one hand on the rein. He was certainly sober as stone, aware, probably, of his vulnerable situation, as responsible for getting his lord home and bedded. Picard drew back from them, raising a hand in farewell. The two horses walked at leisure out at the gate, and the measured clop of their hooves on the cobbles of the Foregate faded gradually into silence.

Along the Foregate all was dark, but for the faintly luminous quality of moonless starlight, the sky sparkling after several misted days, the air on the clear, near edge of frost. In one or two windows a candle showed. Outside the bishop's house, where the gate-pillars drew back from the roadway, the wayside trees gave dark green shadow on either flank.

The two horsemen came at an easy walk, and halted briefly in the road, in front of the gates. Their voices, though pitched low, carried clearly in the great stillness.

'Go in, Simon,' said Domville. 'I have a fancy to take the air a while. Send the grooms to bed.'

'And your chamber attendants, sir?'

'Dismiss them. Say I want no service tonight, nor until an hour past Prime tomorrow, unless I call. Make sure it's understood those are my orders.'

The young man bowed his acquiescence without a word. The movement was just perceptible in the utter hush that surrounded it. The man in the shadows, concealing with disciplined stillness an illicit presence thus near the town, heard the slight rustle of a cloak, and the jingle of harness as a horse stirred. Then Simon wheeled obediently and trotted into the courtyard, and Domville shook his bridle and moved onward towards Saint Giles, first at a walk, then breaking into a brisk and purposeful trot.

A shadow among shadows moved along the grassy border of the road after him, with long, uneven strides that made no sound. For a lame man, going upon one foot mangled by disease, he moved at a surprising speed, but he could not maintain the effort for long. But as long as he could hold the steady hoofbeats within earshot, he followed, along the empty Foregate, past the hospice and church, out along the highway beyond. He recognised the moment when the sound, which had been receding steadily, abruptly fell silent, and judged on which side of the road the rider had turned off on to a grassy track. To that spot he continued, no longer in haste.

To the right of the road the ground fell away towards the valley of the Meole brook, and the mill leat that was drawn off from it. Here open woods and scattered copses clothed the slope, below in the valley the trees grew more thickly. Down through this rolling woodland went a grassy ride, wide enough and smooth enough to be ridden safely in the night, with starlight overhead, and half the leaves already shed. By that path Huon de Domville had descended; here the night was empty of sight or sound of him.

The old man turned, and made his way slowly back to Saint Giles, where all his fellows were within doors and asleep, and only he restless and waking. He did not go in, though the outer door was never locked, in case some unfortunate should come in the chill of the night. Before dawn this night might be chill enough, but it was clean and sweet-smelling, and had the pure stillness proper to solitary thought, and he was not sensitive to cold. Outside the fence, in the angle of the cemetery wall, there was a great pile of dried brushings from the final reaping of the grass slope between the hospital and the road. In a day or two it would be carried within to the barn, to store for fodder and litter for the beasts. The old man wrapped his cloak about him, and sat down there on the grass, drawn well back into the stack to have its softness and warmth about him. The clapperdish that hung at his belt he laid beside him on the ground. There was no human creature stirring about him now to need warning of the presence of a leper.

He did not sleep. He sat with head erect and straight back, his hands folded together at rest within his lap, the maimed left one within the sound right. Nothing else in the night was quite so still.

Joscelin had slept for a while in his bed of hay. Simon had brought him bread and meat and wine as he had promised, and his clothes had dried on him; he had lain in less comfort many a time. Only his mind was uncomforted. It was all very well for Simon to speak calmly of being able to make the excuse that the grey needed exercise, and get him from behind locked doors in a day or two, and so help his friend to escape when the hunt slackened, as it must. What use was that? In one more day, let alone two, Iveta would have been sacrificed, and escape without her played no part in Joscelin's plans. It was good of Simon to provide him this refuge, and sensible, no doubt, to advise him to stay within here until flight was possible. Very well-meant advice, and Joscelin was grateful, but he had no intention of taking it. A respite was most welcome, but would be wasted if it did not lead to action before ten o'clock on the morrow.

And here was he, alone, due to be pursued, if not shot, at sight, without a weapon, without a clear idea in his head, and only a few hours of grace left to him.

It was a simple conclusion, at any rate, that he could do nothing here, and if he was to remove himself elsewhere it would have to be during darkness. Even if he could have been provided with a dagger, and made his way undetected into the house, to Domville's bedside while he slept, he knew he could not have used his advantage. It was all very fine talking wildly about killing, but Brother Cadfael had been perfectly right, he could not do it, not by stealth. As for an honest challenge in a good quarrel, Domville would laugh in his face before tossing him back to the sheriff. Not out of cowardice, either, Joscelin conceded. There were very few things in this world that Domville was afraid of, and very few antagonists in the lists he need be afraid of. I am no bad swordsman, Joscelin told himself judicially, but for all his years he could carve and eat me for his dinner. No, disdain, not caution, would reject me.

Unless . . . Unless I could beard him before abbot and canon and guests and all, and strike him in the face, something his dignity would not bear, something done publicly that must be wiped out publicly in blood. For that he might even ride roughshod over the sheriff and the law, for that he might forgo destroying me in slower ways, and want nothing but my heart spitted on his blade. For that he would forget Iveta and wedlock and all, until he had wiped out the insult. And what is more, if I could bring him to that point, he would be meticulous to the last hair, give me breathing-time, provide me a sword the length of his own, kill me punctiliously, honourably. Do him that justice, with weapons he fights fair, even if he sees no reason to extend that scruple to such matters as lying charges backed with forged evidence.

And who knows . . . Who knows? With Iveta's prayers on my side, and all the weight of my grudge into the bargain—for he has dealt foully by me!—who knows but I might prevail? Then, even if they wrung my neck for his lying charge, *she* would be delivered.

To be honest, he did not think much of that conclusion, and not all for his own sake. For Iveta needed to be delivered not only from this detestable match, but from the guardian who preyed on her and her inheritance like murderous ivy on an oak, and would sell her to the next compliant bidder as nimbly as to this one. But even delay was salvation. Things could change. Picard could die. Only fend off tomorrow!

If he was to accomplish anything he must get out of here, and somehow make his way in hiding back to the abbey, where all must be enacted. No hope at all by the Foregate, the road would be patrolled, the gatehouse and the parish door guarded, so much was certain. On every side but one the abbey grounds were surrounded by a high boundary wall. The remaining side was bordered by the Meole brook, no mean water hemming the gardens, but fordable or swimmable. Waters were no threat to Joscelin. If he could get across the Foregate, he could make his way down into the valley, and so back beyond the brook to the abbey precincts. There were copses and coverts there for shelter. And it was downstream the sheriff would be hunting him first.

He turned, rustling, in his bed of hay, sneezed at the tickling of dust in his nostrils, and hastily smothered the sneeze. A fine object he must look to confront and blaze defiance at a baron of the realm, but it was the only hope he had. And to retain it even as a hope he must get out of here and across the Foregate into the valley while it was still night. With a rueful obeisance in the direction of Simon, who had wished him well, and wanted him to lie here like a hare in its form until danger passed.

He had no means of knowing the hour, but when he eased open the door of the hut, and looked out into the garden, the darkness was hearteningly deep. The dead silence was less pleasing; a breeze in the bushes would have covered a chance footstep. And once he was out of the shelter of the high walls even the darkness grew faintly luminous. But it was now or never, and everything seemed still and silent. He lifted the bar of the wicket door and slipped through, and began to make his way by touch of the wall round the bishop's garden enclosure. A narrow belt of trees and a footpath separated the house from its neighbour, and brought him to the edge of the Foregate. He paused there to listen, and found all still. But by the degree of faint light he now found over the open roadway, it must be nearer dawn than he would have liked. Better make haste.

He made a dash for it across the open, light on his feet for all his size, and was almost into the grass on the further side when a stone rolled under his foot with a brief, grating sound. Somewhere along the Foregate, towards the town, a voice exclaimed aloud, another answered with a muted shout, and feet began to run in his direction. There were guards still patrolling the roads out of the town. Joscelin darted onward, down the steep slope of grass towards the mill stream, and checked and dived into the cover of the bushes as he caught an echoing shout from below him. That way, too, was stopped. Two of the roving pickets between the roads were down there ahead of him, and climbing towards him now in a hurry.

He had not yet been sighted by any of them, but there was only one hope, and that was to put as much space as possible between himself and pursuit as quickly as possible, and that meant by the road, where he could hope to show fleeter than the hunters. He scrambled back in haste and took to the grassy rim of the road, running like a deer towards Saint Giles. Behind him he heard those below in the valley calling to their companions, heard the answering shout: 'The thief's abroad! Come up!'

The two on the road came pounding after, but he had a good start of them, and was confident he could outrun them and find a place to go to earth, short of the guard-post that would certainly be stationed on every road. But the next moment he heard a sound that chilled his blood, the sudden clatter of hooves emerging from grass on to a hard roadway. The two patrols from the valley were mounted.

'After him! He's for the open, ride him down!' bellowed one of the runners.

And there they came at a canter, and these he could not hope to outrun, nor to evade the four of them for long if he turned from the road here. He reached Saint Giles, running frantically, and looking about him wildly for any hiding-place, and finding none. On his left the slope of grass rose to the wattle fence and the cemetery wall. Behind him the pursuit grew triumphantly vocal, though not yet close. The curve of the road had cut him off from their view.

Out of the darkness along the wall an unexpected voice, low but peremptory, called: 'Come! Quickly!'

Joscelin swung towards the invitation instinctively, panting, and half-fell up the grassy slope and into the grasp of a long arm held out to him. A lean, tall figure in a voluminous dark cloak had risen from the ground and was ripping a hasty tunnel open in the stack of drying herbage in the angle of the wall. 'Here!' said the voice featureless as the face. 'Hide here!'

Joscelin plunged head-first into the heap, and drew it about him frantically. He felt the old man resume his seat on the ground, spread his cloak again, and lean well back against the stack, felt the long spine erect and bony through cloak and gown and grass. Certainly old, certainly a man. The lowered voice might have belonged to either, muffled as it was, but the shoulders pressed well back against him were wide as his own. One hand reached back to grip his knee through the rustling stems, and enjoin stillness, and he froze in instant obedience. The man masking him had a special stillness of his own, a calm that eased Joscelin's heart and mind by its benevolent contagion.

They were coming. He heard the hoofbeats draw close, heard the foremost horse abruptly pulled up on its haunches, feet sliding on the gravel. He thought that the watcher by the wall had been seen; there was pre-dawn light enough for that, and they had a straight stretch of road ahead of them, and certainly empty. He heard one man dismount, and held his breath in the certainty that he was about to climb the slope.

'Unclean!' called the old man warningly, and clashed the clapper of his dish loudly against the wooden rim. There was wary stillness. The climber had taken heed.

Down on the road the second man laughed. 'He'd need to be mad to exchange even a gaol for a lazarhouse.' He raised his voice; the old and diseased must also be hard of hearing. 'Hark, you, fellow! We're on the heels of a wretch who's wanted for thieving. He was headed this way. Have you seen him?'

'No,' said the old man. His voice, besides being muffled behind a veil, was slow in articulation, as if speech gave him trouble; but with labour and patience the words emerged clearly. 'I've seen no thief.'

'How long have you been sitting there? Have you seen any man pass by here?'

'The night long,' said the arduous voice. 'And no one has passed by.'

By the sound of it the two on foot had arrived by this time, out of breath. The four conferred in low tones. 'He must have slipped aside into the trees and turned back,' said one. 'Turn and take the right of the road. We'll ride on to the barrier and make sure he's not wormed his way ahead in cover, and then come back and take the left side.'

The horses stirred and stamped again, and trotted ahead. The two on foot must have turned back to retrace their steps among the trees, beating the bushes for their quarry as they went. There fell a long silence, which Joscelin was afraid to break.

'Stretch out and be easy,' said the old man at last, without turning his head. 'We cannot move yet.'

'I have an errand I must do,' said Joscelin, leaning close to the hooded ear to be heard. 'For this respite God knows I thank you with all my heart, but I must somehow get to the abbey before daylight, or this liberty you've kept for me will not be worth keeping. I have a thing I must do there, for someone else's sake.'

'What is that thing?' asked the old man equably.

'To prevent, if I can, this marriage they're making today.'

'Ah!' said the patient, deliberate voice. ''Wherefore? And by what means? You may not stir yet, they will be back, and they will look this way and must see all as before. An old leper who has preferred a night under the stars to the cover of a roof—nothing more.' The grass rustled; it might have been the very slight stir of a sigh. 'You understood what passed there? Are you afraid of leprosy, boy?'

'No,' said Joscelin, and wavered and reconsidered. 'Yes! I was, or I thought I was. I hardly know. I know I am more afraid of failing in what I must do.'

'We have time,' said the old man. 'If you are willing to tell me, I am listening.'

Only to such a one, chance met and instantly trusted, could Joscelin have poured out the whole load that weighed on his heart. Suddenly it seemed the most natural thing possible that he should confide without restraint, keep nothing back of his indignant love, the wrong done him, and the greater wrongs done to Iveta. In the middle of his narration the controlling hand pressed his knee for silence and stillness, as the two mounted men passed by again towards the town. And when they were gone, the last echo of hooves lost along the road, he resumed as if the thread had never been broken.

'And you have planned to hide yourself somewhere about the cloister,' mused the old man, at the end of it, 'and burst forth to challenge your sometime lord to single combat, and so affront him that he shall not be able to deny you and keep his face?'

'It is the only way I can see,' said Joscelin, though put in such clear terms, he did not think too well of its chances.

'Then be in no haste about it,' said Lazarus, 'until daylight comes, for a clapper-dish and a hood and veil can make you faceless and nameless as well as another. One thing I can tell you. Huon de Domville did not lie in his bed this night. He rode out beyond here, turning right from this road, and I have been here every moment since, and unless he knows of another way back, he has not returned. I think he must ride back by the same way he rode out, and until he passes this place, no bridegroom will present himself at the altar. Between us, you and I can make shift to watch for him. If he comes! But how if he never comes?'

It was the strangest night Joscelin had ever passed, and the strangest dawn. Faint mist came with the light, and the rising sun peered through it overhead, while it lay in great swathes in the valley beyond the road. But no Huon de Domville came trotting back towards the bishop's house.

'Stay in hiding,' said Lazarus at length, 'until I come back.' And he rose and went into the hospice, to return presently with a hooded cloak like his own, and a blue linen cloth for a veil. 'You may creep out and put them on. If you are not afraid to wear the habit of a dead man? He is in the cemetery there. When they come to die here, they leave such clothing behind, there's store enough within. The linen they burn, the habits they clean as best they can. A big man he must have been, you'll find it ample enough.'

Joscelin did all that he was bidden, like a child, or a man in so unpredictable a dream that he must rely on his guide. In such a state it no longer seemed strange that he should open his heart to a leper, accept the protection of the leper cloak, and let himself be led into the hospital where the unfortunates were housed, without conscious fear or revulsion. This was the hand that had been held out to him, and he gripped it warmly and gratefully. He did not even ask how he should pass among the

72

inmates. Surely their number must be known, and he was too large to escape notice. Whether Lazarus had already spoken a word in several ears, or whether the poor know by instinct when one of their fellows is in need, and deploy their movements so subtly as to contain and dissemble him, all those men and women mustered about Joscelin and hid him among them as they assembled in the church for Prime.

Round about him he saw all manner of maimings and disfigurements, and found himself possessed unexpectedly by an overwhelming and unaccustomed humility. Not for a long time had he paid such devout attention to the words of the office, or felt himself so truly drawn into a company at worship.

As for the watch on the road, outside, Lazarus had confided it to the little boy Bran, who knew very well the appearance of the man for whom he was to watch. All was being done for Joscelin by others, and as at this moment there was no resistance he could offer, and no repayment he could make, but to bow his head fervently among the rest and give profound thanks for present mercies. And so he did.

5 &

THEY HAD ROUSED IVETA EARLY, FOR SHE HAD AN ELABORATE
toilet to make. Agnes and Madlen bathed, dressed and adorned
her, swept up the gold mane of her hair in a dozen shining
braids, coiled it in a filigree net, and bound it in a gold circlet
stuck with stones. From the coronal a veil of gilt thread hung
round neck and shoulders, over the stiff gold broidery of her
gown. She submitted to all with a mute tongue and an icy face,
so pale that her ivory ornaments looked dun by comparison.
She turned obediently under their hands, bent her head as they
instructed, did all that was demanded of her. When she was
ready they stood her in the midst of the chamber, posed like a
gowned statue for a saint's niche, every fold of her dress
coaxed out to perfection, and ordered her not to move, for fear
of creasing her splendour. She stood as they had placed her and
made no complaint, all the time that they were adorning themselves no less splendidly.

Her uncle came, walked round her with narrowed eyes and

critical grimace, twitched the folds of her veil into more severe symmetry, and expressed himself satisfied. Canon Eudo came, smooth and sanctimonious, complimented her not so much on her beauty or appropriate grandeur as on her great good fortune in this match, and the gratitude she owed her guardians for achieving it for her. The guests came, admired, envied, and went to take their places in the church.

At the hour of ten, on other days earmarked for High Mass, her attendants formed at her back, and she was led forth into the main porch of the guest-hall on Picard's arm, ready to go forth to meet her bridegroom when he came.

There was only one thing amiss with the scrupulous arrangements, which up to this moment had worked to perfection. The bridegroom did not come.

No one, not even Picard, ventured to murmur or look askance for the first ten minutes. Huon de Domville was a law to himself, and though this marriage was certainly profitable to him, he regarded it as a condescension on his part. It was ungracious to come late, but no one doubted that he would come. But when ten more minutes had slipped away, and still no formal procession entered at the gatehouse, and no hoofbeats were heard along the Foregate, there began to be a shifting and murmuring, an uneasy shuffling of feet and then a whispering. Iveta stood in the forefront, and awoke out of her frost to the shivering of doubt all round her, and drew breath in wonder. She gave no sign, only the blood began to stir again in her face, and flush into her set lips, softening them into rose-leaves.

Canon Eudo came floating elegantly from the church, but all his graces could not conceal his agitation. He spoke in low tones with Picard, whose brow was growing black and knotted with anxiety. Cadfael, coming late and in haste from the garden to take his place among the brothers, looked only at the bride, and could not take his eyes from the tiny golden doll they had made of her, not a thread of it real but the small, chill face melting among the gilt, and the quickening spark deep in her iris-purple eyes, making its live way up out of frowning fathoms to the light of day.

She was among the first to catch the hurried clatter of hooves along the Foregate. She turned her eyes without daring to turn her head, as Simon Aguilon, in all his wedding finery, rode into the gateway, dropped his bridle into the porter's hand, and swung hastily down to stride across the great court to the door of the guest-hall, in evident agitation.

'My lord, I pray your pardon! Things have somehow gone amiss, we don't know how . . .' He drew in Canon Eudo, the three heads leaned close, and Agnes hovered with pricked ears and drawn brows. The voices spilled abroad, none the less. Both abbot and prior had emerged from the church, and stood at a dignified distance, in contained displeasure. They could not long be ignored.

'Last night, when we left here to return home—I do his bidding, I do not question, how could I? He said to me that he had a fancy to ride a while, and I should go in, and bid the household go to bed, for he wanted no service that night, nor until he should say the word this morning. And so I did! What else? I thought he would be there asleep this morn, when his chamberlain looked in on him. I slept late myself. They shook me awake a good half-hour past Prime, and said he was not in his bed—nor had been, all night long, for the bed was not pressed.' The young man's voice had risen, all those crowding in could hear. They were silent enough, all intent on that knot of consternation in the midst.

'Father Abbot,' Simon turned to him with a hasty reverence, 'we are greatly afraid that something must have happened to my lord. He has not been home all night, since he sent me in and dismissed all attendance. And very surely he would not be absent or late here, had he his freedom and health to keep the tryst. I fear he may have come by an injury, somehow—a fall, perhaps. . . . Night riding is risky, but he had a fancy for it. It wants only a crippling stone in a hoof, or a fox's earth . . .'

'He left you at the gate of the house?' asked Radulfus. 'And rode on?'

'Yes, towards Saint Giles. But I do not know which way he took, after that, or where he was bound, if indeed he had some purpose in mind. He told me nothing.'

'It would be a first step,' said Radulfus drily, 'to send out along that road for sign or word of him.'

'So we have done, Father, but vainly. The superior at the hospital has seen nothing of him, and we have ridden further along the road without result. Before taking it further I had, of courtesy, to bring word here. But I have spoken to one of the sheriff's sergeants, who was out with a patrol beating the woodlands for the prisoner they lost, and his men will be keeping watch also for any sign of my lord Domville. He has sent a man to tell the sheriff what has happened. Father, you will understand that I dared not be too quick to raise an alarm or question anything my lord does, but I think now it is time there should be a full search for him. He may be lying somewhere hurt and unable to rise.'

'I think as you do,' said the abbot with decision, and turned courteously to Agnes Picard, who stood attentive and alert at her husband's side, one hand closed possessively on Iveta's golden sleeve. 'Madam, I trust this distress may not be long, and that we shall find my lord Domville safe and none the worse, only delayed by some trivial circumstance. But it would be well if you would take your niece within, and have her rest in privacy with you, while these gentlemen—and the brothers of our house, too, if they so choose—go and search for the bridegroom.'

Agnes made brief, anxious acknowledgement, and swept the girl away with her, out of sight. The doors of their apartments closed on them. Iveta had not spoken one word.

They saddled up, mounted and rode, all the men among the wedding guests, all the grooms and pages from the bishop's house, a squad of men-at-arms from the castle, many of the younger brothers and novices on foot, and one of the boy pupils whose long ears had overheard the news, and who had slipped into hiding before he could be herded away into school. He might pay for his truancy later, but he thought it well worth the risk.

Those mounted chose to ride along the Foregate to where Domville had parted from his squire, and been seen continuing towards Saint Giles. Thence they split into two parties, since the roads forked there, and spread out into the verges on either side of either highway. Those afoot took at once to the byways, some threading their way through the woods down-river, some going round by the mill-pond into the valley of the Meole brook, and so upstream through meadows and copses.

Cadfael joined these last. They spread out in a long line, to cover as wide a swathe as possible, and made their way upstream on both sides of the brook from the limit of the abbey grounds. A mounted man would use only good open country or the well-trodden paths and rides in this richly wooded countryside, and to look for him in the first reaches was pointless, if he had begun from his own gateway. They proceeded briskly, therefore, until they had left the abbey precincts well behind, and were strung out across the valley just below the hospital. They could see the little turret of the church just above the bushes at the crest, where the road ran.

From this point they went more slowly and thoroughly, stretching their line to take in more ground. They knew every path here, and threaded each for some distance as they came to it. No doubt others on the opposite side of the Foregate had reached much the same point, and were proceeding in the same way, but as yet there had been no shout anywhere to direct or call off the hunt.

By this time they were probably half a mile beyond Saint Giles, and the sloping fields and light, scattered copses had thickened into woodland. The climb to the road here was steep, and for some distance, until the gradient grew gentler, no paths descended to cross their line. Then they came, as they had known they would, to a broad green ride, a good, smooth plane of turf that came down from the road and narrowed slightly as it entered the denser woods. South-west from the road it ran, twice fording the bends of the brook, which here was narrow and stony, and wandered away, Cadfael recalled, towards the fringe of the Long Forest, a few miles distant.

They had just emerged on to this green track when the truant schoolboy, who had been running in circles ahead of them in his zeal, came rushing back along the path in great excitement, waving an arm towards the groves behind him.

'There's a horse grazing back there in a clearing! Saddle and harness and all, but no rider!'

And he whirled and darted back, with all of them hard on his heels. The path continued clear and well-used, closely hemmed by trees, and then expanded into a small, lush meadow; and there, placidly cropping the grass under the bordering trees, Huon de Domville's tall black horse strolled unalarmed, and raised a mildly wondering stare as so many men suddenly bore down on him. All his harness was in order, nowhere any disarray, but of his rider there was no sign.

'If he'd been near his own home stable,' said the excited boy, proudly possessing himself of the bridle, 'he'd have gone back to it, and they'd have been warned. But he was on strange ground, so when he got over his fright, he wandered.'

It was good sense, and he was all eagerness to press on. But there might well be that ahead that was not good for a child to see. Cadfael looked at Brother Edmund the infirmarer, who was next to him, and saw the same thought reflected back to him. If horse and rider had parted by reason of some shock or alarm, and they met the horse first, then Huon de Domville had probably been on his way back when mischance befell him; and if he had lain out all night, it meant he was in no good case. A tough, determined man, he would not let minor injury hold him helpless.

'A startled horse bolts forward, not back,' pursued the voluble imp, glowing, 'isn't that right? Shall we go on?'

'You,' said Cadfael, 'may have the credit for taking this beast back to the bishop's house, and telling them there where you found him. Then go back to your lessons. If you make a good story of it you may escape punishment for running away.'

The boy looked first dismayed, and then mutinous, and began to argue.

'Hop!' ordered Cadfael briskly, cutting off his objections. 'You may ride him. Here, up with your foot . . . so!' He cupped a hand, and hoisted the boy into the saddle before he had time to decide whether to be aggrieved or flattered. But the feel of the fine beast under him did the trick. His face became one complacent beam, he gathered the reins importantly, ignored the stirrups that were far too long for him, dug his heels into the satin sides, and chirruped at his mount as casually as if he rode such beasts every day.

When they had watched him far enough along the ride to be sure that he was competent, and would do as he had been bidden, they turned and went on. The glade ended, trees closed in again on the track. Here and there, in places where the grass was thin and the ground soft, they saw the mark of a hoof. They had gone perhaps another quarter of a mile before Brother Edmund, who was leading, suddenly halted.

'He is here.'

The thick, powerful body lay sprawled on its back, head against the roots of a great oak, arms spread. The trees grew close here, and the deep shadows swallowed the rich colours of his clothing, so that the upturned face stared out of a green darkness, suffused with blood, open eyes bulging and reddened. The brutal, muscular quality of the face seemed to have melted and run like wax from a candle. As well the child had been sent back before he could run ahead of them and stumble over this in valiant innocence, and sicken in too early knowledge of good and evil.

Cadfael put Edmund aside and went forward, dropping to his knees beside the motionless body, and in a moment Edmund followed him, and crouched on the other side. He was accustomed to easing old men into their deaths, but deaths as gentle as affectionate care and the company of friends could make it, and this abrupt severing of a vigorous life appalled and daunted him. The two novices and the lay brother who had followed them drew near and stood silent.

'Is he dead?' asked Brother Edmund fearfully, and understood at once that it was a foolish question.

'Dead some hours. Around dawn, it might be. He's cooling but not cold.' Cadfael lifted the heavy head on his hand, and felt the sticky foulness of congealed blood on his fingers. High at the back of the head, behind and above the left ear, the bald crown bore a ripped bruise, which had oozed blood from a dozen scratches, now drying. Where his head had lain, and for a hand's-length above, the bole of the oak bore smeared traces of the impact. Cadfael felt delicately over and round the bruise, and the skull seemed to him intact, there was no depression under his touch.

'He was thrown from his horse, and heavily,' ventured Edmund, watching, 'and fell on to this oak-bole. Could such a fall kill him?'

'It could,' said Cadfael distractedly, but did not see fit as yet to make plain that it had not.

'Or if he lay out, not regaining his senses—the chill of the night . . .'

'He has not been here all night long,' said Cadfael. 'The dew of the mist is under him. And if he was thrown, you see he was thrown backwards, not forwards, out of the saddle. The horse did not stumble.' For the body lay diagonally half across the path, head against the tree on the right, his feet towards them as they approached from the brook. 'It was in the early morning, and he was hurled backwards. He was certainly riding back then to his own household. The path is good, at least for a man who knows, but I should guess there was also some light already, for I think he was riding briskly, to come down so heavily.'

'His horse reared,' suggested Edmund. 'Some small night creature started under his feet, and shocked him . . .'

'That could be.' Cadfael laid Domville's head carefully back, and the broken crown rested at the foot of the grazed and bloodied streak on the bole. 'He has not moved since the fall,' he said with certainty. 'Only the heels of his boots, see, have scored deep through the grass, as though in some convulsion.'

He rose to his feet, leaving the body just as it lay, and began to move about the ride, eyeing it from many angles. One of the novices, sensibly enough, had turned back to meet the sheriff's men, who would certainly be despatched from the bishop's house as soon as the boy brought his news. They would need a litter, or a door lifted from its hinges, to carry the dead man back. Cadfael also retraced his steps some dozen yards along the path, and began to work his way back to where the body lay, viewing all the trees on both sides with great care, at a level above his own modest height, as Edmund noted without understanding.

'What is it you're looking for, Cadfael?'

Whatever it was, he had found it. Some four paces from the dead man's feet he had halted, fixing his eyes first on the trunk on his right, well above his own head, and then transferring the same intent stare to the tree opposite.

'Come and see. Come, all, and bear me witness when I tell it.'

On either trunk at the same level there was a thin, scored line, scarring the fine ridges of the bark.

'A rope has been stretched between these trees, throat-height to a man of middle stature and well-mounted, though even at breast-height it would have fetched him down. It was light enough for a canter on so good a pathway, I fancy, for surely he was going briskly. You see how far it toppled him. We shall find the mark of it on his throat.'

They stared, appalled, and had no word to say, as they followed him in awed silence back to where the body lay, and he turned back the collar of the coat, and bared Domville's neck.

For the dark-red slash of the cord was not all they found under the beard, on the thick, sinewy flesh. There, plain to be seen, were the wreathing, blackened bruises of two human hands, and the two thumbs, overlapping, had left a great, mangled stain on the Adam's-apple, and possibly crushed the gristle within.

They were still gaping in horrified silence when they heard urgent voices approaching along the ride, the sheriff's loudest among them. The intimation of disaster had gone before, but as yet its magnitude was a secret among these few.

Cadfael drew the collar close over the evidence of strangulation, and turned with his companions to meet Gilbert Prestcote and his officers.

When the sheriff had viewed everything Cadfael had to show him, they brought a litter, and lifted Huon de Domville on to it, drawing the folds of his cloak over his face. At the spot from which they raised him they fixed a cross bound from two sticks, to enable them to find and search the place again at need. Then they carried him back, not to the bishop's house but to the abbey, to be laid in the mortuary chapel there and made decent for burial by the monks of Saint Peter's, who should have witnessed his marriage.

The child Bran, who could pass for any urchin of the Foregate, briefly, at least, and with discretion, simply by shedding his leper cloak, came back from a wary foray along the road, to report to the two tall, veiled men who sat together with their clapper-dishes under the cemetery wall: 'They have found him. I saw them carrying him back. They've taken him past the house. I dared not go further.'

'Alive or dead?' asked the slow, calm voice of Lazarus from behind the faded blue face-cloth. The boy knew death already, no need to shield him.

'His face was covered,' said Bran, and sat down beside them. He felt the silence and tension of the other, the new man, the one who was known to be young and whole, and wondered why he trembled.

'No words,' said Lazarus tranquilly. 'You have your breathing-space. So has she.'

Within the great court of the abbey the men-at-arms laid down the litter they carried, and from all sides, in haste and anxious clamour that died abruptly into silence and stillness, all those bound up in this matter came flooding, to form a mute, wide-eyed audience all about the bier. They halted at an awed distance, all but the sheriff and his men, and Abbot Radulfus, who advanced with authority. From the guest-hall Picard burst forth, obstinately hopeful, to freeze at sight of the shrouded figure and covered face. The women followed fearfully. The little golden image moved as though she could barely sustain the weight of her finery, yet she came, and did not turn her eyes away. No doubt of it now. Shocking though it might be, this death was life to her. Why, why had she so belied herself yesterday?

'My lord abbot,' said Prestcote, 'this is very ill news we bring, for my lord Domville is found indeed, but as you see him. These brothers of your house found him, thrown from his horse on the woodland path that leads out towards Beistan. His horse was grazing unharmed, and is back in his stable. Huon de Domville was thrown against an oak tree, and is dead. It seems that he was on his way home when this thing happened. Father, will you receive him and have body and soul cared for, until due arrangements can be made? His nephew is of his party here, and the canon is also his kinsman . . .'

Simon hovered, wordless. He inclined his head and swallowed hard, eyeing the body on the litter.

'This is a very ill turn for such a day to take,' said Radulfus heavily, 'and we extend our sorrow and fellow-feeling to all those thus bereaved. And naturally, our hospitality for as long as may be needed, the services of our order, and the privacy of our guest-halls. It is a time for quietness and prayer. Death is present with us every day of our lives, it behoves us to take note of its nearness, not as a threat, but as our common experience on the way to grace. There is no more to be said. It is better to accept the will of God, and be silent.'

'With respect, Father,' Picard spoke up in a voice thin as steel, yet very civil and respectful. Cadfael had been trying to read the man's face, and made little headway; there was dismay there, certainly, and rage, and frustration, but instant calculation, too. 'With respect, I say, should we so tamely accept that this *is* the will of God? Huon de Domville knows this region, he has a hunting-lodge no great way off, near the Long Forest. He has ridden lifelong without mishap, by day or by night, are we to believe he uses less skill and less awareness suddenly on his wedding-eve, when you and I both know he rode from here sober and unwearied? He told his squire he would take the air a little before sleeping. Surely that was all he intended. Now in a moment we have him brought back dead, a man in his prime and in his full powers! No, I do not believe it! There is some evil-dealing here, and I must know more before I can be satisfied.'

It seemed that Prestcote had deliberately delayed the full assault of his news, in order to see if any among his hearers showed signs of gratification at the likelihood that the death would pass as an accident. If so, and if he discovered anything, for all the narrowed glances with which he was sweeping the ring of shocked faces, he was more successful than Cadfael, who was pursuing the same quest. Nowhere could he discover any shadow of guilt or fear in any face, only the expected and obligatory grief and dismay.

'I have not said his death was accidental,' said the sheriff, bluntly now. 'Not even his fall was chance. He was fetched down out of the saddle by a rope stretched across the path between two trees, at a level that took him in the throat. But it was not the fall that killed him. Whoever laid the ambush for him was present to complete his work, while Domville lay senseless. A man's two hands round his throat killed him.'

The whole circle shifted as though a rough wind had shaken them, and drew hard, audible breath. The abbot raised his head to stare.

'You are saying this was murder?'

'As cold and thorough as ever was committed.'

'And we know by whom!' Picard leaned forward, blazing up in malevolent triumph like a thorn fire. 'Did I not say it? This is the work of that thieving youth who was dismissed my lord Domville's service. He has taken his devil's revenge by killing his lord. Who else? Who else had any grudge? Joscelin Lucy did this!'

Light flashed suddenly on darting gold at his back, and there stood Iveta confronting him, yesterday's sacrificial lamb become a spitting yellow wildcat. Dilated iris eyes glittered like amethyst. Her voice rose high and challenging, even triumphant, even derisive, as she cried:

'It's false! You know, you all know, that *cannot* be true! Have you forgotten? He of all men *must* be innocent of this— he's behind locked doors in Shrewsbury castle these two days— and that charge as false as this!—but thank God for it, the sheriff's own gaoler is witness he cannot have done murder.'

Understanding fell upon Brother Cadfael somewhat after the fashion of a great blow on the head, and left him dazed, unable to catch at first the full implications of what she had said. Not so hard now to guess the meaning of her resolute composure when questioned by the abbot. They had cased her up securely within, and kept her from knowing anything of Joscelin's escape, when it would have been comfort and joy to her. Now, when it destroyed all her comfort, they would turn on her and hurl it in her face. They were at it already, both the Picards, Agnes the shriller and more savage of the two.

'Fool girl, he is *not* prisoner. He broke free before ever they got him over the bridge, he's at large with his grudge . . .'

'Thief he was, and now a hunted wolf in the woods, and has murdered your bridegroom! *And will hang for it!*'

All the brightness, all the valour, was stricken from her face.

She hung a moment quite still, and just once her lips formed a protesting 'No!' that made no sound. Then her cheeks blanched whiter than snow. She put up a hand to her heart, and fell down like a shot bird, in a little crumpled heap of gold.

The maid Madlen came rushing officiously, all the women crowded in upon the small, spilled body, Picard gave a cry rather of exasperation than concern, and stooped to gather her up by the wrist and haul her to her feet. She was a reproach and an embarrassment, they wanted her hustled away out of sight and out of mind. Cadfael could not forbear from interfering, before they stifled her among their skirts, or tugged a wrist out of joint. He plunged into the midst of them and spread his arms to press them back from her.

'Peace, let her breathe! She has swooned, don't lift her yet.'

Brother Edmund, versed in such collapses, seconded him valiantly on the other side, and with Abbot Radulfus looking on, the guests could hardly reject the help and authority of those who tended the sick within these walls. Even Agnes stood back, though with a chill and wary face, as Cadfael went on his knees beside the girl, and straightened her tumbled limbs to lie at ease, her head raised on his arm. 'A cloak to fold under her head! And where is Brother Oswin?'

Simon threw off his cloak and rolled it eagerly into a pillow. Oswin came running from among the staring novices.

'Go and fetch me the little flask of mint and sorrel vinegar from the shelf by the door, and a bottle of the draught of bitter herbs. And be quick!'

He laid her head down gently on the pillow Simon had made for it, and took her wrists into his hands and began to chafe them steadily. Her face had the pinched, bluish white of ice. Oswin came back at the same devoted gallop, and moreover, had brought the right medicines. There was hope of him yet. Brother Edmund knelt on the other side, and held the little bottle of vinegar, hot and sharp with mint and sorrel, to her nostrils, and saw them dilate and flutter. A small convulsion like a cough heaved her childish breast, and the steel-sharp lines of cheekbones and chin gradually softened. Over her oblivious head her uncle, having abandoned her to her physicians, returned to his vengeance with renewed venom.

'Can there be any doubt? He broke loose without weapons, and with no means of getting any. Only a man deprived of other means needs to kill with his bare hands. He is a big, strong rogue, capable of such an act. No one else had any grievance against Huon. But *he* had a grudge, and a bitter one, and he has taken to extremes to have his revenge. Now it is mortal! Now he must be hunted down like a mad dog, shot down at sight if need be, for he's perilous to anyone who approaches him. This is a hanging matter.'

'My men are beating the woods and orchards for him at this moment,' said Prestcote shortly, 'and have been ever since a patrol reported flushing a man out of cover into the Foregate early this morning. Though it was not yet light, and they got but the briefest glimpse of him, and for my part I doubt if it was Lucy. More likely some rogue in a small way pilfering from hen-houses and backyards by night. The hunt goes on, and will until we take him. Every man I can spare is out already.'

'Make use of my men also,' offered Picard eagerly, 'and of Huon's. We are all of us bound now to hunt down his murderer. There's surely no doubt in your mind that Joscelin Lucy *is* his murderer?'

'It seems all too clear. This has all the marks of an act of desperate hate. We know of no other present enemy of his.'

Cadfael worked unhurriedly upon Iveta, but listened to all that passed, the abbot's few words and reserved silences, Picard's vindictive urgings, the sheriff's measured dispositions for the continued and extended hunt, all the deployment of the law closing round Joscelin Lucy. In the middle of it he noted that faint colour was returning to Iveta's face, and watched the first delicate flutterings of her eyelids, the shadow of long dark-gold lashes quivering on her cheekbones. Dazed purple eyes opened at him, and gazed in uncomprehending terror. Her lips parted. As if by chance he laid a fingertip upon them, and briefly closed his own eyes. Joscelin's peril, far more effectively than her own, had made her wits quick. The eyelids, veined like harebells, closed again and remained closed. She lay like one still senseless, but showing signs of returning life.

'She is beginning to stir. We may take her in now.'

He rose from his knees and lifted her in his arms, before Picard or Simon or any other could forestall him.

'She should lie at rest for some hours, after she comes round. It was a bad swoon.' He marvelled how little there was of her, and was convinced her finery weighed more than she did; yet this fragile creature had roused herself to heroic defiance for the sake of Joscelin, she who was so tamed and resigned for herself. Even the charge of theft and a cell in the castle had seemed comfort and joy to her when they served to ward off the infinitely worse charge of murder. Now, when she got her wits back, and remembered, she would be torn in two between terror for his life, since this killing was indeed a hanging matter, and hope for his escape, since thus far he was still at liberty. Hope offered itself and snatched itself away again from Iveta de Massard.

'Madam, if you will show the way . . .'

Agnes gathered her splendid skirts and swept before him into the guest-hall, to her own apartments. It could not be said, Cadfael reflected, that she felt no concern for her niece, since her niece was the greater part of her fortune, and for that she felt a strong defensive care. But her prevailing emotion towards the girl Iveta herself was impatience and displeasure. By this hour she should have been safely married off, a commodity profitably disposed of. However, she was still eminently saleable, she still had all her father's great honour in lands and titles, down to the sword and helmet of the paladin Guimar de Massard, chivalrously restored by the Fatimids of Egypt: the one item of her inheritance, possibly, which Picard did not covet.

'You may lay her here.' By the narrow way she eyed him,

Agnes had not forgotten that he was the brother of whose ready prevarications she had complained to the abbot; but that hardly mattered now, since Joscelin Lucy was quarry for a hunt to the death, and no threat to her peace of mind any longer. 'Is there anything needs to be done for her?'

Iveta lay on her covered bed, sighed and was still. All that gold, as though she had been minted.

'If you would be kind enough to find me a small cup, to take a draught of this decoction of herbs when she is with us again. It's a good, bitter restorative, and wards off further fainting. And I think there should be some warmth in the room. A small charcoal brazier would serve.'

These recommendations she took seriously, perforce. He had given her enough to do to remove her from the room, though for perhaps five minutes at best. Her maids had waited in the hall. She swept out to set them to work.

Iveta opened her eyes. The same brother! She had known his voice, and stolen that one glance to make certain. But when she tried to speak, tears rose to hamper her utterance. But he was listening close; he heard.

'They never told me! They said the theft could be pressed to his death . . .'

'I know,' said Cadfael, and waited.

'They said—unless I did all perfectly, spoke the right words, made all above suspicion . . . Huon would have his life . . .'

'Yes . . . Hush now, softly! Yes, I know!'

'But if I did all well, he should go free . . .'

Yes, she had been ready to sell herself, body and will and hopes and all, to see Joscelin delivered. She had her own bravery.

'Help him!' she said, huge eyes like purple flowers overblown, and closed her small hand, fine-boned like a little bird, but with a little bird's strong and compelling grip, on Cadfael's hand. 'He has not stolen or killed . . . I know!'

'If I can!' breathed Cadfael, and stooped to conceal her from Agnes in the doorway. She was very quick, she lay back in mute acceptance, eyes veiled, the hand was empty and limp as before. Not for several more minutes did she raise her lids again and look up, answer faintly and wonderingly when Agnes asked her, with genuine anxiety but little kindness, how she did, and drink the bitter, aromatic draught Cadfael presented to her lips.

'She should be left alone in quietness,' he advised when he took his leave, minded to procure for her, if he could, the solitude she needed, deliverance from the company of people whose very presence was oppression. 'She will sleep. Such seizures are as exhausting as great exertion. If Father Abbot permits, I will look in on her before Vespers, and bring her a syrup that will ensure her a peaceful night.'

That, at least, they might allow her. They had her securely in their power, she could not escape, but at present no more could be done with her or to her. Domville was dead, there would have to be reconsideration now, the field was open to other bidders. It was not deliverance, but it was a respite. Time to give some thought to the circumstances of this violent death, and the fate of the unfortunate young man at whose door it was being laid. There were a great many questions not yet asked, let alone answered.

It was towards noon that one of the men-at-arms combing the copses and gardens behind the houses of the Foregate on the north side came to his sergeant and said brightly: 'There's but one garden left unexamined in all this array, and now I mind me there could be good sense in looking there, too. Bishop de Clinton's house itself!' And when he was cried down with mention of the folly of hiding in the very lion's mouth, he defended his notion earnestly.

'Not such folly, neither! Suppose this fellow's listening to the pack of you now, making mock of the very idea! He'd have the laugh if he's lying low within there, and you refusing to believe it possible. The one place you put out of the question is the one place he might have wit enough to be. And don't forget his horse is within there, and with all this running hither and thither, who's to care whether the stable's left open?'

The sergeant thought the argument worth considering, and authorised the search of the bishop's garden, byres and stables, his orchard, all the ground within his walls. In due course they arrived at the hay-store by the rear wall. They did not find Joscelin Lucy, but they did find plain evidence that someone had lain there in the hay, and left behind him the heel of a loaf and the core of an apple, besides the impress in the fodder of a long young body, clear to be seen. Joscelin Lucy knew this place, and the wicket in the wall was unbarred. No one had any doubt as to who the vanished guest had been.

So the man-at-arms who had insisted on entry here, though he failed of getting the credit for a capture, did well enough out of his suggestion to be commended by his officer, and was not ill-content with the enterprise.

6 &

HUON DE DOMVILLE LAY NAKED BENEATH A LINEN CERE-cloth in the mortuary chapel, and round about him stood the abbot and prior, the sheriff of the county, the dead man's nephew and squire, Sir Godfrid Picard, who should by this time have been his uncle by marriage, and Brother Cadfael.

Simon Aguilon was still cloaked and gloved from his strenuous part in the morning's search, and looked haggard and worried, as well he might, at the responsibility that had fallen on him as the dead man's nearest kin here. Picard was gnawing the black, clipped fringe of his beard, and brooding on his losses and the openings now left to him. Radulfus was quietly and scrupulously intent on what Cadfael was expounding.

The abbot was a man of the world and of the church, of wide experience, but not so wide as to include those manifestations of violence which were an open book to Brother Cadfael, who had been soldier and sailor besides. Rare among men of wide experience, Radulfus knew precisely the gaps that were left, and was willing to be instructed. The honour and integrity of his house was his prime concern, and in that criterion pure justice was implied. As for Prior Robert, his Norman loyalties were outraged, since a Norman lord had been removed by murder. In his own way he required a vengeance just as surely as did Picard.

'The head injuries,' said Brother Cadfael, his palm under the newly laved and combed head, 'would have been no danger, had they been all. But the blow stunned him, and laid him open to assault. Now, see . . .' He drew down the linen cloth below the great barrel of a breast and the massive upper arms. 'He fell asprawl on his back, head against the tree, arms and legs spread. My lord Prestcote here saw him so, and so did Brother Edmund and certain novices of our house. I could not then see what I have seen now, by reason of his clothing. Look here at the inner side of his upper arms, those round black bruisings in the muscle. See those arms spread, and consider what fell upon him, senseless as he was. His enemy knelt here upon these arms, reached here to his throat.'

'And that would not rouse him?' asked the abbot gravely, following Cadfael's blunt brown finger as he traced the prints of murder.

'There was some effort made.' Cadfael recalled the deep pits Domville's boot-heels had scored in the turf. 'But by the body only, as men jerk from wounds when they have no more power to resist them. His senses were out of him, he could not fight his assailant. And these were strong hands, and resolute. See here, where both thumbs, one over the other, were driven in. The apple of his neck is ruptured.'

He had not had the opportunity until now to look more closely at that savage injury. Under the short beard the slash made by the rope drew a dark-red line, from which the beads of blood had been washed away. The black bruises left by the strangler's hands showed up clearly.

'Here is every sign of a madly vindictive attacker,' said Prestcote grimly.

'Or a very frightened one,' Cadfael said mildly. 'Desperate at his own act, an act unlike him, suddenly undertaken and monstrously overdone.'

'You could be speaking of the same man,' said Radulfus reasonably. 'Is there anything more this body can tell us about him?'

It seemed that there was. On the left side of Domville's neck, about where the middle fingers of the right hand must have gripped, and had left their shadowy shape, the bruise was crossed by a short, indented wound, as though a jagged stone had been pressed into the flesh there. Cadfael pondered this small, insignificant thing in silence for a while, and concluded that it might be by no means insignificant.

'A small, sharp cut,' he mused, peering close 'and this hollow wound beside it. The man who did this wore a ring, on the middle or third finger of his right hand. A ring with a large stone in it, to thrust so into the flesh. And it must hang rather loose on his finger, for it turned partially within as he gripped. On the middle finger, surely . . . if it had hung loose on the third he would have shifted it to the middle one. I can think of no other way such an injury can have been made.' He looked up into the circle of attentive faces. 'Did young Lucy wear such a ring?'

Picard shrugged off all knowledge of such matters. After some thought Simon said: 'I cannot recall ever noticing a ring. But neither can I say certainly that he never wore one. I might ask Guy if he knows.'

'It shall be enquired into,' said the sheriff. 'Is there more to be noticed?'

'I can think of nothing. Unless it is worth wondering where this man had been, and on what errand, to find him on that path at such an hour.'

'We do not know the hour,' said Prestcote.

'No, true. It is not possible to say how long a man has been dead, not within a matter of hours. Yet the turf under him was moist. But there is another point. All the signs show—very well, let us be wary of reading too confidently, they *seem* to show!—that he was riding back towards his house when he was waylaid. And the trap set for him was laid, and waiting before he came. Therefore whoever set it, and thereafter killed him, knew where he had gone, and by what road he must return.'

'Or must have followed him in the night, and made his plans accordingly,' said the sheriff. 'We are sure now that Lucy made his way to the hay-store in the bishop's garden and hid there, but after dark he came forth, and may well have lurked to keep watch on his lord's movements, with this fell intent in mind. He knew Domville would be supping here at the abbey, for all the household knew it. It would not be difficult to wait in hiding for his return, and to see him riding on alone and dismissing his squire provided the very chance revenge needed. Small doubt but Lucy is our man.'

There was no more then to be said. The sheriff returned to his hunt, convinced of his rightness; and on the face of it, Cadfael allowed, no blame at all to him, for the case was black. Huon de Domville was left to the care of Brother Edmund and his helpers, and his coffin bespoken from Martin Bellecote, the master carpenter in the town, for whether he was to find his burial here or elsewhere, he must be decently coffined for his journey to the grave, and with suitable grandeur. His body had no more now to tell.

Or so Brother Cadfael thought, until he consented to recount the circumstances of death and enquiry to Brother Oswin in the workshop, over the sorting of beans for the next year's seed. Oswin listened intently to all. At the end he said with apparent inconsequence: 'I wonder that he should ride in a late October night without a capuchon. And he bald, too!'

Cadfael stood at gaze, contemplating him with wonder across a handful of seed. 'What was that you said?'

'Why, for an old man to go bare-headed in the night . . .'

He had put his finger firmly on the one thing Cadfael had missed. Domville had not ridden away bareheaded from the abbey gatehouse, that was certain. Cadfael himself had seen him depart, the fine crimson capuchon twisted up into an elaborate hat, gold fringe swinging, and yet he had not thought to look for it where the body lay fallen, or question its absence.

'Child,' said Cadfael heartily, 'I am always underestimating you. Remind me of it when next I breathe down your neck over your work, for I shall deserve it. He did indeed have a capuchon, and I had better be about finding it.'

He asked no permission, preferring to consider that the morning's leave to join in the search might reasonably be extended to cover a further stage in the same quest. There was still time before Vespers if he hurried, and the place was marked with their improvised cross.

The turf under the oak still retained the vague shape of Domville's body, but already the grasses were rising again. Cadfael prowled the pathway with his eyes on the ground, penetrated into the trees on both sides, and found nothing. It was a sudden shaft of sunlight through the branches, filtering through thick underbrush, that finally located for him what he sought, by picking out the glitter of the gold fringe that bordered the cape of the capuchon. It had been flung from its wearer's head when he was thrown, and buried itself in a clump of bushes three yards from the path, its fashionable twisted arrangement making it all too easy to dislodge in such a shock. Cadfael hauled it out. The turban-like folds had been well wound, it was still a compact cap, with one draped edge left to swing gracefully to a shoulder. And in the dark crimson folds a cluster of bright blue shone. Somewhere in his nocturnal ride Huon de Domville had added to his adornments a little bunch of frail, straight stems bearing long, fine green leaves and starry flowers of a heavenly blue, even now, when they had lain all day neglected. Cadfael drew the posy out of the folds, and marvelled at it, for though it had commoner cousins, this plant was a rarity.

He knew it well, though it was seldom to be found even in the shady places in Wales where he had occasionally seen it. He knew of no place here in England where it had ever, to his

97

knowledge, been discovered. When he wanted seed to make powders or infusions against colic or stone, he had to be content with the poor relatives of this rarity. Now what, he wondered, viewing its very late and now somewhat jaded flowers, is a bunch of the blue creeping gromwell doing in these parts? Certainly Domville had not had it when he left the abbey.

It was a pity there was no time to go further, since he must be back to attend Iveta and go to Vespers. He was beginning to be very curious indeed about Domville's nightly ramblings. Had not Picard mentioned by the way that the baron had a hunting-lodge near the Long Forest? From the Foregate this path might well be the most direct way to that lodge. True, the place might lie anywhere along some miles of the forest borders, but it would be well worth following the road the dead man had taken. But not today, that was out of the question.

Cadfael tucked the little bunch of blue and the capuchon in the breast of his habit, and made his way back. No doubt it was his duty to hand over both, with due explanations, to the sheriff, but he was not at all sure that he was going to do so. The capuchon, certainly, that added nothing to what was already known. But this small knot of fading beauty was eloquent indeed. Where that grew, Domville had been, and there surely could not be more than one such place in all this shire. He knew of only three in Gwynedd, where it had its home, here he was astonished to find even one. And Prestcote was an honest and just man, but arbitrary in his decisions, and already convinced of Joscelin's guilt. Who else had a grudge against the baron? Cadfael was not convinced. Loose talk about killing did not delude him. There are people who are capable of murder by stealth, and people who are not, and nothing would persuade him to the contrary. Every man may be driven to kill, but not every man can be driven to kill by cunning, the knife in the back, the rope across the path.

He went back dutifully to the abbey, delivered the capuchon to the sergeant Prestcote had left at the gatehouse, and went to fetch the poppy syrup for Iveta from his workshop.

This time they did not leave him alone with her for a moment. The maid Madlen, plainly Agnes's creature to the hilt, stood over them sharp-eyed and prick-eared, all he could give the girl was the reassurance of his continued partisanship by his very presence, and the ministrations he offered. At least they could exchange looks, and interpret what they saw. And he could ensure that she should sleep, and sleep long, while he pondered how best to help her. Also to help Joscelin Lucy? She would not be grateful for a partisanship that did not extend to her lover, for whose life she had been willing to barter all her own future happiness.

Cadfael went to Vespers with the little fading cluster of blue still in his habit.

Brother Mark had been vaguely but persistently troubled, all that day, by the feeling that his grasp on the whole body of his flock at the hospice had somehow been disrupted. It had begun at Prime, when all the household, except the one or two young children, came together in the church. It was not that he ever counted them. If any were sicker or more out of mood than normally, they could remain at rest, no one drove them, so the number need never be the same. Moreover, during even this brief office there were some who for good reason must ease their discomfort by movement, and therefore the whole mass shifted and changed a little. It was rather that he was haunted by a sense of unexpected bulk, a limitation of the light within the church, which at all times was dim and cramped. There were six or seven big men among his charges, but he knew the manner and gait of them all, the little halts and stoops that identified even the veiled ones among them.

Once or twice during Prime he had thought he detected one lofty, shrouded head and covered face that had an alien look, but always he lost it again. Not until the end did it dawn on him that he was losing it because all his afflicted household was so disposing its people as to swallow up the intruder.

Intruder seemed a hard word where the doors were open to

all, yet had the newcomer been truly a leper, here arrived at one more halt in a lifetime's pilgrimage, he would have announced himself, and there would have been no need for this mysterious shifting and dissembling. Yet what whole man in his right mind would choose to hide here? He would have to be desperate.

Mark had almost persuaded himself that he was dreaming. But when he doled out the bread and oatmeal and small ale at breakfast, though again he did not count—for who counts what is given to the unfortunate?—by the end of it he knew that his supplies were depleted beyond what he had expected. Someone among his children had drawn food for another mouth.

He knew, of course, that the sheriff's men were beating the woods and gardens between Saint Giles and the town, and before noon the news of Huon de Domville's death had reached him. The isolation of the outcasts here never kept out the news. Whatever happened in town or abbey was known at once in the hospice, down to the very manner of the baron's death, and the outcry raised against the escaped squire as his murderer. But Brother Mark had work to do, and had not thought much about the rumours. There were all his morning medical duties first, and not until the last dressing was renewed and the last sore anointed did he give much consideration to the discrepancy that was troubling him. Even then there were other matters to be attended to, recording gifts made to the hospital, arranging for a party of the able-bodied to go gleaning for the winter wood-pile in the manor of Sutton, a right granted them by the late lord and continued by his son, helping to prepare the midday meal, checking the superior's accounts, and a dozen other things. Only in the afternoon was he at leisure to pursue some of the duties he had appropriated to himself of his own will, such as reading the office privately to one old man who was too ill to leave his bed, and giving a lesson to the boy Bran. Very easy lessons they usually turned out to be, more than half play, but for all that, the child was thirsty for letters, and drew in learning like mother's milk, as naturally as breathing.

Mark had made a little desk for him, the appropriate size for his spindly eight years, and on this day he trimmed a leaf of old, cleaned vellum for his use, leaving the frayed strips he had removed on his own desk close by. The schoolroom was a cramped corner of the hall, close to a narrow window for light. Sometimes they ended using up the rest of the leaf in children's drawing games, at which Bran could usually win. The leaf could always be cleaned and used again and again, until it wore too thin and frayed away.

Mark went out to find his pupil. The day was clear, but the sunlight moist and mild. Many of the lepers would be out along the fringes of the highroads with their clapper-dishes, keeping their humble distance from all traffic, but crying their appeal to those who passed. But close to his accustomed place beside the cemetery wall Lazarus was sitting, tall, straight-backed, head erect in its shrouding hood and veil. Close beside him, leaning comfortably upon his thighs, was Bran, both hands raised with spread fingers holding a web of coarse thread, with one side of it caught in his teeth. The man's hands shared the spread of the web. They were playing the old game of cat's-cradle, and the boy was bubbling with laughter round the cord he nibbled.

It was pleasant and cheering to see old age and childhood in harmony together, and Brother Mark hesitated to break into their concentration. He was about to withdraw and leave them to their game, but the child had caught sight of him, and let fall his tether to call out hastily: 'I'm coming, Brother Mark! Wait for me!'

He unwound his fingers from the web, said a blithe farewell to his playmate, who unlaced the thread without a word, and ran willingly to slip his hand into Mark's, and skip beside him into the hall.

'We were only filling up the time, till you were ready for me,' said the boy.

'Are you sure you wouldn't rather stay out and play, while the weather's mild like this? You may, of course, if you wish. We can learn in the dark evenings, all the winter long by the fire.'

'Oh, no, I want to show you how well I can do the letters you taught me.'

He had towed Brother Mark indoors, and was at his desk and smoothing the fresh sheet of vellum proudly before him, and still it had not dawned on Mark what he had just witnessed. It was the sight of the thin, careful hand gripping the quill that finally brought enlightenment. He drew in breath so sharply that Bran looked up quickly, in the belief that he must be doing something either very badly, or unexpectedly well, and Mark made haste to reassure and praise him.

But how could he have failed to recognise what he was seeing? The height matched, the erect carriage was right, the width of the shoulders under the cloak—everything was as it should be. Except that both hands from which Bran had been in the act of lifting their web of thread had all their fingers, and were smooth, supple and shapely, a young man's hands.

Nevertheless, Brother Mark said never a word to the superior of the hospital, or to any other, of what he had discovered, nor did he make any move to confront the interloper. What impressed him most, and caused him to hold his hand, was the unanimity with which his afflicted flock had opened to receive the fugitive, surely with barely a word said, and nothing explained, and had closed about him in the silent solidarity of shared misfortune. Not lightly would he presume to turn back that tide, or dispute the rightness of that judgment.

The hunters came back from their fruitless search with the fall of darkness. Guy, a very reluctant conscript, tramped into the chamber he shared with Simon, kicked off his boots, and lay back on his bed with a great gusty sigh of exasperation.

'Well for you, that you escaped that penance! Hours of draggle-tailing it through the bushes and peering into cottage pig-styes, and scaring out moulting hens. I swear I stink of muck! Canon Eudo came bustling back from the church and hunted us all out, but his zeal didn't run as far as volunteering for the foul work himself. He went back to his prayers—may they do the old man's soul some good!'

'And you've seen nothing of him? Of Joss?' asked Simon anxiously, pausing with one arm in the sleeve of his best cotte.

'If I had, I should have looked the other way, and kept main quiet about it.' Guy smothered a huge yawn, and stretched his long legs at ease. 'But no, never a glimpse. The sheriff's got a cordon round the town that should keep in even a mouse, and they're planning a slow drive further out on the north side to-morrow, and if that fails, on the brook side the next day. I tell you, Simon, they're set on taking him. Did you hear they even ransacked the grounds of this house? And found he, or some fellow, had been hiding in one of the outhouses down by the wall?'

Simon completed the donning of his coat, glumly thoughtful. 'I heard it. But it seems he was long gone. If it *was* he.'

'Do you think he may be already out and away? Why should we not at least leave the old man's stable unlocked tonight? Or move Briar to the open one in the court? A small chance is better than none.'

'If we even knew where he might be . . . But I've been thinking,' agreed Simon, 'that at least we'd better have the poor beast out into daylight again, and find him some exercise. Who knows, if I was seen riding him, and Joss got word of it, he might get in touch.'

'I see you no more believe in this charge than I do,' observed Guy, lifting his rumpled head to give his friend a sharp glance. 'Nor in that wretched business of the necklace in his saddle-bag, either. I wonder which misbegotten dog among the servants got his orders to hide it there! Or do you suppose the old man saw to it himself? He was never afraid of his own dirty work, as long as I've known him.' Guy had been in the baron's service from twelve years old, beginning as a page fresh from his father's house, and had even acquired a kind of detached affection for his formidable lord, who had never had occasion to turn formidable to him. 'But still, it was a foul way to make away with him,' he said. 'And I do still wonder. . . . If Joss was mad with rage—and he had reason to be—I would not be ready quite to stake my soul he did not kill him. Even that way!'

'But I would,' said Simon with certainty.

'Ah, you!' Guy rose indulgently and clapped his fellow on the shoulder. 'Where others hold opinions, you *know!* Be careful you don't trip yourself some day by trusting too far. And now I look at you,' he added, twitching the collar of Simon's best coat into immaculate neatness, 'you're very fine tonight. Where are you off to?'

'Only to the Picards at the abbey. A common courtesy, now the worst of the day's over and the dust settling. They came close to becoming his kin, they'll have to be allowed a part in the mourning for him. It costs nothing to defer to the man as elder and adviser until my uncle's buried. There'll be messages to send out to my aunt in the nunnery at Wroxall, and one or two distant cousins. Eudo can make himself useful doing the scribing, he has the right flowery style.'

'I warn you,' said Guy, rising lazily to go and demand hot water for his ablutions, 'the sheriff and Eudo between them will drive you out with the rest of us to take part in their sweep tomorrow. They're bent on hanging him.'

'I can always look the other way, like you,' said Simon, and departed to do his duty by one who had almost become a kinsman, and had hoped by this time to have a kinsman's rights.

Iveta lay in her bed, with Brother Cadfael's poppy draught measured and ready to her hand, and his promise that it would bring her sleep like a small, warm core of comfort in her mind. But she did not want to sleep yet. There was a kind of passive pleasure in being here alone in the room, even though she knew that Madlen was within call. They had so seldom left her alone all these weeks, the oppression of their presence had been like a shadow cutting her off from the sun. Only yesterday, and only for those meagre minutes, and even then with an eye on her from the distance, had they sent her out to dispose herself where she must be noticed, and might be questioned, so that she might give the right answers, and display the right assured calmness of consent in her hateful destiny. And all the time they had known that Joscelin was not a prisoner, but somewhere at liberty, even if his liberty was that of a hunted man.

That was over. She could not be cheated like that again. Two things at least she could cling to: he was not taken, and she was not married.

She caught the sound of a hand at the door, and shrank within herself, wary and still. But when the door opened, and Agnes appeared, it was with a face almost benign, and a voice almost solicitous, surely for the benefit of the visitor who came in at her shoulder. Iveta stared in astonishment at the transformation.

'Still awake, child? Then here is a good friend enquiring after you. May he come in for a few moments? You are not too tired?'

He was in already, Simon in his best, and on his best behaviour for her aunt and uncle; and his best behaviour must have made its impression, for he was actually allowed to be alone with her. Agnes was withdrawing, smiling her benevolence in her best public manner. 'Only a few minutes. She should not exert herself longer tonight.'

She was gone, and the door had closed after her. Simon's pleasant, boyish face shed its wariness instantly, and he came striding to Iveta's bedside, pulled up a stool, and sat down beside her. She raised herself gladly on her pillows, the gold mane of her hair loose over the shoulders of her linen gown.

'Softly!' he warned, finger to lip. 'Speak low, your dragon may be set on to listen. I'm let in briefly to pay my respects and enquire how you are. God knows I was sorry to see you so shocked. Did they never tell you he broke free?'

She shook her head, almost too full to speak. 'Oh, Simon, is there news? Not . . .'

'Not good nor ill,' he said quickly, in the same low and rapid whisper. 'Nothing has changed. He's still at liberty, and pray

God he will be. They'll be hunting for him, I know. But so shall I,' he said meaningly, and took the small hand that groped out blindly towards him. 'Take heart! They've searched all day, and no one has laid hand or eye on him yet, who knows but he's away out of the circle long since. He's strong, and bold . . .'

'Too bold!' she said ruefully.

'And still has friends, for all they've charged against him. Friends who don't believe in his guilt!'

'Oh, Simon, you do me so much good!'

'I would I might do more, for you and for him. But take comfort, all you need do is be patient and wait. One threat is gone from you. Now, if he continues free, there's no urgency, you *can* wait.'

'And truly you don't believe he ever stole? Nor that he has killed?' she pleaded hungrily.

'I *know* he has not,' said Simon firmly, with all the self-assurance with which Guy had goodnaturedly charged him. 'The only wrong he has done is to love where love was not allowed. Oh, I know!' he said quickly, seeing her flinch and turn her face aside. 'Forgive me if I'm presumptuous, but he's my friend and has spoken with me as a friend. I *do* know!' He cast an uneasy glance over his shoulder, and smiled wry reassurance at her. 'Your aunt will be beginning to frown. I should go. But remember, Joss is not friendless.'

'I will,' she said fervently, 'and thank God and you for it. You'll come again, Simon, if you can? You can't imagine how you comfort me.'

'I'll come,' he promised, and stooped hurriedly to kiss her hand. 'Goodnight now! Sleep well, and don't be afraid.'

He was on his way to the door when Agnes opened it, still benevolent, but watchful all the same. This young man was Huon de Domville's nephew, and partook of the deference accorded his uncle in life. But the watch on Iveta would never be wholly relaxed until she was profitably disposed of, and the gains secured.

The door closed. Iveta was ready now for sleep, the load on

her heart greatly lightened. She drank Brother Cadfael's potion, honeysweet and heavy, and blew out her candle.

When Madlen came prowling suspiciously, Iveta was already asleep.

After Compline Brother Cadfael asked audience of Abbot Radulfus, in his own study in the abbot's lodging. It was a good hour for grave conversation, a day of many passions over at last, the night's needful composure closing in.

'Father, I have told you all I know of this matter, but for one thing. You know that I have knowledge of herbs. In the capuchon I brought back and delivered to the sheriff this evening, I found a herb which I know to be exceedingly rare, even in Wales, where it does habit in some places. Here I had never before met with it. Yet Huon de Domville, in his last night in this world, was where this herb grows. Father, I think this circumstance of the greatest importance, and it is my wish to find this place, and discover what business the dead man had there, on his marriage eve. I believe it may have a bearing on his death, the manner of it, and the maker of it.'

He had the little faded posy in his palm, a drying bunch of thin stems, thread-like green leaves and wilting, starry flowers, still surprisingly blue.

'Show me,' said the abbot, and gazed with wondering attention. 'And you can say where such a thing grows, and where it does not grow?'

'It grows in a few, a very few places, where the chalk or limestone crops out. I have never before seen it in England.'

'And by this you believe you can divine where our murdered man spent his night?'

'We know the path by which he was returning. By that same path he surely went, when he left his squire at the gate. It is my wish, if you give leave, to follow that path, and find this flower. I believe lives—innocent of anything beyond youth, folly and anger—may hang upon so small a thing.'

'Such things have happened times without number,' said Abbot Radulfus. 'Our purpose is justice, and with God lies the privilege of mercy. You have leave, Brother Cadfael, to pursue this as long as may be needful. You have my trust.'

'God knows I value it,' said Cadfael truly. 'And you have, and shall have, mine. Whatever I may find, I submit to you.'

'Not to the sheriff?' asked Radulfus, and smiled.

'Surely. But through you, Father.'

Brother Cadfael went to his bed in the dortoir, and slept like an innocent babe safely cradled, until the bell rang for Matins.

7 &

WHEN CADFAEL EMERGED FROM PRIME, THE FOLLOWING morning, Prestcote was already abroad marshalling his renewed hunt on the northern side of the Foregate. This time they would make a great, slow sweep for some three miles out, so exhaustive that barely a weasel or a hare would elude their net. The sheriff was determined to fetter his quarry this time, and reasonably sure that he had not already slipped through the cordon, which had been strengthened overnight. Picard was out with all the men of his household marshalled at his back, and Canon Eudo was probably exhorting Domville's people at the bishop's house to the same forced service. And though some, no doubt, turned out reluctantly, nevertheless there is something infectious about the zeal of a hunt, that would have most of these beaters in full cry if ever they scented their quarry.

Not for the first time, Brother Cadfael wished heartily that he had Hugh Beringar here, to temper the chill of Prestcote's proceedings. The deputy sheriff had room in his head and conscience for healthy doubts of his own omniscience, and was always perversely suspicious of what seemed a foregone conclusion to others. But Hugh Beringar was in the north of the shire, at his own manor of Maesbury, and certainly would not consent to move from there these coming few weeks, for his wife was near her time with their first child, and that is a peak of experience in any young man's life. No help for it, this matter would have to be settled under Gilbert Prestcote's direction. And at that, thought Cadfael fairly, we're luckier than many a shire. He's an honest, fair-minded man, if he is too urgent for quick resolutions and summary justice, and not inclined to look too far beyond the obvious. Nevertheless, show him a provable truth, and he'll accept it. Provable truths are what we need.

Meantime, he took some care over giving Brother Oswin his tasks for the day. Only a week ago, he would have found him enough rough digging and outdoor work to keep him occupied, and prayed heartily that the great maladroit need not even set foot in the workshop. Today he handed over to him some early winter pruning, but also the tending of a batch of wine just beginning to work, and the making of an ointment for the infirmary. They had made the same ointment together once, the process fully explained as they went. Cadfael nobly refrained from repeating and underlining every stage, and left Oswin with only the most modest and trusting recapitulation.

'I leave the workshop in your hands,' he said firmly. 'I place full confidence in you.'

'And God forgive me the lie,' he muttered to himself when he was out of earshot, 'and turn it to truth. Or at least count it as merit to me rather than sin. If I've been setting your teeth on edge, Oswin, my lad, now's your chance to spread your wings on your own. Make the most of it!'

Now he had the day at his disposal, and his starting point must be the spot where Domville had died. He took the quickest way to it, a risky and unorthodox route he had sometimes used on more obscure business of his own. The Meole brook, where it bordered the abbey fields and gardens, was fordable except in flood-time, provided a man knew it well, and Cadfael knew it perfectly. He thus cut off a detour by the roads, at the mere cost of kilting his habit above the knees, and sandals let out water as freely as they let it in. By the time chapter ended at the abbey, he was on the path where the baron had been ambushed, and pushing on along it at a good pace.

This part of the path he knew, it lay directly across a great winding bend of the brook, and he was approaching the second ford which would take him out of the loop, and away through woods and fields towards Sutton and Beistan, sparsely peopled country approaching the great stretch of the Long Forest. He did not think that Domville could have had many miles to go, nor that he had spent the night in the open. A man tough enough for that and worse when there was need, but fond of his comforts when things were going easily.

At Sutton Strange the woods fell back before fields. Cadfael exchanged the time of day with a cottar whose children he had once treated for a skin rash, and enquired if the news of Domville's death had reached the village. It had, and was the chief gossip for miles around, and already the inhabitants were expecting that the hunt for the murderer might reach as far as their homes and byres the next day.

'I heard he had a hunting-lodge somewhere in these parts,' said Cadfael. 'On the edge of the forest is what I heard, but that could mean anywhere along ten miles of country. Would you know of the place?'

'Ah, that'll be the house over beyond Beistan,' said the cottar, leaning comfortably on his garden wall. 'He has rights of warren in the forest, but he came there only rarely, and keeps only a local lad there as steward, and the old woman his mother to take care for the house when it's unvisited. As it mostly is. He has better hunts elsewhere. *Had!* Seems someone set a snare for him, this time.'

'And made a thorough job of it,' said Cadfael soberly. 'How do I best go for this place? Through the village at Beistan?'

'That's it, and cross the old road and bear on between the

hills. You'll find this path makes a straight run of it. You'll be in the edge of the forest there, sure enough, before ever you see the house.'

Cadfael went on briskly, emerging on to a highroad at the village of Beistan, where the path he was following crossed and moved on, dead straight, past a few scattered holdings beyond, and then into fitful stretches of rising heathland and copses between two gentle slopes. After another mile or so it became a forest path once again, closely hemmed in. Where groundrock broke through into view, it was white and chalky, and in the more open glades heathers brushed crisp and prickly against his ankles. It was a long time since he had been so far afoot, and if he had not been on so grave a quest his walk would have been pure enjoyment.

He came upon the hunting-lodge quite abruptly, the trees falling away on either side to show him a low boundary wall of stones, and a squat timber building within, raised on an undercroft, with outhouses lining the rear wall of the enclosure. Among the rough white stones of the wall there were all manner of wild herbs growing, toadflax and ivy, stonecrop and self-heal, known by their leaves even now that hardly any flowers remained. There were orchard trees within the wall, but few and old and gnarled, as though someone had once made a garden here, but now it was neglected and forgotten. Some former lord, perhaps, of Domville's line, with a family of children, to turn this quite pleasant fastness into a favourite home, whereas in recent years a childless elderly man had had no use for it but in the hunting season, and even then preferred fatter forests elsewhere in his widespread honour.

Cadfael crossed to the open gate in the wall, and stepped within. Instantly his eye was caught by a broom-bush on the inner side, in a corner near the gate. For it was an unmistakable broom-bush, and yet in this autumn season it was in flower, and its flowers, scattered and starry, were of a bright and limpid blue instead of gold. He went closer, and saw that the three lowest courses of the wall and the ground beside were matted with proliferating stems, thin, straight, branching into long, narrow leaves. The mat on the ground reached the roots of the broom, and sent up long, frail stalks to clamber through its branches, thrusting up to the light these late, radiant clusters of heavenly blue.

He had found his creeping gromwell, and he had found the place where Huon de Domville had spent the last night of his life.

'You are seeking someone, brother?'

The voice behind him was respectful to the point of being obsequious, and yet had a cutting edge like a well-honed knife. He turned alertly to view the speaker, and found the very same ambiguous qualities. He must have come from the outhouses under the rear wall, a fine, well-set-up fellow about thirty-five years old, in country homespun but with a dignity to him that fell just short of a swagger. He had eyes like pebbles under a sunlit brook, as hard and clear, and as fluid and elusive in their glance. He was brown and handsome and altogether pleasant to the view, but he was not quite easy in his authority, and not quite friendly in his civility.

'You are Huon de Domville's steward at this house?' asked Brother Cadfael with wary courtesy.

'I am,' said the young man.

'Then the mission I have is to you,' said Cadfael amiably, 'though I think it may be unnecessary. You may have heard already, for I find it's known in the countryside, that your lord is dead, murdered, and is now lying in the abbey of Saint Peter and Saint Paul of Shrewsbury, from which I come.'

'So we heard yesterday,' said the steward, his manner somewhat easing at this reasonable explanation for the visit, though not as much as might have been expected. His face remained wary and his voice reserved. 'A cousin of mine brought the word, coming from the town market.'

'But no one has been to you from your lord's household? You've had no orders? I thought Canon Eudo might have sent to let you know. But you'll understand they're all in confusion and consternation yet. No doubt they'll be in touch with you and all his manors when they get round to the proper arrangements.'

'They'll be set first on getting hold of his murderer, no question,' said the man, and moistened his lips, elusive pebble-eyes looking slightly sidelong at Cadfael. 'I shall hear when his kin see fit. Meantime, I'm still in his service until another either confirms me in my stewardship here, or turns me off. I'll keep his property and stock as I should, and turn them over to his heir in good order. Say so for me, brother, and no man need trouble for this place. Let them put their minds at rest.' He veiled his eyes a moment, thinking. 'You did say murdered? Is that certain?'

'Certain,' said Cadfael. 'It seems he rode out after his supper, and was waylaid on his way back. We found him on a path that leads in this direction. It was in my mind he might have been here, seeing this grange is his.'

'He has not been here,' said the steward firmly.

'Not at all, since he came to Shrewsbury three days ago?'

'Not at all.'

'Nor any of his squires or servants?'

'No one.'

'So he did not lodge any guests here for the wedding feast. You keep his lodge alone?'

'I see to grounds and stock and farm, my mother keeps the house. The few times he ever hunted here, he brought his own body servants and cooks and all. But the last time's a good four years gone.'

Now he was lying as roundly and freely as he breathed. For there were the starry blue flowers that grew here, and could hardly be found anywhere else in the shire. But why so determined to deny that Domville had been here? Any wise man may go to ground when there's a death-hunt up, true, but this young man did not seem the sort to take fright easily. Yet clearly he was determined that no thread should connect this place or anyone in it with the murder of his lord.

'And they've not so far laid hand on his slayer?' No mistake, he would have been glad to have the quarry snared, the hue and cry over, the malefactor safe in prison, and all enquiry at an end.

'Not yet. They're out after him in force. Ah, well,' said Cadfael, 'I'd best be getting back, then, though to tell the truth, I'm in no hurry. It's a fair day, and a good long walk is a pleasure. But would there be a cup of ale and a bench to sit a while, before I set off?'

He had half-expected reluctance, if not some ingenious refusal, to let him into the house; but the young man almost visibly changed his mind, and decided that it would be his best course to invite this monk freely within. Why? To have him see for himself that there was no one here to account for, and nothing to hide? Whatever the motive, Cadfael accepted with alacrity, and followed his host through the open doorway.

The hall was dim and silent, the scent of timber rich and heavy. A little, brisk old woman, very neat and plain, came bustling from the room beyond, and halted in surprise, if not downright alarm, at sight of a stranger, until her son, with slightly suspect speed and emphasis, accounted for the guest.

'Come through, brother, we may as well sit in the best comfort. We very seldom have gentlefolk here to make use of the solar. Mother, will you bring us a stoup? The good brother has a long walk back.'

The solar was light and bright, and furnished with considerable comfort. They sat down together over the ale and oatcakes the old housekeeper brought, and talked of the weather and the season, and the prospects for the winter, and even of the sad state of the country, torn two ways between King Stephen and the empress. Shropshire might be at peace just now, but peace was precarious everywhere in this divided land. The empress had been allowed to join her half-brother Robert of Gloucester in Bristol, and others were throwing in their lot with her, Brian

FitzCount, the castellan of Wallingford, Miles, the constable of Gloucester, and others besides. It was rumoured that the city of Worcester was being threatened with attack from Gloucester. Devoutly they agreed to hope that the tide of war would come no nearer, perhaps even spare Worcester.

But for all this innocuous talk, Brother Cadfael's senses were on the alert; and it might, after all, have been a miscalculation on the steward's part to invite him in, so that he could see for himself how all was empty, well-kept and innocent. For it certainly was not the old woman who had brought that faint, indefinable perfume into the room. Nor had the one who distilled it been gone from here very long, for such a fragrance would have faded away within a few days. Cadfael had a nose for floral essences, and recognised jasmine.

There was nothing more to be discovered here within. He rose to take his leave and give thanks for his entertainment, and the steward went out with him dutifully, no doubt to make sure that he set off back to the abbey without deceit. It was pure chance that the old woman should be coming out of the stables in the yard just as they emerged, and had let the door swing wide open behind her before she was aware of them. Her son was deft and quick to spring across and close it, shooting the bar home. But he had not been quite quick enough.

Cadfael gave no sign of having noticed more than he should, but said his farewell cheerfully at the gate, beside the broombush that bore blue flowers instead of gold, and set off at a swinging pace back along the path by which he had come.

There was a horse in that stable certainly not built to carry Huon de Domville's lusty weight, or sustain a day's hunting even under one of his retinue. Cadfael had glimpsed the small, delicate white head and curious face peering out, the arched neck and braided mane, and the light, ornate harness hanging on the inner side of the swinging door. A pretty little white jennet, such as a lady would ride, and such elaborate and decorative accoutrements as would be provided for a lady. Yet he would have been prepared to swear that there was no lady there at the hunting-lodge now. There had been no warning of his approach, no time to hide her away. He had been brought in expressly to see for himself that she was not there, that no one was there but the usual custodians.

Why, then, however dismayed she might be at the thought of being hunted out of her privacy, displayed as having some dark connection with Domville's death, perhaps even suspected of collusion in it, why should she choose to depart on foot, and leave her mount idle behind? And where, on foot, in such a remote solitude, could such a lady go?

He did not return directly to the abbey, but continued along the green ride until it emerged on the Foregate, and made his way to the bishop's house. The great courtyard, usually such a bustle, was quiet indeed on this afternoon, for even the grooms and able-bodied servants had been drafted into the hunt as beaters, and were out somewhere in the woods. Only the older men were left here, which suited Cadfael well enough, for the oldest servants were the most likely to know all their lord's private business, whether they ever acknowledged it or not, and the absence of the busy and sharp-eared young made confidences more likely.

He sought out Domville's chamberlain, who had, it seemed, been in his master's service many years, and moreover, had the shrewd good sense to see the force of telling unvarnished truth, now that Domville himself was gone. There was no one else here to be feared, complete frankness would serve his turn best with the sheriff. There would be an inevitable interregnum, and then a new master. The servants were under no suspicion, and had nothing to fear, why conceal anything that might be of significance?

The chamberlain was a man well past sixty, grey-haried and staid, with illusionless eyes and the withdrawn, resigned dignity of most old servants. His name was Arnulf, and he had answered all the sheriff's questions without hesitation, and was willing to answer as candidly any others that Cadfael or any man might put to him. An age had come to an end with his lord's death, he would have to trim his service to quite another rule now, or go into retirement and take his ease.

Nevertheless, the first question Cadfael asked was one Arnulf had certainly not foreseen.

'Your lord had the name for a womaniser. Tell me this, had he a mistress of such importance—or perhaps a new sweetheart so absorbing—that he could not do without her even for these few days while he married the Massard heiress? Someone he might bring along with him, and install within reach, but apart?'

The old man gaped, as if such forthright words came curiously from one in a Benedictine habit, but after narrow scrutiny appeared to find, after all, nothing so surprising about it. His manner relaxed noticeably. They had a language and an experience of life in common.

'Brother, however you may have hit on it, yes, there is such a woman. They come in all kinds, women. I was never a great one for them myself, I've had troubles enough without courting more. But *he* could not go far or long without them. They came and went, with him. By the score! But there's this one who is different. She stays. Stable as a wife. Like an old gown or a pair of shoes, easy and comfortable, someone he need not make speeches for, or put himself out to flatter and please. I had a feeling always,' said Arnulf reflectively, scrubbing in his beard with thin fingers, 'that wherever he went, she wouldn't be far away. But I know nothing of any plans to bring her here. Not that he ever made use of me in such matters. I helped him into his shirts and hose, and pulled off his boots after hunting, and slept close to fetch him wine in the night if he called. Not for his women. That's another service. What of her? There's been no word of her here. I did wonder.'

'Nor of a palfrey,' asked Cadfael, 'pure white, mane and all? A pretty little lady's jennet out of Spanish stock, I should say by the glimpse I got of her. With a gilded bridle hanging on her stable door.'

'I know the one,' said Arnulf, startled. 'He bought it for her. I was not supposed even to know these things. Where have you seen it?'

Cadfael told him. 'The horse, but not the woman. She left her palfrey and her perfume behind, but she's gone.'

'Well,' allowed Arnulf reasonably, 'I suppose she might well want to avoid being tangled in a matter of murder, and certainly if she was there, and he found on that path, as they tell, it would seem that he rode to her when he sent young Simon in and went on alone. She might well take fright and think it better to vanish.'

'She has also very loyal servants there,' said Cadfael drily, 'who are exerting themselves to convince me and all the world she never was there at all. By this time I daresay that young fellow has moved the jennet away to a safe place.'

It had occurred to him, somewhat belatedly, that the steward might have good reason to do as much for his own sake, as well as the lady's. If she had been in attendance there all this while, waiting for a visit from her lord and keeper, she might well have passed the time pleasantly enough with a younger, handsomer, altogether more personable man who was there to hand. And he, for his part, might have a healthy fear of having the association known, in case it should bring him into suspicion of having made away with his lord for the woman's sake, in jealousy and despite. It was but one step further to wonder if he had not done that very thing. Say that Domville came that night, after the young man had been blessed with the woman's favours to the point where he thought of her as his. Say that he was cast out into the night while they were together, and had nothing to do but brood and grieve, until it came to him that his lord's way home lay clear, and if he removed the act far enough from the lodge, near enough to Shrewsbury, he left the field wide open for any man to be judged the killer. It was possible! It could have happened so. Much depended on the woman. Cadfael wished that he knew more of her.

'The question now is, since she left her mount behind, where could she go from that remote place, on foot?' It was also, why should she choose to go afoot, but that he did not say, that was a more obscure problem.

'The manor where he usually kept her—her home, you might say—is well away in Cheshire.' Arnulf considered, and visibly stirred himself to recall things long neglected or forgotten. 'But it was somewhere in these very parts he found her. Some rustic beauty, a young girl then, twenty years and more ago, that must have been. Yes, more. She used to be known as Avice of Thornbury, they say her father was the village wheelwright there. They were free folk, I recollect, not villeins.' So the village craftsmen usually were, but tied to their tofts just as surely as the villeins to the land. 'Most likely she still has kin there,' said Arnulf. 'Would that be far? I'm strange in these parts.'

'No,' said Cadfael, enlightened, 'it is not far. Thornbury I know. There she could have gone on foot.'

He went away from the bishop's house with much to think about. The vanishing lady became ever more interesting. Since it was more than twenty years that she had been Domville's patient, permanent mistress, so firmly established as to have the respectability and the calm subservience of a wife, she must be fully forty years old, some years senior to that young steward at the hunting-lodge, but no doubt she must still have the charms to dazzle him, if she so wished. Yes, he could have fallen victim to desire and jealousy, and seen fit to rid himself of the old, hard man who was her owner and stood between. But the revelation of her probable years had other implications. So far gone towards middle age, a woman was unlikely to strike up another such comfortable liaison, now Domville was dead. That consideration could well have caused her to reflect that her own people were hardly more than a mile away, and that with them she could vanish, and be hidden for as long as she felt the need to hide.

But why, why should she leave behind a valuable horse, her own property, the gift of her lord? She could just as well have ridden to Thornbury as walked.

Today was more or less spent, he must go back ready for Vespers, and see what prodigies of destruction or genius Brother Oswin had performed in his absence.

But tomorrow he would find her!

At Saint Giles two young men were fretting over their personal problems. Brother Mark had long since made up his mind that the tall leper who matched Lazarus in all particulars but the completeness of his hands was indeed the fugitive squire for whom the sheriff was hunting with such formidable numbers and such ferocious determination. He was therefore caught up in a moral dilemma of some complexity.

He had heard the story of the supposed theft of the bride's necklace, but it was as suspect to him as to Brother Cadfael. Too many men, in all manner of circumstances, had been dragged to ruin and death simply by inserting such valuables into their baggage. It was all too easy a way of wiping out an enemy. He simply did not believe in it. Nor, having observed Huon de Domville, would he willingly have surrendered any man to his vengeance, which was likely to be mortal.

But the murder, that was another matter. He found it all too credible that a young man so wronged, if that accusation had indeed been false, should be driven to brood on revenge even against his nature, and to extremes. Where then was right? And yet the ambush, and the finishing of a stunned man, stuck fast in Mark's humble, unknightly craw. Such a vengeance no man could sanction. He was wrought to the limit, and he could not put off his burden upon any other shoulders. He alone knew what he knew.

He thought of approaching the intruder directly and asking for his confidence, but such a move demanded a privacy hardly to be found in this enclosed community. Not until he was certain of guilt would he make any move that should draw attention to the fugitive. Every man should be adjudged innocent until there was proof against him, and all the more where very suspect and malicious charges had already been thrown at him, and rang leaden as false coin.

If I can find occasion to be alone with him, unobserved of any, Brother Mark decided, I will speak openly and judge as I find. If I cannot, or until I can, I will watch him as best I may, mark all that he does, challenge him if he attempts any ill, stand ready to speak in his defence if he does none. And pray that God may see fit to make use of me for truth, one way or the other.

The object of his concern was sitting with Lazarus at a discreet distance from the highway but within view, some quarter of a mile along the road that led towards the river crossinq at Atcham. One of the begging bowls they held, at least, was legitimate, but they made no appeals to any of those who passed by, and used their warning clappers only if some charitably disposed soul showed signs of approaching too closely. They sat cross-legged and shrouded in the bleached autumnal grass under the trees. The attitudes were easily learned.

'Just as you are,' said Lazarus, 'you might walk away through their cordon and go free. They will not believe any man so brave or so mad as to walk in a dead leper's gown, or be themselves so brave or so mad as to risk stripping you to find out.' It was a long speech for him, by the end he stumbled, as if his maimed tongue tired of the effort.

'What, run and save my own skin and leave her still captive? I do not stir from her,' said Joscelin vehemently, 'while she is still in ward to an uncle who plunders her substance, and will sell her for his own profit. To a worse than Huon de Domville, if the price is right! What use is my freedom to me, if I turn my back on Iveta in her need?'

'I think,' said the slow tongue beside him, 'that if truth be told, you want this lady for yourself. Do I belie you?'

'Not by a hair!' said Joscelin with passion. 'I want this lady for myself as I never have wanted and never shall want anything else in this great world. I should want her the same if she lacked not only lands, but shoes on her feet to walk those lands, I should want her if she were what I am feigning to be now, and what you—God be your remedy!—truly are. But for all that, I'd be content—no, grateful!—only to see her safe in the care of a worthy guardian, with all her honours upon her, and free to choose where she would. Surely I'd do my best to win her! But lose her to a better man, yes, that I would, and never complain. Oh, no, you do not belie me! I ache with wanting her!'

'But what can you do for her, hunted as you are? Is there ever a friend among them you can rely on?'

'There's Simon,' said Joscelin, warming. 'He doesn't believe evil of me. He hid me, out of goodwill, it grieves me that I quit the place without a word to him. If I could get a message to him now, he might even be able to speak with her, and have her meet me as she did once before. Now the old man's gone—but how can that ever have come about!—they may not watch her so closely. Simon might even get me my horse . . .'

'And where,' asked the patient, detached voice, 'would you take this friendless lady, if you got her out of ward?'

'I've thought of that. I'd take her to the White Ladies at Brewood, and ask sanctuary for her until enquiry could be made into her affairs, and a proper provision made for her. They would not give her up against her will. It would go as far as the king, if need be. He has a good heart, he'd see her justly used. I would a long sight sooner take her to my mother,' burst out Joscelin honestly, 'but it would be said I coveted her possessions, and that I won't endure. I have two good manors coming to me, I covet no man's lands, I owe no man, and I won't be misprised. If she still chooses me, I'll thank God and her, and be a happy man. But I care most that she should be a happy woman.'

Lazarus reached for his clapper-dish, and set the clapper woodenly clouting, for a plump, solid horseman had halted his pony and turned aside from the road towards them. The rider, nonetheless, smiled from his distance and tossed a coin. Lazarus gathered it and blessed him, and the good man waved a hand and rode on.

'There is still goodness,' said Lazarus, as if to himself.

'Praise God, there is!' said Joscelin with unaccustomed humility. 'I have experienced it. I have never asked you,' he said hesitantly, 'if you have ever had wife and child. It would be great waste if you had always been solitary.'

There was a lengthy silence, though silences at Lazarus's side were neither rare nor troublesome. At last the old man said: 'I had a wife, long dead now. I had a son. He was blessed, in that my shadow never fell upon him.'

Joscelin was startled and indignant. 'I don't find you a shadow. Never speak so! Any son of yours might properly joy in his father.'

The old man's head turned, the eyes above the veil shone steadily and piercingly upon his companion. 'He never knew,' said Lazarus simply. 'Hold him excused, he was only an infant. It was my choice, not his.'

Young and blunt and blundering as he was, Joscelin had learned in haste to understand where he might not pass, and must not and need not wonder. It astonished him, when he looked back, to discover how far his education had progressed in these two days among the outcasts.

'And there is a question you have never asked me,' he said.

'Nor do I ask it now,' said Lazarus. 'It is a question you have not asked me, either, and since a man can hardly say anything but no to it, what sense is there in asking?'

In the mortuary chapel of the abbey, after Vespers, Huon de Domville was coffined, in the presence of Prior Robert, Canon Eudo, Godfrid Picard, and the dead man's two remaining squires. Picard and the two young men had ridden in from the fruitless day's hunting, tired and irritable, still cloaked and gloved, with no captured malefactor to show for their trouble, though whether that was a matter for regret to anyone here but Picard and Eudo seemed to be in some doubt.

The candles on the altar and at the head and foot of the bier guttered gently in a chill draught, and the shadows of those present quivered hugely on the walls. Prior Robert's long white hand took the aspergillum, and shook a few drops of holy water delicately over the dead, and the candle-light caught their flight and turned them to sparks, kindled and dying in the air. Canon Eudo followed, and looking round for the only other kinsman present, handed the aspergillum to Simon, who stripped off his gloves hastily to take it. He stood looking down at his uncle's body with a sombre face as he dipped the brush of sweet herbs, and sprinkled holy water in his turn.

'I had not thought to do this for many a year yet,' he said, and turned to hold out the aspergillum to Picard and withdraw again into the shadows.

The green sprays shook some drops of water on the back of his hand as he relinquished them, and Picard watched them fall, and saw the young man shake them off as if startled at their coldness. There was something fascinating in the way the light of the candles picked out so sharply every detail of those ministering hands, cut off at the wrist by dark sleeves. So many severed hands moving and acting with a life of their own, the only pallors in the enfolding dimness. From Prior Robert's pale, elegant fingers to Guy's smooth brown fist, last of the ministrants, they performed their ritual dance and held all eyes. Only when the act of reverence was done could all those present look up, and find relief in the more human pallor of strained and solemn faces. It seemed that everyone drew a deep breath, like swimmers surfacing.

It was over. The five of them separated, Prior Robert to a brief session of prayers for the dead before supper, Canon Eudo to the abbot's lodging, the two young men to walk their jaded horses back to the bishop's house and see them tended, stabled and fed before seeking their own supper and rest. As for Picard, he bade them all a very short goodnight, and withdrew to the guest-hall, and there drew Agnes with him into their own chamber, and closed the door against all the rest of the household, even those most trusted. He had matter of importance to confide to her, and it was for no other ears.

The little boy Bran had begged and brought away with him from his lesson the strips of worn vellum trimmed from the sheet on which he practised his letters. He got credit with his teacher for wanting them, though his purpose was not quite what Mark supposed. In the dortoir, where he should long ago have been asleep, he crept to Joscelin's side with his prizes, and whispered the secret into his ear.

'For you wanted to send a message. Lazarus told me. Is it true you can write and read?' He was in awe of anyone who had such mysteries at his finger-ends. He nestled close to Joscelin's side, to be heard and to hear in the most private of whispers. 'In the morning you could use Brother Mark's ink-horn, no one will be watching his desk. If you can write it, I could carry it, if you tell me where. They don't notice me. But the best piece of the leaf is not very big, it would have to be a short message.'

Joscelin wrapped the folds of his cloak round the skinny little body against the chill of the night, and drew him into his arm. 'You're a good, gallant ally, and I'll make you my squire if ever I get to be knight. And you shall learn Latin hand, and reckoning, and matters far beyond me. But yes, I can write a sort of fist that will serve. Where's your vellum?' He felt the meagre width but sufficient length of the strip that was pressed eagerly into his hand. 'It will do very well. Twenty words can say much. Bless you for a clever imp as ever was!'

The head from which Brother Mark's pellitory dressing had erased even the last drying sore of under-feeding and dirt burrowed comfortably into Joscelin's once-privileged shoulder, and he felt nothing but amused and indulgent affection. 'I can get as far as the bridge,' boasted Bran sleepily, 'if I keep to the back ways. If I had a capuchon I could get into the town. I'll go wherever you say . . .'

'Will your mother be missing and wanting you?' Joscelin breathed into the boy's ear. The woman, he knew, had given up all care for the world, and waited only to leave it. Even her son she abandoned thankfully into the hands of Saint Giles, patron of the diseased and shunned.

'No, she's asleep . . .' So, almost, was her busy and contented child, for whom the excitement of study and the small intrigues of friendship opened the world that was closing on her.

'Come, then, shift close, and go to sleep. Creep inside, and get my warmth.' He turned to let the searching face find a nest in the crook of his shoulder, and was startled by the pleasure he got from its delighted confiding. Long after the child was asleep he lay awake wondering that so much of his interest and energy should be directed elsewhere when his own neck was threatened, and so much of his thought devoted to excluding this small, neglected soul from whatever peril he himself had incurred, by his folly or his fate. Yes, he would write, he would try to find a way of getting his message to Simon, but not by involving the innocent lying easy in his arm.

Joscelin also slept, and with mutual drowsy movements accommodated his guest all night long. Somewhere apart, Lazarus lay wakeful far into the night, long since having discarded his need for sleep.

8 🐚

JOSCELIN AROSE BEFORE DAWN, WITH SCRUPULOUS CARE NOT
to awake his bedfellow, who lay now in his abandoned ease and
warmth with limbs flung abroad as if discarded. The voluminous leper-cloak Joscelin left draped over the child, for the
early air was chilly, and moreover, he dared not draw nearer the
town wearing it, though the risk of approaching without its
cover was surely as great. He would have to rely on keeping out
of sight, and also drew some comfort from the fact that the previous day's drive must have virtually exhausted the possibility
of taking the sheriff's quarry on the northern side of the Foregate, and therefore, or so at least he hoped, the watch would be
concentrated elsewhere.

He stole out through the hall, and picked up Brother Mark's
ink-horn and quill from the desk. He would not wait for light
from dawn, and could make none here, but in the church the
constant light on the altar, however meagre, would be enough
for his young eyes and few words. He had already worked out

in his mind what he would write, and managed it legibly, if none too neatly, on his strip of vellum. The quill needed trimming, and tended to spit, but he had no knife to correct it. He was come to the condition of those now his comrades, but that his skin and limbs were whole; otherwise he had nothing but what he stood up in, no possessions of any kind at his disposal.

'Simon, for friendship do me two things, tether Briar in cover across the brook from the abbey, and bid Iveta to the herb-garden after Vespers.'

It would be enough, if he could find some way to get it to the right hands. But if he could not, he must withhold it, since he had written Simon's name. He regretted now the natural impulse to give his missive an address, in case it fell astray, for how could he implicate his friend in his own troubles? But he had no means of cutting off the offending name. It must go as it was, or stay, and destroy the only plan he had. It behoved him to be even more wary and even more audacious, in his attempt to reach the right man.

He went out into just such a pre-dawn dimness and stillness as when he had run from his hiding-place in the bishop's grounds. Warily he made his way behind the hospice and towards the town, keeping well away from the road, where trees and bushes afforded him cover. When he came to the gardens and backyards of houses he was forced further from the highway, but he had time enough to move with caution. No one would stir at the bishop's house until the first light came, no one would quit the courtyard until it was full day, and the gentlefolk had broken their fast. He reached the narrow, tree-shaded path that emerged on the Foregate beside the bishop's boundary wall, and paused to choose his ground. Only by climbing could he see over the wall, and if he must take to the trees it had better be where he could view both the inner and the outer sides of the courtyard, recognise known figures, and watch all the activity about the stables.

He chose his place with care, in the bole of an oak, stretched along a limb still covered well enough to hide him, but affording him views on both sides, and a quick and easy drop to the ground should he have to move in haste. Then there was nothing to be done but wait, for the dawn was still only a grudging pallor in the east. He would miss his breakfast, today nobody need steal for him.

Dawn came at last, in its own good time. The house, the containing wall, the stables and byres and storehouses within, all took shape very gradually out of darkness, and put on colour and life. Sleepy servants, bakers and grooms and dairy-maids, first crept, and then bustled, out about their business. Loaded trays of loaves appeared from the bakehouse, carried indoors by scullions. The morning loitered a further while, and the gentry began to make their appearances, Canon Eudo the first of them, bound for the second Mass of the day, then, some little while later, Simon and Guy together, none too eager, and deep in sombre talk. The grooms were leading out, surely, most of the horses in the stables. It seemed that the morning's hunt was already ordered and preparing to muster.

Muster they did, Guy resigned but sullen among them, and file out from the gate to turn along the Foregate towards the town. But Simon did not mount with them. He was still standing on the steps of the hall, looking after them, and apparently waiting for something. The bishop's own stable was round a corner of the house and out of Joscelin's view, but he pricked his ears to the sound of hooves, urgent and lively, coming round thence into the courtyard. In a moment more he saw his own Briar, silvery grey blotched with darker grey, frisk indignantly out into the open air of the morning, tugging a sweating and voluble groom with him. Simon came down from the steps to meet them, ran a hand over gleaming grey neck and shoulder, and held the silvery head between his palms a moment, in an appreciative caress. Joscelin's heart warmed to him. With all this coil of troubles, he had still spared a thought for the active beast shut up in a stall, and haled him out for exercise. The words he spoke to the groom as he turned back to re-enter the house were not distinguishable at this distance, but his gestures towards horse and gateway had said plainly enough: 'Saddle him up and lead him out for me.'

Joscelin waited long enough to see for himself that the groom was about that very business, and then dropped out of his tree, and moved cautiously forward in cover of the bushes until he could see the outside of the gates. And here they came, Briar mischievously lively, impatient for action. The groom led him out, and hitched him indifferently to one of the rings in the wall beside the mounting-block, and there left him to wait for his rider. It could not have turned out better. As soon as the man had gone back into the yard, and was tramping across the cobbles to the stable, Joscelin was out of cover and darting along the wall to caress and soothe a startled and delighted Briar. There was no time for dalliance, and at first he cursed the chance that a couple of horsemen came jingling along the Foregate at that moment, and he was forced to turn his back on the road and stand stolidly holding the bridle until they passed, as though he had been one of the grooms waiting for his master. But the enforced delay gave time for Briar to feel reassured, and stand in charmed quietness, while Joscelin hurriedly knotted his strip of vellum securely in the silvery forelock.

The riders had passed, for the moment the Foregate here was empty, and there was no one on the path between the trees. Joscelin tore himself away from his favourite perforce, shutting his ears to the protesting whinny that pursued him, and ran like a bolting hare back into cover, and did not stop until he had worked his way some distance back towards Saint Giles.

It was done, he dared not stop to see whether it took immediate effect, for now it was broad day, and growing populous on the roads, and he had better hide himself as quickly as possible in his leper's gown, so much stronger a defence than any weapon, since no one would willingly draw near enough to be contaminated. He could only pray that Simon would find the message—surely before he had been astride Briar long he must notice the knotted mane!—and act on it faithfully. There was at least a safeguard of sorts, Joscelin reflected, for if he made his way to the copses opposite the abbey fields at the time appointed, and failed to find Briar secreted there, he could draw off again, on the assumption that his plea had gone astray, or never been detected. Draw off, and try something else, but never give up, never until Iveta was in better hands, and properly treated.

Meantime, this day of all days, he must remain until evening tamed and exemplary about Saint Giles, taking no risks, drawing no attention to himself.

In the spinney at the edge of the hospital grounds he paused to look ahead before venturing close, suddenly aware of his perilous nakedness without the cloak, now that it was light. And out of the bushes arose a small, hurtling figure with a trailing dark garment bundled under one arm, and embraced him about the thighs with the other arm, reproaching him bitterly in a breathy undertone: 'You never woke me! You went away and left me! *Why* did you?'

Startled and touched, Joscelin sat on his heels and embraced the child heartily in return. 'I was not sleeping, and you were, so soundly it would have been shame to disturb you. And it's done, and I'm back, so hold me excused. I know you'd have done as well or better, never think I didn't trust you . . .'

Bran thrust the gown at him sternly. 'Put it on! And here is the face-cloth . . . How would you have got back into the hospice without it?' He had brought a hunk of bread, too, to make up for the missed breakfast. Joscelin broke it in two, and gave him back the greater half, shaken clean out of his preoccupations by an irresistible tenderness that filled him with a wild urge to laughter.

'What should I do without you, my squire? You see I'm barely fit to be let out without my keeper. Now I promise you I'll let you bearlead me all this day—except for your lesson-time with Brother Mark, of course! We'll do whatever you please. You shall call the tune.'

He shrouded himself obediently in the adopted vestments, and they consumed the bread together in silent content before he draped the linen cloth again about his face. Hand in hand they emerged solemnly from the trees, and made their way decorously back into the precincts of Saint Giles.

Simon had trotted an exuberant Briar almost to the abbey gatehouse before he noticed the knotted forelock and reaching to discover the cause, with some displeasure at such poor grooming, felt the coiled strip of vellum hard under his fingers. He eased to a walk, which did not please his mount, while he disentangled the roll, and uncoiled it curiously.

Joscelin's none too practised fist, further complicated by poor light for the writing, and an unbiddable quill, cut to another man's hand, was nevertheless readable. Simon shut the coil hurriedly in his palm, as though someone might be paying too close attention, and looked back over his shoulder, and all about him, belatedly searching for some sign as to how this sudden message had been placed here for him, and where his elusive correspondent might be. Far too late! He might be anywhere. There was no way of laying hand on him or getting word to him, except by doing what he asked, and setting a scene to which he would certainly come.

Simon put the leaf away carefully in the pouch at his belt, and rode on very thoughtfully. Beyond the gatehouse, towards the bridge that crossed the Severn into the town, the sheriff's forces were beginning to mass. In the great court of the abbey the usual business of the day proceeded. The lay brothers were coming forth briskly to the main gardens at the Gaye, and going about the affairs of the grange court and the stock. Brother Edmund bustled between the herbarium and the wards of his infirmary, and Brother Oswald the almoner was distributing doles to the few beggars at the gate. Simon rode in soberly through the gates, and handed over Briar to a groom. At the guest-hall he asked audience with Godfrid Picard, and was promptly admitted.

Iveta was sitting with Madlen in her own chamber, listlessly sewing at a piece of decorative tapestry for a cushion. It was true that she could go forth now if she wished, but not beyond the gatehouse, She had tried it once, very fearfully, and been turned back by one of her uncle's men, civilly but with a faint, furtive grin that made her cheeks burn. And what was the use of going forth only within this closed ground, however pleasant it might have been in other circumstances, when Joscelin was only God knew where, and she had no means of reaching him? Better to sit here and hold her breath, and listen for a wind of freedom, with word of him. The brother who had warded off the lightnings once, and once conjured her back kindly into a bleak world, he was one friend, even if she had not spoken with him of late. And there was also Simon. He was loyal, he did not believe in the charges made against Joscelin. If the chance ever offered, he would help them.

Iveta stitched away and sat very still, all the more after she had caught the faint sound of voices raised in the next room. Even the inner walls here were solid, and held out sound, she did not think Madlen had noticed anything to arouse her interest. Accordingly Iveta carefully suppressed her own. But it was no mistake. Her uncle was quarrelling with someone. She detected it by the vicious vehemence of his voice rather than by any loudness, indeed it was purposefully quiet, and words quite indistinguishable. The other voice was younger, less cautious, more furiously defensive, surely astonished and aghast, as if this fell on him out of a clear sky. Still no words, only the thread of significant sound, two voices clashing in bitter conflict. And now she thought she caught an intonation in the second voice which provided a name that could only dismay her. What could have happened between her uncle and Simon? For surely that was Simon's voice. Was her uncle growing suspicious of every young man who came near her? She knew only too well that he had a treasure to guard, herself, the great honour she bore like a millstone round her neck, the use that could be made of her, the profit that could accrue from her. Yet only a day or so ago Simon had been welcome, privileged, smiled upon by Aunt Agnes.

Madlen sat stolidly stitching at a linen coif for herself, and paid no heed. Her ear was older and duller; if she heard the hum of conversation, that was all.

And even that had ceased. A door closed. Iveta thought she caught a renewed murmur next door, urgent and low. Then the door of her own chamber opened, after a round, confident rap, and Simon entered as of right. Iveta was lost, she could only stare; but he had the right note.

'Goodmorrow, Iveta!' he said easily. And to the maid: 'Give me leave a little while, Mistress Madlen!'

Madlen had Agnes's smiles and becks well in mind, he was still privileged to her. She took up her sewing, made her reverence complacently, indulgent as on the last occasion, and left the room.

The door had barely closed on her when Simon was on his knee beside Iveta, and leaning close. And for all his disciplined calm, he was flushed and breathing hard, his nostrils flaring agitatedly.

'Listen, Iveta, for they'll not let me in to you again. . . . If she tells them I'm here with you now, they'll hunt me out . . . I've word for you from Joss!' She would have questioned, dismayed and anxious, but he laid silencing fingers on her lips, and rushed on, low and vehemently: 'Tonight, after Vespers, he bids you come to the herb-garden. And I'm to have his horse waiting on the other side of the brook. Don't fail him, as I shall not. Have you understood?'

She nodded, almost speechless with wonder and joy and alarm all mingled. 'Oh, *yes!* Oh, Simon, I would do anything! God bless you for his loyal friend! But you . . . What can have happened? Why, why turn against *you?*'

'Because I spoke up for Joss. I said he was neither murderer nor thief, and in the end I would see him vindicated, and they'd have to take back all they've said against him. They'll have no more of me, I'm cast off. But here's his message . . . look!'

She knew the scrawl, and read, quivering. She fondled the slip of vellum as if it had been a holy relic, but closed Simon's hand over it again, though reluctantly.

'They might find it . . . you keep it. I'll do his bidding, and thank you a thousand times for all your goodness. But oh, Simon, I'm sorry that between us we've brought you to grief, too . . .'

'Grief, what grief?' he whispered fiercely. 'I care nothing for them, if I have *your* goodwill.'

'Always, always . . . more than goodwill! You have been so good to me, what should I have done without you? If we break free . . . if we can . . . we'll find you. You will always be our dearest friend!'

She was clinging to the hand with which he had hushed her, trying to express by touch the gratitude for which words seemed inadequate, but he made a warning grimace and withdrew his hand quickly, rising and standing back from her in one lissome movement, for there was a footstep at the door, a hand at the latch. 'The herb-garden!' he whispered, and noted the answering flash of her eyes, at once resolute and terrified.

'I'm glad to see you so much restored,' he was saying formally as the door opened. 'I could not take my leave without paying my respects.'

Picard came into the room with deliberate pace, his narrow, subtle face cold, his voice colder still, though carefully civil.

'Still here, Messire Aguilon? Our niece is keeping her room, and should not be disturbed. And I had thought you were in haste to return to your household and make ready. You're pledged to join the sheriff's forces this day, I hope you mean to keep your word.'

'I shall do what is required of me,' said Simon shortly. 'But not on my friend's horse! But rest assured, my lord, I shall join the sheriff's line as I'm ordered, and in good time.'

Agnes had appeared at her lord's shoulder, tightlipped, with narrowed eyes glittering suspicion. Simon made a deep reverence to Iveta, a stiff and formal one to Agnes, and marched out of the room. Two heads turned to watch him out of the hall in grim silence, and when he was gone, turned with the same chill unanimity to study Iveta. She bent her head meekly over her embroidery, to hide the defiant joy she could not quite banish from her face, and said never a word. The concentrated silence lasted long, but at length they went away, shutting the door upon her. They had asked nothing. She thought they were satisfied. When had she ever shown any spirit on her own account? They did not know, they had no means of understanding, what prodigies she felt she could do now, for Joscelin.

Brother Cadfael had set out, immediately after breaking his fast, on a mule borrowed from the abbey stables, and by the time Iveta received Joscelin's message he had passed Beistan, and was in the open woodland near the hunting-lodge. To reach the hamlet of Thornbury it was not necessary to keep to the path that led to the lodge, he struck off somewhat to the right, westward into the edges of the Long Forest. Between lodge and village the distance was hardly more than a mile, yet still it remained a mystery why a woman should abandon a good horse, and choose to remove herself there on foot.

The trees fell back as he approached the village, and left open to the sun a pleasant bowl of green meadows and striped ploughland, compact and well cared for. Scattered among the surrounding woods there were a few small, new assarts cut out of the forest by enterprising younger sons. And in the midst the low, timbered buildings clustered, fronds of blue smoke and the scent of wood fires hanging over them like a veil. Small, remote and poor, a place for hard-working men, but for all that, with plentiful fuel all around, and excellent poaching, which Cadfael judged might well be a communal enterprise here. Plentiful timber of all kinds, too, for the wheelwright's craft. Elm, essential for the stock, oak, to provide the cleft heartwood for the spokes, with the grain unbroken, and springy, supple ash to make the curved felloes of the rim, they were all here to hand.

Cadfael halted his mule at the first cottage, where a woman was feeding hens in her yard, and asked for the wheelwright.

'You're wanting Ulger?' she said, leaning a plump arm on her fence and viewing him with friendly curiosity. 'His toft's the far end there, past the pond, you'll see it by the timber stacks on your right hand. He has a wagon in for a new wheel, he'll be hard at it.'

Cadfael thanked her and rode on. Beyond the pond, where ducks gossiped and plunged, he saw the stacked wood seasoning, and came at once to the toft, a large undercroft well stocked with tools and materials, a room and a garret above, and in the yard before the house, a wagon standing, propped short of one wheel. The broken halves of it lay on the ground, several spokes shattered, the iron rim salvaged and perhaps to be used again. A new elm stock, already fully provided with spokes, lay star-like on the grass, and the wheelwright, a thick-set fellow of about forty-five years, bearded and muscular, was working away with an adze on a length of well-curved ash for the felloes, shaping with the grain of the wood.

'God bless the work!' said Cadfael, halting his mule and lighting down. 'I think you must be Ulger, and it's Ulger I'm seeking. But I looked for an older man.'

The wheelwright rose and abandoned his adze, moving at ease in his own kingdom. He looked at his visitor with amiable curiosity, a round-faced, good-natured soul, but with a dignified reserve about him, too. 'My father in his time was also Ulger, and also wheelwright to this and many another hamlet round here. Belike you had him in mind. God rest him, he died some years back. The toft and the office are mine.' And he added, after a rapid and shrewd scrutiny: 'You'll be from the Benedictines at Shrewsbury. By this way and that way, we do get word.'

'And we have our troubles, and you hear of them,' said Cadfael. He slipped the mule's bridle over a fence-pale, and shook out his habit and stretched his back after the ride. 'I tell you truth as I would be told truth. Huon de Domville was murdered early on his wedding-day, and at his hunting-lodge none so far from here he kept a woman. He was on his way from her when he died. And she is no longer at the hunting-lodge. They called her Avice of Thornbury, daughter to that Ulger who must be also your father. In these parts he found and took up with her. I do not think I tell you anything you did not already know.'

He waited, and there was silence. The wheelwright faced him with countenance suddenly hard and still, for all its native candour, and said no word.

'It is no part of my purpose or my need,' said Cadfael, 'to bring upon your sister any danger or threat. Nevertheless, she may know what justice needs to know, and not only for retribution, but for the deliverance of the innocent. All I want is speech with her. She left behind her at Domville's lodge her horse, and I believe much more that was hers. She left afoot. It is my belief that she came here, to her own people.'

'It is many years,' said Ulger, after a long silence, 'since I had a sister, many years since I and mine were her own people to Avice of Thornbury.'

'That I understand,' said Cadfael. 'Nevertheless, blood is blood. Did she come to you?'

Ulger regarded him sombrely, and made up his mind. 'She came.'

'Two days ago? After the news came from Shrewsbury of Huon de Domville found dead?'

'Two days ago, late in the afternoon she came. No, the news had not reached us then. But it had reached her.'

'If she is here with you,' said Cadfael, 'I must have speech with her.' He looked towards the house, where a sturdy, comely woman moved out and in again as he gazed. In a corner of the yard a boy of about fourteen was fining down cleft oak spokes for some lighter wheel. Ulger's wife and son. He saw no sign of another woman about the toft.

'She is not here,' said Ulger. 'Nor would she be welcome in my house. Only once or twice have we seen her since she chose to go for a Norman baron's whore, a shame to her kin and her race. I told her when she came that I would do for her all that a man should do for his sister, except let her into the house she abandoned long ago for money and ease and rich living. She was not changed nor put down. Make what you can of her, for I'm in many minds about her. She said calmly and civilly that she wanted nothing from me and mine but three things—the loan of my nag, a plain peasant gown in place of her fine clothes, and some hours of my son's time to guide her where she was bound, and bring back the horse safely. She had three miles to go, and her fine shoes were not fit for the way.'

'And these three you granted her?' said Cadfael, marvelling.

'I did. She put off her finery here in the undercroft, and put on an old gown of my wife's. Also she stripped off the rings from her hands and a gold chain from her neck, and gave them to my wife, for she said she had no more need of them, and they might pay a part of her debt here. And she mounted my nag, and the boy there went with her on foot, and before night he rode the horse back to us here. And that is all I know of her, for I asked nothing.'

'Not even where she was bound?'

'Not even that. But my son told me, when he returned.'

'And where is she gone?'

'To a place they call Godric's Ford, west from here and a short way into the forest.'

'I know it,' said Cadfael, enlightened. For at Godric's Ford there was a small grange of Benedictine nuns, a cell of the abbey of Polesworth. So Avice had made for the nearest female sanctuary in her need, for safe hiding under the protection of a powerful and respected abbey until Huon de Domville's murderer was known and taken, his death avenged, his mistress forgotten. From that secure haven she might be quite willing to speak out anything she did know to the purpose, provided she herself remained inviolable in her retreat.

So he was thinking, as he thanked Ulger for his help, and mounted to ride on to Godric's Ford. A very natural course for a discreet woman to take, if she feared she might be drawn into a great scandal and the complex web of a crime.

And yet . . . ! And yet she had left her jennet behind and gone afoot. And yet she had put off her finery for a homespun gown, and stripped the rings from her fingers, to pay a part of her life's debt to the kin she had deserted long ago. . . .

The grange at Godric's Ford was a decent long, low house in a broad clearing, with a small wooden chapel beside it, and a high stone wall enclosing its well-kept kitchen garden and orchard of fruit trees, now graced with only half their yellowing leaves. In a butt of newly dug ground within the wall a middle-aged novice, comfortably rounded in form and face, was planting out cabbage seedlings for the next spring. Cadfael observed her as he turned in at the gate and dismounted, and with his eye for competence and industry approved the confidence of her manner and the economy of her movements. Benedictine nuns, like Benedictine monks, think well of manual labour, and are expected to expend their energies as generously in cultivation as in prayer. This woman, rosily healthy, went about her work like a good, contented housewife, pressing the soil firm around her transplants with a broad foot, and brushing the loam from her hands with placid satisfaction. She was agreeably plump, and not very tall, and her face, however rounded and well-fleshed, yet had solid, determined bones and a notable firmness of lip and chin.

When she became aware of Cadfael and his mule, she straightened her back with the right cautious gradualness and a true gardener's grunt, and turned upon him shrewd brown eyes under brows quizzically oblique, very knowing eyes that took him in from cowl to sandals in one sweeping glance.

She left her plot, and came unhurriedly towards him.

'God greet you, brother!' she said cheerfully. 'Can any here be of service to you?'

'God bless your house!' said Cadfael ceremoniously. 'I am seeking speech with a lady who has recently sought sanctuary here within. Or so I reason from such knowledge as I have. She is called Avice of Thornbury. Can you bring me to her?'

'Very readily,' said the novice. In her russet apple cheek a sudden, startling dimple dipped and rose like a curtsey. Beauty, in its most mature and tranquil manifestation, flashed and faded with the change, leaving her demure and plain as before. 'If you're seeking Avice of Thornbury, you have found her. That name belongs to me.'

In the dark little parlour of the grange they sat facing each other across the small table. Benedictine monk and Benedictine nun-in-the-making, eyeing each other with mutual close interest. The superior had given them leave, and closed the door upon them, though the postulant's manner was of such assured authority that it seemed surprising she should ask anyone's permission to speak with her visitor, and even more surprising that she did so with such becoming humility. But Cadfael had already come to the conclusion that in dealing with this woman there would be no end to the surprises.

Where now was the expected image of the Norman baron's whore, spoiled, indulged, kept in state for her beauty? Such a creature should have laboured to keep her charms, with paints and creams and secret spells, starved to avoid growing fat, studied the arts of movement and grace. This woman had subsided placidly into middle age, had let the wrinkles form in her face and neck without disguise, and the grey invade her brown hair. Brisk and lively she still was, and would always be, sure of herself, feeling no need to be or seem other than she was. And just as she was she had held Huon de Domville for more than twenty years.

'Yes,' she said immediately, in answer to Cadfael's question. 'I was at Huon's hunting-lodge. He would always have me close, wherever he went. I have travelled the length and breadth of his honour many times over.' Her voice was low and pleasant, as serene as her person, and she spoke of her past as the most respectable of housewives might, after her man was dead, recalling quiet, domestic affection, customary and unexciting.

'And when you heard of his death,' said Cadfael, 'you thought best to withdraw from the scene? Did they tell you it was murder?'

'By the afternoon of that day it was common knowledge,' she said. 'I had no part in it, I had no means of guessing who had done such a thing. I was not afraid, if that's what you may be thinking, Brother Cadfael. I never yet did anything out of fear.'

She said it quite simply and practically, and he believed her. He would have gone further, and sworn that in her whole life she had never experienced fear. She spoke the very word with a kind of mild curiosity, as if she put her hand into a fleece to judge its weight and fineness.

'No, not fear—reluctance, rather, to play a part in any notorious or public thing. I have been discreet more than twenty years, to become a byword now is something I could not stomach. And when a thing is ended, why delay? I could not bring him back. That was ended. And I am forty-four years old, with some experience of the world. As I think,' she said, eyeing him steadily, and the dimple coming and vanishing in her cheek, 'you also can claim, brother. For I think I do not surprise you as much as I had expected.'

'As at this time,' said Cadfael, 'I cannot conceive of any man whom you would not surprise. But yes, I have been abroad in the world before I took this cowl of mine. Would it be foolish in me to suppose that it was your gift of astonishment that took Huon de Domville's fancy in the first place?'

'If you'll believe me,' said Avice, sitting back with a sigh, and folding plump, homely hands upon a rounding stomach, 'I hardly remember now. I do know that I had wit enough and gall enough to take the best that offered a wench of my birth, and pay for it without grudging. I still have both the wit and the gall, I take the best of what is offered a woman of my years and history.'

She had said far more than was in the words, and knew very well that he had understood all of it. She had recognised instantly the end of one career. Too old now to make a success of another such liaison, too wise to want one, perhaps too loyal even to consider one, after so many years, she had cast about her for something to do now with her powers and energies. Too late, with her past, to contemplate an ordinary marriage. What is left for such a woman?

'You are right,' said Avice, relaxed and easy. 'I made good use of my time while I waited for Huon, as often I have waited, weeks together. I am lettered and numerate, I have many skills. I need to use what I know, and make use of what I can do. My beauty is no longer with me, and never was remarkable, no one is likely to want or pay for it now. I suited Huon, he was accustomed to me. I was his feather-bed when other women had plagued and tired him.'

'You loved him?' asked Cadfael, for her manner with him was such that it was no intrusion to put such a question. And she considered it seriously.

'No, it could not be said that I loved him, that was not what he required. After all these years, certainly there was a fondness, a habit that sat well with us both, and did not abrade. Sometimes we did not even couple,' confided the postulant nun thoughtfully. 'We just sat and drank wine together, played chess, which he taught me, listened to minstrels. Nodded over my embroidery and his wine, one either side the fire. Sometimes we did not even kiss or touch, though we slept snugly in the same bed.'

Like an old, married lord and his plain, pleasant old wife. But that was over, and she was one who acknowledged the realities. She had sincerely regretted her dead companion, even while she was thinking hard, and rubbing her hands in anticipation of getting to work upon a new and different enterprise. So much intelligent life must go somewhere, find some channel it can use. The ways of youth had closed, but there were other ways.

'Yet he came to you,' said Cadfael, 'on his wedding eve.' And the bride, he thought but did not say, is eighteen years old, beautiful, submissive, and has great possessions.

She leaned forward to the table, her face mild and inward-looking, as though she examined honestly the workings of the human spirit, so obdurate and yet so given to conformity.

'Yes, he came. It was the first time since we came to Shrewsbury, and it turned out the last time of all. His wedding eve . . . Yes, marriage is a matter of business, is it not? Like concubinage! Love—ah, well, that's another matter, apart from either of them. Yes, I was expecting him. My position would not have been any way changed, you understand.'

Brother Cadfael understood. The mistress of twenty years standing would not have been dislodged by the equally purchased heiress twenty-six years her junior. They were two separate worlds, and the inhabitant of the alternative world had her own legitimacy.

'He came alone?'

'Yes, alone.'

'And left you at what hour?' Now he was at the heart of the matter. For this honourable whore had certainly never conspired at her lord's end, nor even cuckolded him with his steward, that jealous, faithful, suspicious soul who clove to her out of long-standing loyalty, surely well-deserved. This woman would have both feet firmly on the ground in dealing with those accidentally her servants, and respect them as they would learn to respect her.

She thought carefully about that. 'It was past six in the morning. I cannot be sure how far past, but there was the promise of light. I went out with him to the gate. I remember, there were already colours, it must have been nearing the half-hour. For I went to the patch of gromwell—it went on flowering so late this year—and plucked some flowers and put them in his cap.'

'Past six, and nearer the half than the quarter of the hour,' mused Cadfael. 'Then he could not have reached the spot where he was ambushed and killed before a quarter to the hour of Prime, and probably later.'

'There you must hold me excused, brother, for I do not know the place. For his leaving, as near as I dare state, he rode away about twenty minutes after six.'

A quarter of an hour, even at a speed too brisk for the light, to bring him to the place where the trap was laid. How long to account for the final killing? At the very least, ten minutes. No, the murderer could not have quit the spot before at least a quarter to seven, and most probably considerably later.

There was only one vital question left to ask. Many others, which had been puzzling him before he encountered her, and began to find his way past one misconception after another to the truth, had already become unnecessary. As, for instance, why she had discarded all her possessions, even her rings, left her jennet behind in the stable, denuded herself of all the profits of one career. Haste and fear, he had thought first, a bolt into hiding, putting off without coherent thought everything that could connect her with Huon de Domville. Then, when he found her already in a novice's habit, he had even considered that she might have been stricken into penitence, and felt it needful to give up all before venturing into the cloister to spend the latter half of her life atoning for the former. Now he could appreciate the irony of that. Avice of Thornbury repented nothing. As she had never been afraid, so he felt certain she had never in her life been ashamed. She had made a bargain and kept it, as long as her lord lived. Now she was her own property again, to dispose of as she saw fit.

She had put off all her finery as an old soldier retiring might put off arms, as no longer of use or interest to him, and turn his considerable remaining energies to farming. Which was just what she proposed to do now. Her farm would be the Benedictine conventual economy, and she would take to it thoroughly and make a success of it. He even felt a rueful sympathy for the handful of sisters into whose dovecote this harmless-looking falcon had flown. Give her three or four years, and she would be the superior here. Give her ten, and she would be abbess of Polesworth, and moreover, would further reinforce that house's stability and good repute, as well as its sound finances. After her death she might well end up as a saint.

Meanwhile, though by this time he was assured of her forthrightness and reliability, she had a right to know that by doing her duty as a citizen she might find her privacy somewhat eroded.

'You must understand,' said Cadfael scrupulously, 'that the sheriff may require you to testify when a man stands trial for his life, and that innocent lives may hang on the acceptance of your word. Will you bear witness to all this in a court of law, as you have here to me?'

'In all my life,' said Avice of Thornbury, 'I have avoided one sin, at least. No, rather I was never tempted to it. I do not lie, and I do not feign. I will tell truth for you whenever you require it.'

'Then there is one matter more, which you may be able to solve. Huon de Domville, as you may not have heard, dismissed all attendance when he rode to you, and no one in his household admits to knowing where he might have gone. Yet whoever waylaid and killed him on that path had either followed him far enough to judge that he must return the same way—or else, and far more likely, knew very well where he was bound. Whoever knew that, knew that you were there at the hunting-lodge. You have said that you always used great discretion, yet someone must have known.'

'Plainly I was not left to travel unescorted,' she pointed out practically. 'I daresay some among his old servants had a shrewd idea I should never be far away, but as for knowing where . . . Who better than the one who brought me there at Huon's orders? Two days before Huon and his party came to Shrewsbury. I was always entrusted to one confidant, and only one. Why let in more? For the last three years it has been this same man.'

'Give him a name,' said Brother Cadfael.

9 🐦

THE SHERIFF HAD CONFINED HIS MORNING DRIVE TO THE nearer woods on the southern side of the Meole brook, his line spread like beaters for a hunt, each man just within sight of his neighbours on either hand, and all moving slowly and methodically forward together. And they had netted nothing for all that time and trouble. Nobody broke cover to run from them, nobody they sighted bore any resemblance to Joscelin Lucy. When they drew off to reform and break their fast they had made contact all along their line with the patrols watching the town's borders. The lepers at Saint Giles had come out curiously to watch their activities at the prescribed distance. Gilbert Prestcote was not pleased, and grew markedly short to question or address. Some others were better satisfied.

'The lad's surely away home out of this long ago,' said Guy hopefully to Simon, as they dismounted at the bishop's house to eat a hasty dinner. 'I wish for my life, though, we could be certain of it. I could enjoy the hunt for him if I could be quite sure there's no fear of finding! It would be no hardship to see Picard's face grow blacker and blacker, and a delight if his horse put a foot in a badger's sett and threw him. The sheriff has his work to do, and no avoidance, but Picard has no such duty. Office is one thing, but venom's another.'

'He truly believes Joss killed the old man,' said Simon, shrugging. 'No wonder he's hot after him. All his own plans gone for nothing, and he's a man who'll have his revenge at all costs. Will you believe he's turned against me? I opened my mouth out of turn, and told him flatly I believed Joss never did theft or murder, and he flared at me like wildfire. I'm not welcome to him or his lady any more.'

'Do you tell me?' Guy gaped and sparkled. 'And do you know you're drawn next to him in the line after dinner, when we head further out? Keep a weather eye on Picard, lad, and never turn your back on him, or he might be tempted, if he's at odds with you. I wouldn't trust that temper of his too far, and there's thicker cover where we're bound.'

He was not very serious, merely exuberant in his relief that his comrade and friend was still at liberty. His attention at the time was on his trencher, for the October air was keen, and provided a healthy young man with a voracious appetite.

'The looks he gave me when he turned me out of Iveta's room,' admitted Simon ruefully, 'you could be right! I'll keep an eye on him, and be faster in the draw than he. We're to make our own way back as we please, when the light goes. I'll ensure I'm far enough ahead of him to keep clear of his blade. In any case,' he said, with a swift private smile, 'I have something important to see to before Vespers. I'll make certain he's not there to put a bolt through *that*.' He sat back from the table satisfied. 'Where are you drawn, this time?'

'Among the sheriff's sergeants, for my sins!' Guy grimaced and grinned. 'Is it possible someone has suspected my heart may not be in it? Well, if I turn a blind eye, and they miss taking me up on it, I'm safe enough, they'll see to that. The sheriff's a decent man, but vexed and frustrated, with a murdered magnate on his hands, and King Stephen beginning to look this way. No wonder he's blowing bitter cold.' He pushed back the bench on which he sat, and stretched, drawing breath deep. 'Are you ready? Shall we go? I'll be main glad when we get home this night, and nothing trapped.'

They went out together, down into the valley below Saint Giles, where the beater line was drawing up afresh, to press onward at the same deliberate speed through thicker copses and woodlands, moving south.

From a hillock on the southern side of the highroad, overlooking the broad valley below, two tall, shrouded figures watched the hunters muster and deploy. Over the meadows the strung line showed clearly, before it moved methodically forward and began to thread the open woodlands ahead, each man keeping his dressing by his neighbour on the right, each man keeping his due distance. The air was very faintly misty, but with sunlight falling through the mist, and as the hunters moved in among the trees their clothing and harness winked and flashed through the leaves like motes of bright dust, scintillating and vanishing, reappearing to vanish again. As they swept slowly south, the watchers above as slowly turned to maintain their watch.

'They will keep up this drive until dark,' said Lazarus, and at length swung about to view the deserted fields from which the hunt had been launched. All was quiet and still there now, the stir, the murmur, the play of colours all past. Two threads of silver made the only sparkles of light in the muted sunbeams, the nearer one the mill leat drawn off to feed the abbey pools and mill, the further one the Meole brook itself, here in a stony and broken bed, and looking curiously small by comparison with its broad flow by the abbey gardens, barely a mile downstream. Geese dabbled in a shallow inlet on the southern side. Upstream from them the child minding them fished in a little rock-fringed pool.

'It's well-timed,' said Joscelin, and drew deep and thoughtful breath. 'The sheriff has emptied the valley of all his armed men for me, yes, surely until twilight. Even then they'll come home out of temper and out of energy. It could not be better.'

'And their mounts ridden out,' said Lazarus drily, and turned his far-sighted, brilliant eyes on his companion. The absence of a face had ceased to trouble Joscelin at all. The eyes and the voice were enough to identify a friend.

'Yes,' Joscelin said, 'I had thought of that, too.'

'And few remounts to be had, seeing he has called out almost every man he has, and commandeered almost every horse.'

'Yes.'

Bran came darting down the slope of grass towards them, dived confidently between the two, and took possession of a hand of each. It did not trouble him at all that one of the hands lacked two fingers and the half of a third. Bran was putting on a little flesh with every day, the nodes in his neck had shrunk to insignificance, and his fine fair hair was growing in thickly over the scars of old sores on a knowing small head.

'They're away,' he said simply. 'What shall we do now?'

'We?' said Joscelin. 'I thought it was high time for your schooling with Brother Mark? Are you given a day's holiday today?'

'Brother Mark says he has work to do.' By his voice, Bran was not greatly impressed by the argument, since in his experience Brother Mark never ceased working except when he was asleep. The child was even inclined to be a little offended at being put off, if he had not had these two other elect companions to fall back on. 'You said you'd do whatever I wanted today,' he reminded sternly.

'And so I will,' agreed Joscelin, 'until evening. Then I also have work to do. Let's make the most of the time. What's your will?'

'You *said,*' observed Bran, 'you could carve me a little horse out of a piece of wood from the winter pile, if you had a knife.'

'Unbeliever, so I can, and perhaps a little gift for your mother, too, if we can find the right sort of wood. But as for the knife, I doubt if they'd lend us one from the kitchen, and how could I dare take the one Brother Mark uses to trim his quills? More than my life's worth,' said Joscelin lightly enough, and stiffened to recall how little his life might indeed be worth if the hunt turned back too soon. No matter, these few hours belonged to Bran.

'I have a knife,' said the child proudly, 'a sharp one my mother used to use to gut fish, when I was little. Come and let's look for a piece of wood.' The gleaners in the forest had come back well laden, the fuel-store was full, and could spare a small, smooth-grained log to make a toy. Bran tugged at both the hands he held, but the old man slid his maimed member free, very gently, and released himself. His eyes still swept the crowns of the trees below, where even the quiver and rustle of the beaters' progress had ebbed into stillness.

'I have seen Sir Godfrid Picard only once,' he said thoughtfully. 'Which man in the line was he, when they set out?'

Joscelin looked back, surprised. 'The fourth from us. Lean and dark, in black and russet—a bright red cap with a plume . . .'

'Ah, he . . .' Lazarus maintained his steady survey of the woods below, and did not turn his head. 'Yes, I marked the red poll. An easy mark to pick out again.'

He moved forward a few yards more from the highroad, and sat down in the grass of the slope, with his back against a tree. He did not look round when Joscelin yielded to the urging of Bran's hand, and they left him to his preferred solitude.

Brother Mark had indeed work to do that day, though it could as well have waited for another time, if it consisted of the accounts he was casting up for Fulke Reynald. He was meticulous, and the books were never in arrears. The real urgency lay in finding something to do that could enable him to look busily occupied in the open porch of the hall, where the light was best, and where he could keep a sharp eye on the movements of his secret guest without being too obvious about it. He was well aware that the young man who was no leper had been missing from Prime and from breakfast, and had reappeared innocently hand in hand with Bran, somewhat later. Clearly the child had taken a strong fancy to his new acquaintance. The sight of them thus linked, the boy skipping merrily beside the long strides that so carefully but imperfectly mimicked the maimed gait of Lazarus, the man with bent head attentive, and large hand gentle, had moved Mark to believe, illogically but understandably, that one thus kind and generous of his time and interest could not possibly be either thief or murderer. From the first he had found it hard to credit the theft, and the longer he considered this refugee within his cure—for he could pick him out now without difficulty—the more absurd grew the notion that this young man had avenged himself by murder. If he had, he would have plodded away in his present guise, clapping his clapper industriously, and passed through the sheriff's cordon long ago to freedom. No, he had some other urgent business to keep him here, business that might mean greater peril to his own life before he brought it to a good conclusion.

Yet he was on Mark's conscience. No one else had detected him, no one else could answer for him, or answer, if it came to the worst, for sheltering him and keeping silent. So Mark watched, had been watching all this day since the truant's return. And so far the young man had made it easy for him. The whole morning he had kept company with Bran, and been close about the hospital, lending a hand with the work of stacking the gleaned wood, helping to bring in the last mowing from the verges of the road, playing drawing games with the child in a patch of dried-out clay in a hollow where water lay when it rained—good, smooth clay that could be levelled over again and again as a game ended in laughter and crowing. No, a young fellow in trouble who could so blithely accommodate himself to a pauper child's needs and wants could not be any way evil, and Mark's duty of surveillance was rapidly becoming a duty of protection, and all the more urgent for that.

He had seen Joscelin and Lazarus cross the highroad and

seek their vantage-point over the valley, to watch the afternoon hunt set forth, and he had seen Joscelin return with Bran dancing and chattering and demanding at his side. Now the two of them were sitting under the churchyard wall, blamelessly absorbed in the whittling of a lump of wood brought from the fuelstore. He had only to take a few steps out from the doorway to see them, Bran's fair head, with its primrose down of new hair, stooped close over the large, deft hands that pared and shaped with such industrious devotion. Now and again he heard gleeful laughter. Something was taking shape there that gave delight. Brother Mark gave thanks to God for whatever caused such pleasure to the poor and outcast, and felt his heart engaged in the cause of whoever brought such blessings about.

He was also human enough to feel curiosity as to what marvels were being produced there under the wall, and after an hour or so he gave in to mortal frailty and went to see. Bran welcomed him with a shout of pleasure, and waved the whittled horse at him, crude, spirited, without details, but an unmistakable horse, one and a half hands high. The carver's hooded and veiled head was bent over a work of supererogation, gouging out from another fistful of wood the features of a recognisable child. Eyes unwarily bright and blue flashed a glance upwards now and then to study Bran, and sank again to the work in hand. In two whole hands, unblemished, smooth, sunburned, young. He had forgotten to be cautious.

Brother Mark returned to his post confirmed in an allegiance for which he had no logical justification. The little head, already live before it had any shaping but in the face, had enlisted him beyond release.

The afternoon passed so, the light faded to a point where artistry was no longer possible. Mark could not see his figures, which in any case were completed, and he was sure that Joscelin Lucy—he had a name, why not acknowledge it?—could not see to continue his carving, and must have abandoned or finished his little portrait of Bran. Just after the lamps were lighted within, the boy burst in, flourishing it for his tutor's approval with small, excited shrieks of joy.

'Look! Look, Brother Mark! This is me! My friend made it.'

And it was he, no question, rough, baulked here and there by the obstinate grain of the wood and an inadequate knife, but lively, pert and pleased. But his friend who had made it had not followed him in.

'Run,' said Brother Mark, 'run and show it to your mother, quickly. Give it to her, and she'll be so cheered—she's down today. She'll like it and praise it. You go and see!' And Bran nodded, and beamed, and went. Even his gait was becoming firmer and more gainly now he had a little more flesh on him and was eating regularly.

Brother Mark rose and left his desk, as soon as the boy was gone. Outside the light was dimming but still day. Almost an hour yet to Vespers. There was no one sitting under the churchyard wall. Down the grassy slope to the verge of the highroad, without haste, as one taking the late air, Joscelin Lucy's tall, straight figure moved, paused at the roadside to see all empty, crossed, and slipped down to where the old man Lazarus still sat alone and aloof.

Brother Mark forsook his desk, and followed at a discreet distance.

Down there beneath Lazarus's tree there was a long pause. In the shadows two men stirred, there were words exchanged, but few; plainly those two understood each other very well. Out of the dimness where a hooded figure had stooped and vanished, another figure emerged, outlined against the pallidly luminous sky, tall, lissome, young, unshrouded and uncowled, in blessedly dark and plain clothing that melted away into shade as he moved. He leaned to the tree again. Mark thought that he stooped to a hand, since there was no cheek offered him. The kiss proper by rights between blood-kin was certainly given.

The leper gown remained among the shades. Evidently he would not take the repute of Saint Giles with him into whatever peril he was going out to encounter. Joscelin Lucy, owner here of nothing in the world but what he was and what he wore, stepped out and dropped away down the slope with long, light strides, into the valley. Half an hour now to Vespers, and still dangerously light in the open.

Brother Mark determined now on his duty, made a wary circle round the old man's sheltering tree, and followed. Down the steep slope, a light, springy leap over the mill leat for Joscelin, a more awkward and ungainly jump for Mark, and on to the brook. Gleams of light flashed out of the stony bed. Mark got his sandalled feet wet, his vision uncertain in this light, but made the further shore without more damage, and set off along the brookside meadows with the tall young figure still in view.

Halfway along the floor of the valley towards the abbey gardens, Joscelin drew off from the brook into the fringes of woodland and copse that closed in on the meadows. Faithfully, Brother Mark followed, slipping from tree to tree, his eyes growing accustomed now to the fading light, so that it did not seem to fade at all, but remained constant and limpid, free as yet of the nightly mist. Looking to his right, Mark could see clearly the outlines of his monastery against the last rosy light of the sunset, roofs and towers and walls, looming above the brook, the serene rise of the peasefields, and the walls and hedges of the enclosed gardens beyond.

The twilight came; even on the open sward colours put on their final lucent glow before the dusk washed them all into soft shades of grey. Among the trees all was shadow, but Mark, cautiously slipping from bush to bush, could still discern the one shadow that moved. His ear caught also the sounds of movement ahead, deep among the trees, an uneasy stirring and sidling, and then suddenly a soft, anxious whinnying, hastily hushed, he thought, by a caressing hand. A voice whispered, hardly as loudly as the rustle of leaves, and the same hand patted gently at a solid, sleek shoulder. There was joy and hope in the sounds, as clearly as if the words had carried to him.

From his hiding-place among the trees, some yards away, Brother Mark saw dimly the looming pallor that was the head and neck of a horse, silver-grey, an inconvenient colour for such a nocturnal enterprise. Someone had kept faith with the fugitive, and brought his mount to the tryst. What was to happen next?

What happened next was the small sound of the bell for Vespers carried clearly but distantly across the brook.

At about this same hour Brother Cadfael was also brought up short by the apparition of a light grey horse, and halted his mule to avoid startling it away, while he considered the implications.

He had not hurried away from Godric's Ford, feeling it incumbent upon him to give the superior at least a credible account of his errand here, and he had found the ruling sister hospitable and garrulous. They had few visitors, and Cadfael came with the recommendation of his cloth. She was in no hurry to part with him until she had heard all about the frustrated wedding party at the abbey, and the excitement that had followed. Nor was Cadfael disposed to refuse a glass of wine when it was offered. So he took his leave somewhat later than he had expected.

Avice of Thornbury was still at work in the garden when he mounted and rode, tramping the soil firm round her seedlings as vigorously and contentedly as before, and the plot almost filled. With the same purposeful energy she would climb the steps of the hierarchy, as honest and fair-minded as she was ambitious, but ruthless towards weaker sisters who would fall before her for want of her wits, vigour and experience. She gave Cadfael a cheerful wave of her hand, and the dimple in her cheek dipped and vanished again. He mused on the irrepressible imprint of former beauty as he rode away, and wondered if she would not have to find some way of suppressing a quirk that might be so disconcerting to bishops, or whether, on the contrary, it might not yet prove a useful weapon in her armoury. The truth was, he could not choose but respect her. More to the point, such evidence as she gave, with her unmistakable forthrightness, no one would dare try to refute.

He made his way back steadily but without haste, letting the mule choose his own pace. And at about the hour of Vespers he was jogging in deepening twilight along the green ride, not far from the spot where Huon de Domville had died. He recognised the oak as he passed, and it was some minutes later, with the lighter spaces of the meadows already in view between the trees, that he became aware of rustling movements on his right, keeping pace with him at a little distance. Caution prompted him to halt the mule and sit silent, straining his ears, and the sounds continued, with no attempt at stealth. That was reassuring, and he resumed his way quietly, still listening. Here and there, where the bushes thinned, he caught the silvery pallor of the beast that moved with him. A horse, slender and built for speed, pale as a spirit flickering between the branches. In Holy Writ, he thought, it was Death who rode the pale horse. Death, however, appeared to have dismounted somewhere. No one was riding this grey, his elaborate saddle was empty, his rein loose on his neck.

Cadfael dismounted in his turn, and led his mule gently aside towards the apparition, coaxing softly, but the grey, though he had drawn close to them for company, took fright at being approached, and started away into the thicker woods beyond. Patiently Cadfael followed, but as often as he drew near the grey horse cantered away to a distance again, leading him still deeper into the woods. Here the hunters had surely threaded their paths during the afternoon, and through these copses they must have returned only very recently, as the light failed, each man making his own way back. One of them had either been thrown, failed to recapture his startled horse, and ended the journey ignominiously on foot, or else . . .

Suddenly the grey horse appeared ahead, entire and graceful, in the comparative light of a small, grassy clearing, and the faint radiance of starlight, stooped his head for a moment to crop at the turf, and as Cadfael closed in, tossed heels and mane once more, and made off into the trees on the other side. And this time Cadfael did not follow.

In the small arena of grass a man lay on his back, curled black beard pointing at the sky, long black hair flung up from his head, arms spread abroad, crooked and clawing, one at grass, the other at air. A brocaded cap lay in the grass above his head, visible only by reason of its white plume. And aside by some yards from his empty right hand, something long and thin managed to catch out of the dimness enough light to cast a metallic gleam. Brother Cadfael groped cautiously and found a hilt, and a lean blade the length of a man's hand and wrist. He smoothed a finger along it, and finding it unblooded, left it where it lay. Let it speak clearer by a better light. Now in the dusk there was little he could do, beyond feeling after the beat of the blood and the hammer of the heart, and finding neither. On his knees beside the dead man, peering close and avoiding his own shadow, he concentrated upon the face, and even in the dimness knew it congested and gaping, the eyes starting, the tongue protruding and bitten.

Like Huon de Domville, Godfrid Picard had been met in the way, riding home, and had not survived the meeting.

Brother Cadfael left everything here as he had found it, abandoned the half-Arab grey to his own wilful devices, and rode for the abbey at the best pace the surprised mule could be induced to raise.

10 🐚

IVETA HAD HAD ALL DAY TO COMPOSE HER MIND AND LEARN cunning. Necessity is a great teacher, and it was necessary that by the evening of this day she should be so despised that no one should think it worthwhile to watch her every move, provided she could not pass the gate. In any case, where could she go? Her lover was hunted for his life, her only known friend was banished, even the monk who had been kind to her had not been seen within the precinct since early morning. Where could she go, to whom could she appeal? She was utterly alone.

She had played the part all day, the more thoroughly and convincingly as her rebellious heart rose to the thought of the evening. In the afternoon she complained of a headache, and thought the air would do her good, if she might walk in the garden, and since Madlen was required to work on a gown of Agnes's in which the silver embroidery was fraying, and needed expert repair, she was allowed to go unescorted. Agnes curled a disdainful lip as she gave permission. So tame a creature, what harm could possibly be expected from her?

Iveta went with slow step and languid manner, and even sat for a while on the first stone bench in the flower-garden, in case anyone should be sent spying on her; but as soon as she was sure no one was observing her she skipped nimbly enough through the pleached hedge into the plot beyond, and over the little footbridge to the herb-garden. The door of the workshop stood wide open, and someone was moving about within. Iveta began to believe in success. Of course Brother Cadfael must have an assistant. Medicines might be urgently needed in his absence. Someone must know where to find things, and how to use them, even if he lacked Brother Cadfael's experience and skills.

Brother Oswin was in the act of gathering up the shards of two of the clay saucers they used for sorting seeds, and started guiltily at the sound of footsteps in the doorway. These trifles were the first things he had broken for three days, and as the stock was plentiful, and the dishes themselves easily and quickly replaced, he had hoped to do away with the fragments undetected, and say nothing about the relapse. He turned defensively, and was stricken dumb by the unexpected vision in the doorway. His rosy, guileless face gaped, round-eyed and open-mouthed. It was a question which of them blushed more deeply, Oswin or the girl.

'Pardon if I intrude,' said Iveta hesitantly. 'I wanted to ask . . . Two days ago Brother Cadfael gave me a draught to bring me sleep, when I was not well. He said it was made from poppies. Do you know it?'

Oswin gulped, nodded his head vigorously, and managed speech. 'This is the potion, here in this flask. Brother Cadfael is not here today, but he would wish . . . If I can serve you? He would wish you to have whatever you need.'

'Then may I have such a dose again? For I think tonight I shall need it.' It was no lie, but it was a deliberate deception, and Iveta blushed for it, when this yellow-headed youth, rounded and innocent as a new chick, was offering his services so trustingly. 'May I take double the dose with me? Enough for two nights? I remember how much he bade me take.'

Brother Oswin would have given her all the resources of the workshop, he was so dazzled. His hand shook somewhat as he filled a small vial for her, and stoppered it, and when she put out her hand, just as shyly, to take it from him, he remembered his duty and lowered his eyes before her, rather late in the day for his peace of mind.

It was all over very quickly. She whispered her thanks, looking over her shoulder nervously as though she thought someone might be watching, and hid the vial in her sleeve a good deal more adroitly than Oswin had handled it. His hands and feet seemed to have reverted to their hobbledehoy clumsiness of some years back, in his pimply boyhood, but for all that, the look she gave him in departing made him feel tall, confident and gainly. He was left pensive in the doorway, looking after her as she flitted across the foot-bridge, and wondering if he had not been hasty in deciding that he had a vocation. It was not too late to change his mind, he had not taken his final vows yet.

This time he did not lower his eyes until she vanished along the pleached alley. Even then he stood for some minutes, still pondering. There were drawbacks in any course of life, he supposed sadly. Neither inside nor outside the cloister could a man have everything.

Iveta fled back to her stone bench, sheltered from the breeze, and was sitting there with folded hands and apathetic face when Madlen came out to reclaim her. Iveta rose submissively and went back with her to the guest-hall, and sewed unenthusiastically at the piece of embroidery that had been her cover for weeks, even though her needle was not so industrious that she need unpick at night what she worked during the day, like a certain Dame Penelope, of whom she had once heard tell from a passing jongleur in her father's house, long ago.

She waited until it was almost time for Vespers, and the light fading outside. Agnes had put on the newly mended gown, and

Madlen was tiring her hair for the evening. While Sir Godfrid Picard hunted with savage determination for a fugitive murderer, it was his wife's part to maintain the appearance of ritual devotion, attend all the needful services, and retain the good opinion of abbot, prior and brothers.

'It's time you were making ready, girl,' she said, snapping a glance at her niece along a brocaded shoulder.

Iveta let her hands lie in her lap, indifferent, though she kept her wrist pressed firmly upon the vial in her sleeve. 'I think I won't come tonight. My head is so heavy, and I haven't slept well. If you'll be my excuse, madam, I'll eat supper now, with Madlen, and go early to bed.' Naturally if she stayed away, Madlen would inevitably be left to keep guard on her, but she had made her own provision for that.

Agnes shrugged, her fine, steely profile disdainful. 'You are very vapourish these days. Still, stay if you prefer. Madlen will make you a posset.'

It was done. The lady went forth without a qualm. The maid set a small table in Iveta's bedchamber, and brought bread and meat and a brew of honeyed milk and wine, thick and sweet and hot, ideal to drown the heavy sweetness of Brother Cadfael's poppy syrup. She went and came two or three times before she sat down with her charge, ample time to draw a beaker of the innocent brew, and replace it with the whole contents of Oswin's vial. Ample time to stir it and be sure. Iveta made a pretence of eating, and declined more of the drink, and was gratified to see Madlen finish the jug with obvious pleasure. Nor had she eaten much, to temper the effect.

Madlen removed the dishes to the kitchen of the guest-hall, and did not return. Iveta waited almost ten minutes in feverish anxiety, and then went to investigate, and found the maid propped comfortably on a bench in a corner of the kitchen, snoring.

Iveta did not wait for cloak or shoes, but ran in her soft leather slippers, just as she was, out into the dusk, across the great court like a hunted leveret, half-blindly, and along the dark green alley in the garden. The silver streak of the leat gleamed at her, she felt her way along the hand-rail of the bridge. The sky was starry over her, still half-veiled as in the day, but pallidly luminous beyond the veil. The air was chill, fresh, heady, like wine. In the church they were still chanting, leisurely and intently, thank God! Thank God and thank Simon! The only loyal friend . . .

Under the deep eaves of the herbarium workshop Joscelin was waiting, flattened against the wall in the black shade. He reached both arms to her and caught her to him, and she wound her own slight arms about him passionately. They hung silent a long moment, hardly breathing, clinging desperately. Utter silence and stillness as though the leat, and the brook, and the river itself had stopped moving, the breeze ceased to breathe with them, the very plants to grow.

Then the urgency swept back to swallow everything, even the first stammering utterances of love.

'Oh, Joscelin . . . It *is* you. . . .'

'My dear, my dear . . . Hush, softly! Come, come quickly! This way . . . take my hand!'

She clung obediently and followed blindly. Not by the way she had come. Here they were over the leat, only the brook remained to be crossed. Out from the closed garden into the fringe of the pease-fields, new-ploughed at this season, that ran down to the Meole. Under the hedge he paused a moment to view the empty dusk and listen with stretched ears for any betraying sound, but all was still. Close to his ear she whispered: 'How did you cross? How will you manage with me. . . .?'

'Hush! I have Briar down the field—did Simon not tell you?'

'But the sheriff has every way closed,' she breathed, shivering.

'In the forest . . . in the dark? We'll get through!' He drew her close in his arm, and began to descend the field, keeping close to the dark shelter of the hedge.

The silence was abruptly torn by a loud, indignant neighing, that halted Joscelin in mid-stride. Below at the water's edge the bushes threshed wildly, hooves stamped, a man's voice bellowed. Confused shouting broke out, and from the covering bulk of the hedge Briar lunged into the open, dragging one man with him. Other moving shadows followed, four at least, dancing to avoid being trampled as they sought to subdue and calm the rearing horse.

Armed men, the sheriff's men, ranged the bank between them and freedom. Escape that way was lost, Briar was lost. Without a word Joscelin turned, sweeping Iveta with him in his arm, and began to retrace his steps in furious haste, keeping close to the bushes.

'The church,' he whispered, when she sought to question in terror, 'the parish door . . .' Even if they were still at Vespers, everyone would be in the choir, and the nave of the great church unlighted. They might yet be able to slip through unseen from the cloister, and out by the west door which alone lay outside the precinct wall, and was never closed but in time of great danger and disorder. But even then he knew it was a very meagre hope. But if it came to the worst, there could be sanctuary within.

Rapid movement betrayed them. Down by the water, where Briar stood now snorting and quivering, a voice bellowed: 'There he goes, back into the garden! We have him in a noose! Come on!' And someone laughed, and three or four men began to surge up the slope, without undue haste. They were quite sure of their prize now.

Joscelin and Iveta fled hand in hand, back through the herb-garden, over the leat, along the alley between the black, clipped hedges, and out into the perilous open spaces of the great court. No help for it now, there was no other way left to them. The gathering darkness might hide identities, but could not hide the haste of their running. They never reached the cloister. An armed man stood blocking the way. They swung towards the gatehouse, where torches were already burning in their sconces on the wall, and two more men-at-arms drew together before the gate. From the garden emerged their pursuers, content and at leisure. The foremost of them swaggered into the flickering light of the torches, and showed the grinning, complacent face of that same astute or well-informed fellow who had suggested to his officer the searching of the bishop's grounds, and been commended for it. He was in luck again. The sheriff and all but a meagre handful of his men out scouring the woods, and the remnant left behind were the ones to run the quarry to ground!

Joscelin drew Iveta into the corner of the guest-hall wall, where the stone steps ascended to the doorway, and put her behind him. Though he was unarmed, they took their time and were cautious of moving in upon him until their circle was drawn tight. Over his shoulder, without taking his eyes from the deployment of his enemies, he said with grim calm: 'Go in, love, and leave me. No one will dare stop you or touch you.'

Instinctively she gasped into his ear: 'No! I'll not leave you!' and as quickly understood that she hampered him at this desperate pass, and turned with a sob to scramble up the steps to the doorway, as he ordered. No further! Not a step! Only far enough to free his arms and stand out of his way, but close enough still to experience in her own flesh whatever befell him, and demand her share in whatever followed, penalty or deliverance. But even the moment's hesitation had undone him, for he had turned his head in furious entreaty to order: 'Go, for God's sake . . .' And the distraction had given his enemies their best opportunity, and they were on him from three sides like hounds unleashed.

None the less, it was no easy victory over an unarmed man. Until then all had passed in astonishing silence, suddenly there was chaotic noise, the sergeant hallooing on his men, porters, novices, lay brothers, guests, all coming on the run to find out what was happening, voices demanding, others answering, a clamour to rouse the dead. The first man to lunge at Joscelin had misjudged either his own timing, or his quarry's speed of recovery, and ran full tilt into a large fist that sent him reeling, and unbalanced two of his fellows. But from the other side two more got a hold on Joscelin's clothing, and though he jabbed an elbow hard into the midriff of the one who had him by the full of his cotte, and doubled him up retching, the other was able to hold on to his fistful of the dangling capuchon, and twist and tighten it with intent to strangle his opponent into submission. Joscelin wrenched forward, and though he failed to free himself, the cloth tore, and restored him room to breathe, and he kicked backwards at the officer's shins, and raised an aggrieved roar. The man released his hold to hop and rub at his bruises, and Joscelin took his brief chance and lunged after, not at the man but at the hilt of his dagger. It rose into his hand sweetly, smooth as oil, and he made a wide sweep about him, the blade flashing in the torchlight.

'Now, come on! Buy me dear, you'll not get me cheaply!'

'His own choice!' yelled the sergeant. 'Draw on him now, it's on his own head!'

Then there were swords out, half a dozen minor lightnings gleaming and vanishing in the dusk. The hubbub sank into a strange, breathless silence. And into the silence, from the cloister, swept the whole brotherhood, startled at the end of Vespers to find so offensive a disturbance in their own peaceful enclave. An outraged voice, loud and authoritative, thundered across the court:

'Stand! Let no man move or strike!'

Everyone froze into stillness, and only dared turn to face the speaker with slow and submissive care. Abbot Radulfus, that austere, dry, stern but composed man, stood at the edge of the battlefield, where the red torchlight caught him, and blazed like an excommunicating angel, fiery-eyed in a face sharp and cold as ice. Prior Robert at his shoulder looked faded and negligible by comparison, with all his noble Norman hauteur and dignity. Behind them the brothers stared and fluttered, and waited for the lightnings to strike.

Iveta's legs gave way under her, and she sat down on the top step and rested her head on her knees in the weakness of relief. The abbot was here, there would not be killing, not yet, not yet, only law, and the killing that law countenances. One step at a time now, and don't look beyond. She prayed passionately without words for a miracle.

When she managed to still the trembling that ran through her whole body, and lifted her head to look again, the entire great court seemed to be full of people, and more were pouring in even as she looked about her. Gilbert Prestcote had just reined in and dismounted within the gates. The members of the hunt, making their ways back at their own speed, were coming in by ones and twos, startled and wondering at what they found here at home, after raising no quarry through all the surrounding countryside. In the flickering light it took the sheriff some moments to recognise in the dishevelled and embattled young man drawn back against the wall of the guest-hall the suspected murderer and thief he had wasted two full days pursuing through the woods.

He came striding forward in haste. 'My lord abbot, what's this? Our wanted man here at bay within your walls? What is happening here?'

'That is what I am bent on discovering,' said Radulfus grimly. 'Within my walls indeed, and within my jurisdiction. By your leave, Sir Gilbert, it is my right here to enquire into such an unseemly brawl as this.' He cast a glittering look about him at the ring of armed men. 'Put up, every man of you. I will not have drawn steel here on my ground, nor violence done to any.' The same fiery glance lit upon Joscelin, braced and wary in his corner, dagger in hand. 'And you, young man—it seems to me I had occasion to use similar words to you once before, and to warn you that this house also has a punishment cell, and you may find yourself within it if you so much as touch hilt again. What have you to say for yourself?'

Joscelin had regained his breath enough to speak up for himself with spirit. He spread his arms to show there was no scabbard of sword or dagger upon him. 'I brought no weapon within your walls, Father. See how many circle me! I have borrowed what offered, to keep my life, not to take any other man's. My life and my liberty! And for all that these may say against me, I have never stolen or killed, and so I'll maintain within or without your jurisdiction, as long as I have breath.' He was running out of it by then, partly from his exertions, and partly from the choking force of his anger. 'Would you have me offer my neck tamely to be wrung, when I have done no wrong?'

'I would have you abate your tone to me and to these secular authorities,' said the abbot sternly, 'and submit to the law. Give back the dagger, you see it cannot avail you now.'

Joscelin stared back at him for a long moment with grim face and hostile eyes, and then, abruptly, held out the hilt of the dagger to its owner, who took it warily, and was only too glad to slide it into its sheath and back away out of the ring.

'Father,' said Joscelin, and it was a challenge, not an appeal, 'I am in your mercy here. Your justice I might trust more than I trust the law, and I am where your writ runs, and I have obeyed you. Examine me, of all that ever I did, before you give me up to the sheriff, and I swear to you I'll answer all truthfully.' He added quickly and firmly: 'All, that is, as concerning my own acts.' For there were those who had helped and been good to him, and he would do nothing to bring them into question.

The abbot looked at Gilbert Prestcote, who met the glance with a considering smile. There was no great urgency now, the fellow was trapped, and could not escape. There was nothing to be lost by conceding the abbot's prior authority here. 'I bow to your wishes in the matter, Father, but I maintain my claim to this man's person. He is charged with theft and murder, and it is my duty to hold him fast and produce him in time for trial on those charges. And so I shall—unless he can satisfy both you and me, here and now, of his innocence. But let all be done openly and fairly. Question him, if you so please. It would be helpful also to me. I would prefer to turn the key on a manifestly guilty man, and have your own doubts, if you entertain any, set at rest.'

Iveta was on her feet by then, running anxious eyes over every face that showed fitfully in the flickering light. Horsemen were still riding in one by one at the gatehouse, and staring in open-mouthed wonder at the scene within. She caught sight of Simon at the back of the crowd, newly arrived and startled and bewildered like the rest, and Guy behind him, just as dumbfounded. Not everyone here was an enemy. When she met the sharp black eyes of Agnes, there at Prior Robert's shoulder as they had emerged from Vespers, she did not lower her own eyes. This time she had ventured so far out of her old self that there could be no returning. It was not she who showed uneasiness, not she who punctuated a glare of naked dislike with frequent and hurried glances towards the gatehouse, noting each new arrival, and unsatisfied with all. Agnes was waiting and hoping for her husband to come, and resume his authoritative role, which in his absence she felt slipping out of her own fingers. Agnes was afraid of what might yet transpire here while her lord was not there to master it.

Iveta began to descend the steps up which she had groped blindly at Joscelin's entreaty. Very slowly and stealthily she came, stair by stair, not to break the tension below.

'You must be aware,' said Radulfus, surveying Joscelin with face still as grave, but not now so angry, 'that you have been sought by the law ever since your escape into the river, after arrest. You have said you will answer truthfully for your actions. Where have you been hiding all this time?'

Joscelin had promised truth, and must deliver it. 'Under a leper's cloak and veil,' he said bluntly, 'in the hospital at Saint Giles.'

A stir and murmur went round the great court, almost a gasp. Guests and brother alike stared in awe at a creature so desperate as to choose such an asylum. The abbot neither gasped nor stirred, but accepted the answer gravely, his eyes intent on Joscelin's face.

"Into that sanctuary, I think, you could hardly have penetrated without help. Who was it stretched out a hand to you?'

have said I was hiding there,' said Joscelin steadily. 'I

have not said I needed or received any help. I answer for my own actions, not for those of others.'

'Yes,' said the abbot thoughtfully, 'it seems there were others. For instance, I doubt if you thought to hide on your own lord's premises, as it seems for a while you did, without having a friend willing to give you cover. Also, as I remember, that grey horse I observed being led out of the garden just now—there he stands under guard, like you — is the one you rode when we encountered here once before. Did you recover possession of him without help? I doubt it.'

Iveta glanced over Joscelin's shoulder to where Simon stood, and saw him draw back a pace into deeper shadow. He need not have had any qualms. Joscelin closed his mouth very firmly, met the abbot's measuring stare without blinking, and suddenly, though, still doubtfully, he smiled. 'Ask me of my own deeds.'

'It seems,' interrupted the sheriff sharply, 'that we have need here of someone in authority at Saint Giles. It's a serious matter to hide a wanted murderer.'

From the rear of the crowd in the direction of the gardens, a deprecating voice piped up none too happily: 'Father Abbot, if it please you, I am willing to speak for Saint Giles, for I serve there.'

Every head turned, all eyes opening wide in astonishment at the sorry little figure advancing meekly to stand before Radulfus. Brother Mark's face was smudged with mud, a trailing wisp of pond-weed adorned his straggling tonsure, his habit trickled water from its skirts at every step, and clung to his thin body in heavy, dripping folds. He was ridiculous enough, and yet the soiled, earnest face and devoted grey eyes had still a bedraggled dignity, and if there were some half-hysterical grins and sniggers among the throng at sight of him, Radulfus was not smiling.

'Brother Mark! What can this mean?'

'It took me a long time to find a fordable place,' said Mark apologetically. 'I am sorry I come so late. I had no horse to carry me over, and I cannot swim. I had to draw back twice, and once I fell, but at the third try I found the shallow place. By daylight it would not have taken so long.'

'We pardon your lateness,' said Radulfus gravely, and for all the composure of his voice and his face, it was no longer quite so certain that he was not smiling. 'It seems you had reason to feel you might be needed here, for you come very aptly, if you come to account for how a wanted man came to find refuge in the hospital. Did you know of this young man's presence there?'

'Yes, Father,' said Brother Mark simply, 'I did know.'

'And was it you who introduced and sheltered him there?'

'No, Father. But I did come to realise, at Prime of that day, that we had one man more among us.'

'And held your peace? And countenanced his presence?'

'Yes, Father, that I did. At first I did not know who he was, nor could I always single him out from others of our flock, for he wore the face-cloth. And when I suspected . . . Father, I do not own any man's life, to give it up to any but God's judgment. So I held my peace. If I was wrong, judge me.'

'And do you know,' asked the abbot impassively, 'who it was who introduced the young man into the hospice?'

'No, Father. I do not even know that anyone did. I may have some thoughts as to that, but I do not *know*. But if I did,' owned Mark with candid-eyed humility, 'I could not give you a name. It is not for me to accuse or betray any man but myself.'

'You are two here of like mind,' said the abbot drily. 'But you have yet to tell us, Brother Mark, how you come to be fording the Meole brook, on the heels, as I understand it—if, indeed, I have yet understood any part of it!—of this young fugitive, who was sensible enough to provide himself with a horse for the venture. Had you been following him?'

'Yes, Father. For I knew I might be answerable for harbouring one less innocent and good than I thought him—for which thought I promise I had good reason. So all this day I have watched him. He has hardly been a moment out of my sight. And when he discarded his cloak in the dusk, and set off this way, I did follow him. I saw him find his horse tethered in the copse across the brook, and I saw him cross. I was in the water when I heard the outcry after him. As for this day I can speak for all he has done, and there was no blame.'

'And the day when he came to you?' the sheriff demanded sharply. 'What of his first appearance among your lepers? At what hour?'

Brother Mark, single-hearted in his allegiance, kept his eyes fixed upon the abbot's face for guidance, and Radulfus nodded gravely that he, too, required an answer.

''It was two days ago, at Prime, as I've told you,' said Mark, 'that I first was aware of him. But at that time he was already provided with the leper cloak, and a face-cloth to hide his face, and behaved altogether conformably with the others. I judge, therefore, he must have been in hiding among us at least some quarter to half an hour, to be so well prepared.'

'And as I have heard,' said the abbot thoughtfully, turning to Prestcote, 'your men on patrol in the Foregate, my lord, started a hare that same morning, and lost him in the neighbourhood of Saint Giles. At what hour did they sight him?'

'They reported to me,' said the sheriff, pondering, 'sighting such a fleeing man the best part of an hour before Prime, and certainly they lost him near Saint Giles.'

Iveta descended one more step. She felt herself suspended in a dream, a double dream that filled her with terror when she looked one way, and wild hope when she looked the other way. For these were not the voices of enemies. And still, blessedly, her uncle did not come, to cast into the balance his black animosity, his narrow malice. She was but two steps behind Joscelin now, she could have stretched out her hand and touched his unkempt flaxen hair, but she was afraid of shattering his braced attention. She did not touch him. She kept an alert eye on the gatehouse, watchful for her chief enemy's return. That was why she was the first to mark Brother Cadfael's arrival. Only she and Agnes were looking that way.

The little mule, which had enjoyed an unhurried day, was resentful at being urged to speed at the end of it, and manifested his displeasure by halting inside the gatehouse and refusing to budge further. And Brother Cadfael, who had been demanding some effort of him until that moment, sat to gaze in mute astonishment as his eyes lit upon the scene in the great court. She saw his rapid glance rove over all those intent faces, she could almost feel him stretch his ears to pick up the words that were passing. He saw Joscelin standing braced and alert at the foot of the steps, saw sheriff and abbot eyeing each other sombrely, and the draggled little figure of the young brother who, for Iveta, spoke with the unwitting tongue of a minor angel, the kind of angel who would descend with disarming apologies, and of whom no sinner would ever be afraid.

Hastily but quietly, Cadfael dismounted, surrendered the mule to the porter, and advanced to the edge of the crowd, himself still unnoticed. Obscurely encouraged, Iveta descended one more step.

'So it would seem,' said Radulfus reasonably, 'that you were at the hospital, young man, by a quarter of an hour at least before Prime of that day, and perhaps as much as half an hour.'

'I had—acquired my cloak,' agreed Joscelin, a little astray now and treading warily, 'some little time before I went to the church.'

'And you were instructed how to behave?'

'I have attended Prime before, I know the office.'

'Perhaps, but it would take some few minutes of instruction,' persisted Radulfus mildly, 'to pick up the whole order of the day in Saint Giles.'

'I can watch others and do as they do,' said Joscelin flatly, 'as readily as any other man.'

'Granted, Father,' said Gilbert Prestcote impatiently, 'that he was there well before the seventh hour of the morning. That I accept. But we have no way of knowing the hour of my lord Domville's death.'

Brother Cadfael had the whole drift of it by then. Finding his way blocked by spectators so intent that they remained deaf and blind to his civil requests and attempts to make his way through their ranks, he used his elbows sturdily, and butted a path through to the front. And before anyone else could speak up and brush the question of timing aside, he lifted his voice and called loudly as he came: 'True, my lord, but there is a way of knowing when he was last seen alive and well.'

He broke through then, the sudden shout opening a path before him, and emerged face to face with the abbot and the sheriff, both of whom had swung about to face and frown upon the interruption.

'Brother Cadfael! You have something to say in this matter?'

'I have . . .' began Cadfael, and broke off to gaze in vexed concern at the shivering little figure of Brother Mark. He shook his head in distracted compunction. 'But, Father, should not Brother Mark be changing that wet habit, and getting something hot into him, before he takes his death?'

Radulfus accepted the rebuke with penitent grace. 'You are quite right, I should have despatched him at once. Any further testimony he may have to give can very well wait until his teeth stop chattering. There, brother, get yourself dry garments, go to the kitchen, and have Brother Petrus make you a hot posset. Quick, run.'

'If I may ask but one question first,' said Cadfael hastily, 'before he goes. Did I hear, brother, that you have been following yonder lad as he came here? Have you had him under your eye all this while?'

'All the day from morning,' said Brother Mark, 'he has not been more than a few minutes out of my sight. He left the hospice only an hour or so ago, and I followed him here. Is it of importance?' He meant to Brother Cadfael and whatever cause he had in mind, and Cadfael's satisfied nod comforted and warmed him.

'There, run! You did well.'

Brother Mark made his reverence to the abbot, and dripped

and shivered away to the kitchen thankfully enough. If he had done well for Brother Cadfael, he was content.

'And now,' said Radulfus, 'you may explain what you meant by saying you had means of knowing when my lord Domville was last seen alive and in good health.'

'I have found and talked with a witness,' said Cadfael, 'who will testify, whenever the sheriff requires, that Huon de Domville spent the night before his death in his own hunting-lodge, and did not leave it until about a third of the hour after six, next morning. Also that at that time he was in excellent health, and mounted to ride back to his quarters in the Foregate. The path on which we found him is the path he would have to take from that place. And the witness, I dare pledge, is reliable.'

'If what you say is confirmed,' said Prestcote, after a moment's silence, 'this is of the first importance. Who is this witness? Name the man!'

'No man,' said Cadfael simply, 'but a woman. Huon de Domville spent his last night with his mistress of many years, and her name is Avice of Thornbury.'

The shock passed along the ranks of the innocent brethren as a sudden wind-devil whirls through standing wheat in summer, in a great, gusty sigh and a convulsion of rustling garments like shaken stems. On his wedding-eve, to repair to another woman! And after supping with the abbot, at that! To those of lifelong celibacy even the contemplation of a bride, chaste and young, was disturbing. But a kept woman, and visited on the eve of the marriage sacrament, in despite of both the celibate and the marital morality . . . !

The sheriff belonged to a more illusionless world. Not the outrage, only the understandable fact, concerned him. Nor was Abbot Radulfus greatly disconcerted, once the words were spoken. He might have evaded the experiences of the flesh, he had not gone in ignorance of them thus far through a highly intelligent life. The mention of Avice did not shake him.

'You recall, Father,' Cadfael pursued, while he had every

man's attention, 'that I showed you the blue flowers of the gromwell he wore in his cap when he was found. The plant grows at this hunting-lodge, I found it there, and it bears out the woman's story. She herself set it in his cap when he left her. It is nearly two miles from the lodge to the spot where he was ambushed and killed. Your own officers, Sir Gilbert, bear witness that they flushed young Lucy here out of cover in the Foregate more than half an hour before Prime. Therefore he could not possibly have been the man who set the springe for Huon de Domville, and killed him. The baron can have been no more than half a mile from his hunting-lodge, when Joscelin Lucy was being hunted along the Foregate to the hospital.'

Iveta took the last step that brought her to Joscelin's side, and slipped her hand into his, and he gripped it convulsively, unaware that he was hurting her, and drew breath into him so deep and hard that she felt he had drawn in the breath of new life for both of them.

Agnes craned and peered towards the gatehouse, but still did not find what she sought. Her face was sharp and icy with malice, but she said never a word. Iveta had expected a blaze of disbelief, casting doubt upon both Brother Cadfael and his witness, even upon the evidence of the sheriff's men. People can be vague and imprecise about time, it is not so hard to argue about the difference a mere half-hour can make. But Agnes kept silence, containing her aching rage and uneasiness.

Abbot Radulfus exchanged a long and thoughtful look with the sheriff, and turned again to Joscelin. 'You promised me truth. I will ask you now what I have not so far asked. Did you play any part in the death of Huon de Domville?'

'I did not,' said Joscelin firmly.

'There remains the charge he himself brought against you. Did you steal from him?'

'No!' He could not keep the scorn out of his voice.

Radulfus turned back to the sheriff with a faint, wry smile. 'For the murder charge, Brother Cadfael will bring you to speak with this woman, and you will judge for yourself what trust to place in her. As for your own officers, there is no need to question their truthfulness. It seems to me that on this count this man must be held guiltless.'

'If this is confirmed,' agreed Prestcote readily, 'he cannot be the murderer. I myself will take this woman's testimony.' He turned to Cadfael with a question: 'She is still at the hunting-lodge?'

'No,' said Cadfael, not without some relish at the stir his answer would make, 'she is now at the cell of the Benedictine sisters at Godric's Ford, where she has entered the order as a novice, and intends to take full vows.'

It was an achievement to have made even Abbot Radulfus blink; shaking the brotherhood was a routine success by comparison. 'And you esteem her an honest witness?' asked the abbot mildly, recovering his control in an instant, while Prior Robert's patrician nose still looked pinched and blue with shock, and the ranks behind his shoulder still quivered.

'As the day, Father. The sheriff will judge for himself. I am convinced that, whatever else she may be, she has no disguises, and does not lie.'

They would get from her, without conceal, the whole story of her life, of which she was not ashamed, and she could not but impress them. He had no fears on that head. Prestcote was a practical man, he would recognise her quality. 'My lord,' said Cadfael, 'and you, Father, may we now understand that you accept—subject to questioning Mistress Avice and finding her testimony true—that Joscelin Lucy is altogether innocent of Huon de Domville's murder?'

Prestcote had no hesitation. 'That seems certain. The charge cannot stand.'

'Then—bear with me!—you cannot but accept, also, that this day he has been under constant watch by Brother Mark, as Mark himself has told us, and has done nothing to occasion suspicion or blame.'

The abbot was regarding him with searching attention. 'That must also be granted. I think, brother, you have some particular reason for calling attention to it in this way. Something has happened!'

'Yes, Father. Something I should have told you at once, if I had not blundered into these equally grave matters as soon as I rode in. Well for any man who can say that today, all day long, he had a good man watching him and seeing no evil. For there has been violence done once again, in the woods beyond Saint Giles. Not an hour ago, as I was coming home, I happened upon a riderless horse, but could not catch him, and following him, I came upon a clearing where another man lies dead, and as I think, strangled like the first. I can lead you to the place.'

In the horrified hush that fell, he turned slowly to confront Agnes, who stood wild-eyed but still as stone.

'Madam, I grieve to bring you such news, but it is certain, even in the dim light, by the horse he rode . . .'

11 &

THERE WAS A MOMENT OF UTTER SILENCE, WHILE SHE STOOD
blanched and stiff like a woman turned to ice. Then, as
abruptly, she came to life with a piercing scream of rage and
grief, and whirling in a storm of flying skirts, turned her back
upon sheriff, abbot, niece and all, and clove like a fury through
the startled brothers who gave way hastily before her on-
slaught. Not one glance at Joscelin Lucy now, she bore down
on one man, and one man only, raging.

'You . . . you! Where are you, coward, murderer, come
forth and face me! You, you, Simon Aguilon, *you* killed my
lord!'

The ranks scattered before her blazing eyes and levelled arm.

'Stand, damned murderer, face me! Hear me!' The whole
Foregate, surely, must be hearing her and crossing themselves
in superstitious dread, envisaging a demon come after some
prodigious sinner. As for Simon, he stood aghast, too taken
aback, it seemed, even to retreat before her. He stared open-

mouthed, speechless, as she halted challengingly before him, her black eyes huge and flaring redly in the torchlight. Beside him Guy turned a startled stare helplessly from one to the other, and drew back a furtive pace or two from this new and deadly battlefield.

'You killed him! None but you could have done this. You rode off beside him to this hunt, close to him in the line—I know, I heard how it was drawn up. You, FitzJohn, say, let them all hear! Where did this man ride?'

'He was next to Sir Godfrid,' admitted Guy dazedly. 'But . . .'

'Next to him, yes . . . and on the way home, in those thick woods, it was easy to take him by surprise. Late and quiet you come back, Simon Aguilon, and you have made sure he will never come back!'

Sheriff and abbot had drawn close to witness this encounter, startled and appalled like everyone else, and made as yet no attempt to interrupt it. She was past reason. Simon said so, when he could speak at all, swallowing hard, and still breathless.

'For God's sake, what have I done to be so accused? I am altogether innocent of this death, I knew nothing of it . . . I last saw Sir Godfrid Picard three hours ago, well alive, threading the woods like the rest of us. The poor lady is crazed with grief, she strikes at the nearest . . .'

'I strike at *you,*' she cried, 'and would if there were a thousand in between. For *you* are the man! You know it as I know it. Pretence will not save you now!'

Simon appealed wildly to sheriff and abbot, spreading gloved hands. 'Why, why should I so much as think of killing a man who was my friend? With whom I had no quarrel in the world? What possible motive could I have for such a deed? You see she has run mad.'

'Ah, but you did have a quarrel with him,' shrieked Agnes vengefully, 'as well you know. Why? Why? Do you dare ask me why? Because he suspected—he as good as knew—that you had killed your own lord and uncle!'

Wilder and wilder grew the accusations, and yet this time Simon drew in breath sharply, and for an instant was still and pale. He wrenched himself out of shocked silence with a great heave, to defend himself strongly. 'How can that be? Everyone knows that my uncle dismissed me, put off all company and rode out alone. I went to my bed, as I was bidden. I slept late . . . they came to wake me when they found he had not returned . . .'

She swept that aside with a contemptuous motion of her hand. 'You went to your bed, yes, I make no doubt . . . and you left it again to steal out in the night and set your trap. Easy enough to leave unseen and return unseen when your wicked work was done. There are more ways in and out of any house than by the hall door, and who was so privileged in going and coming as you? Who else had all the keys he needed? Who stood to gain by the old man's death but you? And not only in being his heir, oh, no! Deny to these here present, if you dare, that in the evening of the day Huon was brought back dead, you came to my lord, before your uncle was cold you came, to make a bargain with us that you would step into his shoes with my niece, inherit bride, and honour, and all. Deny it, and I'll prove it! My maid was there!'

Simon looked round the ring of watching faces wildly, and protested: 'Why should I not fairly offer for Iveta? My estate would match hers, it is no disparagement. I esteem, I honour her. And Sir Godfrid did not reject me. I was willing to wait, to be patient. He agreed to my suit . . .'

Iveta's hand gripped and clung convulsively in Joscelin's clasp. Her stunned mind went back over those two meetings when Simon had seemed to her the only friend she had in the world, when he had pledged her his help, and Joscelin his loyalty. The first meeting countenanced by a smiling and gracious Agnes, complacently welcoming fortune restored. The second . . . yes, that had been different indeed, he had professed himself disapproved and banished, and the event had borne him out in his claim. What could have happened between, to change everything?

'So he did,' shrilled Agnes, glittering with hatred, 'thinking you the honest man you seemed then. But Huon's throat was bruised and cut—the monk there said it, and my lord heard it, and so did you—bruised and cut by a ring the murderer wore on his right hand. And once you had heard that said, who saw you again without gloves? In season and out! But my husband was at the coffining of Huon de Domville yesterday, and then you were forced—were you not, wretch?—to doff your gloves for once to take the aspergillum. And it was to him you handed it thereafter! He saw—oh, not the ring, no, that you had taken off hastily as soon as the monk here spoke of it, but the pale band where it was wont to be, and the square whiteness under the stone. And he remembered then that you used to wear a ring, just such a ring. And he was fool enough to speak out what he had seen, and what he believed, when you came visiting. He cut off all ado with a man he had cause to think a murderer.'

Yes, so he had. So that was the reason for the change! But not, thought Iveta, grown by force too suddenly into a woman, not because a murderer would not have been acceptable to him, provided no breath of suspicion ever blew his way. No, rather because while suspicion was even possible, he dared not risk contamination. Give him absolute security on that point, and he would have made up his differences quickly enough. And Joscelin had still been the law's quarry, and Joscelin might still have been taken, taken and hanged . . . And she would have been left believing despairingly that she had but one kind friend in the world, and that was Simon Aguilon! He had sworn that the very reason he was banished because he had declared his faith in Joscelin! And he might—given time enough to dull pain—he might even have prevailed! She pressed close to Joscelin's side, and trembled.

'I urged him, I begged him,' moaned Agnes, writhing, 'to sever all ties with such a man. You knew all too well he might feel it his duty to speak out what he suspected, even without proof. You have made certain he never shall. But you have not reckoned with me!'

'Woman, you are mad!' Simon flung up his hands against her, his voice high almost to breaking. 'How could I have set a snare for my uncle, when I did not know where he had gone, or what he intended, much less by what narrow path he must return! I did not know he had a mistress anywhere within this shire, to tempt him to a night's visit.'

Cadfael had stood silent throughout this duel. He spoke now. 'There is one who will say, Simon Aguilon, that you lie, that you did know, none so well. Avice of Thornbury says, and I fancy there will be two other witnesses to bear her out, once they know she is not at risk and asks no silence, that you, and none other, were the trusted escort who conducted her wherever her lord wanted her. You brought her to the hunting-lodge. The way between was well known to you, for you had ridden it. And Huon de Domville admitted but one man at a time to his private amours. For these last three years you have been that man.'

Agnes uttered a long wail of glee and grief together, that drifted eerily on the blown smoke of the torches. She pointed a triumphant hand. 'Strip him! You will see! The ring is on him now, he never would leave it off his person, for another to see and understand. Search him, and you'll find it. And why should he doff it, if it never left mark on a murdered man?'

The men-at-arms had read the sheriff's signs, and closed in silently, a tight ring of leather and steel about the two antagonists. Simon had been too intent on the threat before him to regard the quiet vigilance behind. He loosed a defiant cry of anger and impatience, and swung on his heel to stride away, 'I need not stay to hear such venom!' he spat, too shrilly.

Only then did he see the solid, silent line of armed men, drawn shoulder to shoulder between him and the gate, and baulked like a headed deer. He looked round wildly, unable to believe the collapse of his fortunes.

The sheriff drew a measured pace nearer, and spoke.

'Take off your gloves!'

It was an unlovely thing to see a human creature break and try to run, see him fight like a wildcat when he was hemmed in, and snarl defiance when he was overcome and pinioned. In deference to the abbot they hauled him out through the gates into the Foregate with as little violence as possible, and dealt with him there. He knotted his hands together to baulk the removal of his gloves, and when his hands were naked, the pale circle on the middle finger of his right hand glared like snow on new-ploughed russet soil, the large blot of the stone clear to be seen. He struggled and cursed when they felt about his body, sank his chin grimly into his chest so that they had to force his head back to withdraw the cord from round his neck, beneath his shirt, and expose the ring to view.

When they had hustled him away, four of them holding him and hard-pressed at that, to a cell in the castle, there fell a dreadful, exhausted silence over the great court. Joscelin, great-eyed, shaken and bewildered, folded his arms about Iveta, and quivered in uncomprehending relief, too shocked to question as yet the devious use that had been made of him throughout. Agnes stood rigid, staring balefully as long as her enemy remained in view, and then, released, clutched her head between her hands and wept, but hardly, in solitary and forbidding grief. Who would have thought she could have loved her unendearing husband?

The virago was gone. She let fall her hands and paced slowly, like one walking in her sleep, through the agitated onlookers who moved aside to give her passage. She looked round once upon them all, from the steps of the guest-hall, having passed by Iveta's extended hand as though the girl did not exist, and then she went in, and vanished.

'Later,' said Abbot Radulfus, heavily but calmly, 'she will speak freely. Her testimony is essential. As for her lord—he is dead already. Need we question, since he cannot be questioned?'

'Not in any tribunal of mine, at any rate,' agreed Gilbert Prestcote drily, and turned to his remaining men. 'You, sergeant, before we set off to bring this dead man home, how comes it that you set so apt a watch about the brook here, while we were beating the forest? We had no intimation that ever reached my ears, that a raid might be attempted on these premises.'

'It was after you were all gone forth, my lord,' said the sergeant, 'that Jehan here came to me with the notion that since the squire was set on the lady, he might take the chance when there were but few of us left here, to try to win her away.' He haled forth the clever fellow who had won commendation for an earlier idea, equally justified in the event. The man was not quite so sure of himself, now that things were turned topsy-turvy, and his patron was become the villain in the web, but he stood his ground. 'It was he who said that the fellow, if he had the wit, might hide in his lord's own gardens, you'll remember, and when we searched, we found he had indeed been there, though he was gone when we came to it. This time it seemed just as good sense, so we kept a vigil in secret.'

'Friend,' said Prestcote, eyeing the man-at-arms somewhat ominously, 'your guesses seem to be blessed by heaven, but I fancy hell had more to do with them. When did Aguilon put it into your head to search the bishop's outhouses for our wanted man? At what hour?'

Jehan had the sense to be open about it, though none too happily. 'My lord, it was after my lord Domville's body was brought back here. When he came back to the bishop's house, then he suggested it. He said I was welcome to the credit if we found our man, and he would as lief keep out of it.'

Joscelin shook his head despairingly between his hands, slow still to understand the whole of it. 'But it was he who helped me—he came to find me, he hid me there himself in good-will . . .'

'In very evil will!' said Brother Cadfael. 'Son, you had given him not only the opportunity of hastening his inheritance of a great estate, but also of adding to it this lady's person and lands. For you had provided him a perfect scapegoat, one wronged and angry and bearing a grudge. Yours would be the first and only name that came to mind, when Huon de Domville was waylaid and murdered. But with that in view he had to have you still at liberty, hidden away somewhere safe, until well after the death, and where he could point the hunt to take you when that was done. It was your leaving your sanctuary that baulked his plans and saved your neck.'

'Then tonight,' pursued Joscelin, frowning over this chill treachery as if his head ached, 'you mean he set this trap for me, in cold blood? I thought him my one friend, I asked his help . . .'

'How?' asked Cadfael sharply. 'How did you get word to him?'

Joscelin told them the whole of it, though not one word yet of Lazarus or Bran, or any of those who had truly helped him. That he might tell some day, surely to Iveta, perhaps even to Brother Cadfael, but not here, not now.

'So he knew only that you were somewhere close, but not where. He could not send his trusty foil here to lay hands on you, he could only wait for you to come to the law, and you had set the scene yourself. All he had to do was pass on your message to the lady, and see that your horse was waiting for you as you had asked—or you would not have crossed into the garden here to be seized, would you?—and then say the quiet word to Jehan here. He would not wish to appear in the matter himself, certainly,' said Cadfael wryly, 'since his pose of loyalty to you was his best commendation with the lady. You once safely taken and hanged,' he said, making no bones about it, for the good-natured lad was wrenching hard at belief in such devious treason in one he had trusted, 'I doubt if Godfrid Picard would have baulked at matching his niece with a murderer—a *successful* murderer. It was the peril meantime he could not stomach, in case it reached as far as his own credit, if not his own neck.'

'Speak up, Jehan,' ordered the sheriff, grimly smiling. 'Did

Aguilon again point you the way to commendation and promotion?'

'This morning,' admitted Jehan unwarily, 'he put the notion into my head . . .'

'This morning! Before ever we set forth! And you said no word to me or to your officer until we were out of the way of your intended feat of arms. Promotion is hardly likely to come your way, fellow, for a while. Think yourself lucky to escape a whipping!'

Jehan was indeed thinking himself well out of a perilous corner, to be dismissed so lightly, and made himself scarce without delay.

'We had best be bringing in this dead man,' said the sheriff, turning brusquely back to the task in hand. 'Will you guide us, brother? We'll go mounted, and with a spare horse for Picard's last ride.'

They were away, half a dozen mounted men, Cadfael in no way displeased to be astride a fine, sturdy rouncey again instead of a modest little mule. The abbot watched them out of the gates, and then turned to dismiss, with even voice and calm face, the disturbed and wondering brotherhood.

'Go, compose your minds, wash your hands, and go in to supper. The rule still orders our day. Traffic with the world is laid upon us for chastening, and for the testing of our vocation. The grace of God is not endangered by the follies or the wickedness of men.'

They went obediently. At a glance from Radulfus, Prior Robert inclined his head and followed the flock. The abbot was left confronting, with a faint, contemplative smile, the two young creatures still clinging hand in hand, eyeing him steadfastly but doubtfully. Too much had happened to them too suddenly, they were like children half-awake, not yet clear what, of their recollections and experiences, was real, and what was dream. But surely the dreams had been terrifying, and the reality must needs be better.

'I think,' said the abbot gently, 'you need not be in any anxiety, my son, about that other charge your lord made against you. In all the circumstances, no just man would consider it safe to believe in such a theft, and Gilbert Prestcote is a just man. I cannot choose but wonder,' he said thoughtfully, 'whether it was Aguilon also who hid the necklace in your saddle-bag with the medal of Saint James.'

'I doubt it, Father.' Joscelin took thought to be fair, even now, to a comrade who had done him such grievous wrong. 'For truly I feel he had not thought of murder until I was cast off and accused, and broke away to freedom as I did. It is as Brother Cadfael said, he was presented with his chance and his scapegoat. My lord Domville most likely did his own meaner work this time. But, Father, it is not my troubles that weigh on me now. It is Iveta.'

He moistened his lips, feeling for the best words, and the abbot stood silent and imperturbable, and gave him no help. Iveta, too, had looked up at him in startled alarm, as though she feared he might too nobly and stupidly let go of her when she thought herself fairly won.

'Father, this lady has been vilely misused by those who were her guardians. Now her uncle is dead, and her aunt, even if she were fit to care for her, would not be allowed to keep the administration of so great an honour. It is my prayer that you, Father, will take her into your own guardianship from this day, for with you I know she will be used with gentleness and honour, and be happy as she deserves. If you put forward such a request to the king, he will not deny you.'

The abbot waited some moments, and his austere lips were very drily smiling. 'And that is all? No plea for yourself?'

'None!' said Joscelin, with the fierce humility that looked and sounded what it was, a nobleman's arrogance.

'But *I* have a prayer of my own,' said Iveta indignantly, keeping fast hold of a hand that would have renounced its claim on her. 'It is that you will look kindly upon Joscelin, and use him as my favoured suitor, for I love him, and he loves me, and though I will be obedient to you in everything else, if you will take me, I will not part with Joscelin, or ever love or marry anyone else.'

'Come,' said the abbot, not quite committing himself to a smile, 'I think we three had better sit down to supper together in my lodging, and consider how best to dispose of the future. There's no haste, and much to think about. Thinking is best after prayer, but will be none the worse for a meal and a glass of wine.'

The sheriff and his party brought back Godfrid Picard's body to the abbey before Compline. In the mortuary chapel they laid him straight, and brought candles to examine his injuries. His unblooded dagger, found some yards aside in the grass, where Cadfael had discovered and left it, they slid back into its sheath as they unbuckled his sword-belt, but it cannot be said that much thought had been given to the curious circumstance of its lying thus naked and discarded in the glade.

The man was dead, his murderer, murderer already of one man, and a kinsman at that, was in Shrewsbury castle, safe under lock and key. If there were odd circumstances in this second case, no one but Cadfael noticed them, though for a while they puzzled him as much as they would have puzzled his companions, had they troubled to examine them. A man dies, strangled with a man's hands, yet himself provided with a dagger, and clearly having had time to draw it. To draw, but not to blood it. And those who kill with their hands do so because they are otherwise unarmed.

The night was still. The candles did not flicker, and the light on the dead man's suffused face, bitten tongue and exposed throat was sharp enough to show detail. Cadfael looked closely and long at the marks of the strong fingers that had crushed out life, but he said nothing. Nor was he asked anything. All questions had already been answered to the sheriff's satisfaction.

'We'd best have a mare out tomorrow, to fetch the grey out of the forest,' said Prestcote, drawing up the linen sheet over

Picard's face. 'A valuable beast, that. The widow could sell him for a good price in Shrewsbury, if she's so minded.'

Having completed his duty here, Cadfael excused himself, and went to look for Brother Mark. He found him in the warming-room, rosily restored after a kitchen supper and a change of clothes, and about to take his leave, and walk back to Saint Giles and his duty.

'Wait only a brief while for me,' said Cadfael, 'and I'll bear you company. I have an errand there.'

In the meantime, his errand here was to two young people who had, as he saw when he ran them to earth in the abbot's parlour, of all places, no great need of his solicitude, since they had enlisted a greater patron, and appeared to be on terms of complete confidence with him, partly due, perhaps, to a good wine after extreme stress and rapturous relief. So Cadfael merely paid his respects, accepted their flushed and generous gratitude, exchanged a somewhat ambiguous glance with Radulfus as he made his reverence, and left them to their deliberations, which were certainly proceeding very satisfactorily, but had certain implications for others, not here represented.

Two warm-hearted children, these, radiant with goodwill towards all who had stood by them at need. Very young, very vulnerable, very eager and impulsive now that they were happy. The abbot would keep them on a close rein for a while, her in some sheltered sisterhood or a well-matroned manor of her own, the boy under discreet watch in whatever service he took up, now that he was clean, honourable and his own best guarantor. But Radulfus would not keep them apart, he was too wise to try to separate what God or his angels had joined.

Meantime, there were others to be thought of, and there was need of the coming night, if what Cadfael had divined proved true.

He returned to the warming-room, where Brother Mark, content and expectant, was waiting for him by the fire. He had not sat so long in the warmth since he was a new novice in the order. It had been well worth getting soused in the Meole brook.

'Is everything well?' he asked hopefully, as they set out together along the Foregate in the darkness.

'Very well,' said Cadfael, so heartily that Mark drew pleased and grateful breath, and ceased to question.

'The little lady for whom you prayed God's help, some days ago,' said Cadfael cheerfully, 'will do very well now. The lord abbot will see to that. All I want at the hospital is a pleasant word with your wanderer Lazarus, in case he moves on very soon, before I can come again. You know how they snuff the air and grow uneasy, and up anchor suddenly, and sail.'

'I had wondered,' confided Brother Mark, 'whether he might be persuaded to stay. He has an affection for Bran. And the mother will not live much longer. She has turned her back on the world. Oh, not on her boy—but she feels he has gone beyond her, and has his own saints,' explained one of those saints diffidently, without self-recognition. 'She is certain he is protected by heaven.'

There were those on earth, too, thought Cadfael, who had some interest in the matter. Two grateful, loosened tongues in the abbot's parlour had poured out all their story without reserve, named names confidingly. Joscelin had a mind quick to learn, and a heart tenacious of affections, and Iveta in the fervour of deliverance wanted to take to her heart and hold fast in her life every soul, high or low, whole or afflicted, who had been good to Joscelin.

In the open porch before the hall of the hospice the old man Lazarus sat, mute, motionless, patient, with his erect back braced against the wall, and his legs drawn up beneath him on the bench, crossed after the eastern fashion. Curled up in the circle of the old man's left arm, Bran lay uneasily asleep, with Joscelin's wooden horse clasped to his heart. The small lamp above the door of the hall shed a faint yellow light on his spindly limbs and ruffled fair head, and showed a face smudged with tears. He awoke when Cadfael and Mark entered, starting up dazedly out of his nest, and the long arm withdrew from him silently, and let him scramble down from the bench.

'Why, Bran!' said Brother Mark, concerned and chiding. 'What are you doing out of your bed at this hour?'

Bran embraced him hard, half-relieved and half-resentful, and accused in muffled tones from within the folds of the new and over-ample habit: 'You *both* went away! You left me alone. I didn't know where you were . . . . You might not have come back! *He* hasn't come back!'

'Ah, but he will, you'll see.' Brother Mark gathered the boy to him, and took possession of a groping hand. Its fellow was busy retrieving the wooden horse, momentarily discarded but jealously reclaimed. 'Come, come to bed, and I'll tell you all about it. Your friend is well and happy, and need not hide any more. Everything that was wrong has been put right. Come, and you shall hear it once from me, and he will tell it all over again when next you see him. As you will, I promise.'

'He said I should be his squire, and learn to read Latin hand, and reckon numbers, if ever he came to be knight,' Bran sternly reminded both his present and his absent patron, and allowed himself to be led sleepily towards the inner door. Mark looked back at Cadfael as they went, and at his reassuring nod took the child gently away towards the dortoir.

Lazarus made no movement and said no word when Cadfael sat down beside him. Long ago he had outlived surprise, fear and desire, at least on his own account. He sat gazing out with his far-sighted blue-grey eyes at a night sky now beginning to flow like running water, a lofty, thin stream of cloud carried tranquilly eastwards on a fair breeze, while here on earth the very leaves were still.

'You'll have heard,' said Cadfael, leaning back comfortably against the wall, 'what Mark told the child. It was true, thanks be to God! Everything that was wrong has been put right. The murderer of Huon de Domville is taken, guilty past doubt. That is over. Pity is out of reach, short of penitence, and of that there's none. The man has not only killed his uncle, but vilely betrayed and misused his friend who trusted him, and shamelessly deceived a harried and forsaken girl. That is over. You need trouble no more.'

The man beside him said no word, asked no question, but he listened. Cadfael continued equably: 'All will be well with her now. The king will surely approve our abbot as her new guardian. Radulfus is an austere and high-minded man, but also a human and humane one. She has nothing more to fear, not even for a lover none too well endowed with worldly goods. Her wishes, her happiness, will no longer be brushed aside as of no account.'

Within the great cloak Lazarus stirred, and turned his head. The deep voice, forming words with deliberate, halting care, spoke from behind the muffling veil: 'You speak only of Domville. What of the second murder?'

'What second murder?' said Cadfael simply.

'I saw the torches among the trees, an hour and more ago, when they came for Godfrid Picard. I know he is dead. Is that, too, laid at this other man's door?'

'Aguilon will be tried for the murder of his uncle,' said Cadfael, 'where there is proof enough. Why look further? If there are some who mistakenly set Picard's death to his discredit, how is his fate changed? He will not be charged with that. It could not be maintained. Godfrid Picard was not murdered.'

'How do you know?' asked Lazarus, untroubled but willing to be enlightened.

'There was no snare laid for him, he had all his senses and powers when he was killed, but all his senses and powers were not enough. He was not murdered, he was stopped in the way and challenged to single combat. He had a dagger, his opponent had only his hands. No doubt he thought he had an easy conquest, an armed man against one weaponless, a man in his prime against one seventy years old. He had time to draw, but that was all. The dagger was wrenched away and hurled aside, not turned against him. The hands were enough. He had not considered the weight of a just quarrel.'

'It must, then, have been a very grave quarrel between these two,' said Lazarus, after a long silence.

'The oldest and gravest. The shameful mistreatment of a lady. She is avenged and delivered. Heaven made no mistake.'

The silence fell between them again, but lightly and softly as a girl's veil might float down and settle, or a moth flutter out of the night and alight without a sound. The old man's eyes returned to the steady, measured flow of wisps of cloud eastward in the zenith. There was diffused light of stars behind the veil, while the earth lay in darkness. Behind the coarse veil of faded blue cloth Cadfael thought there was the faintest and most tranquil of smiles.

'And if you have divined so much from this day's deed,' said Lazarus at length, 'have not others the same knowledge?'

'No other has seen what I have seen,' said Cadfael simply, 'and none will now. The marks will fade. No one wonders. No one questions. And only I know. And only I, and the owner of the hands that did the deed, will ever know that of those hands, the left had but two and a half fingers.'

There was a stir of movement within the mound of dark clothes, and a flash of the ice-clear eyes. Out of the folds of the cloak two hands emerged, and were held to the light of the lamp, the right one whole, long and sinewy, the left lacking index and middle finger and the upper joint of the third, the maimed surfaces showing seamed, whitish and dry.

'Having divined so much from so little, brother,' said the slow, calm voice, 'take me with you one step beyond, and divine me his name, for I think you know it.'

'So I think, also,' said Brother Cadfael. 'His name is Guimar de Massard.'

The night hung motionless over the Foregate and the valley of the Meole, and the woods through which the sheriff and his men had hunted in vain, plotting clearly, for those long-sighted eyes, the passage of Picard's bright red cap through the trees, and mapping the way by which, later, he must return. Overhead, in contrast to this terrestrial stillness, the sky flowed steadily away, like one man's floating, fragile life blown across the constant of life itself, to vanish into the unknown.

'Should I know that name?' asked Lazarus, very still.

'My lord, I, too, was at the storming of Jerusalem. Twenty years old I was when the city fell. I saw you breach the gate. I was at the fight at Ascalon, when the Fatimids of Egypt came up against us—and for my part, after the killing that was done in Jerusalem, of so many who held by the Prophet, I say they deserved better luck against us than they had. But there was never brutality or unknightly act charged against Guimar de Massard. Why, why did you vanish after that fight? Why let us, who revered you, and your wife and son here in England, grieve you for dead? Had any of us deserved that of you?'

'Had my wife, had my son, deserved of me that I should lay upon them the load that had fallen upon me?' asked Lazarus, roused and stumbling for once upon the words that tried his mangled mouth. 'Brother, I think you ask what you already know.'

Yes, Cadfael knew. Guimar de Massard, wounded and captive after Ascalon, had learned from the doctors who attended him in captivity that he was already a leper.

'They have excellent physicians,' said Lazarus, again calm and still, 'wiser than any here. And who should better know and recognise the first bitter signs? They told me truth. They did what I asked of them, sent word of my death from my wounds. They did more. They helped me to a hermitage where I might live with my enemy, as I had died to my friends, and fight that battle as I had fought the commoner kind. My helm and my sword they sent back to Jerusalem, as I asked.'

'She has them,' said Cadfael. 'She treasures them. You have not been forgotten in your death. I have always known that the best of the Sarcens could out-Christian many of us Christians.'

'Chivalrous and courteous I found my captors. At all points they respected and supported me through the years of my penance.'

One nobility is kin to another, thought Cadfael. There are alliances that cross the blood-line of families, the borders of countries, even the impassable divide of religion. And it was well possible that Guimar de Massard should find himself closer in spirit to the Fatimid caliphs than to Bohemond and Baldwin and Tancred, squabbling like malicious children over their conquests.

'How long,' he asked, 'have you been on your way home?' For it was a long, long journey across Europe from the midland sea, on broken feet, with a clapperdish for baggage, and nothing more.

'Eight years. Ever since they brought word to my hermitage, from the reports of an English prisoner, of my son's death, and told me there was a child, a girl, left orphaned to her dead mother's kin, wanting any remaining of my blood.'

So he had left his cell, the refuge of years, and set off with his begging-bowl and cloak and veil to make that endless pilgrimage to England, to see for himself, at the prescribed distance, that his grandchild enjoyed her lands and had her due of happiness. He had found, instead, her affairs gone far awry, and with his own maimed hands he had straightened them, and set her free.

'She has her due now,' said Cadfael. 'But for all that, I think she might be happy to exchange her title to all that great honour for one living kinsman.'

The silence was long and cold, as if he trod upon forbidden ground. Nevertheless, he persisted doggedly. 'You are a quenched fire. You have been now for years, I judge. Do not deny it, I know the signs. What God imposed, no doubt for his own good reasons, for reasons as good he has lifted away. You know it. You are a peril to no man. And whatever name you have used all these years, you are still Guimar de Massard. If she cherishes your sword, how much more would she revere and delight in you? Why deprive her now of her true shield? Or yourself of the joy of seeing her happy? Of giving her with your own hand to a husband I think you approve?'

'Brother,' said Guimar de Massard, shaking his hooded head, 'you speak of what you do not understand. I am a dead man. Let my grave and my bones and my legend alone.'

'Yet there was one Lazarus,' said Cadfael, venturing far and in great awe, 'who did rise again out of his tomb, to the joy of his kinswomen.'

There was a long hush while the sailing filaments of cloud were the only things that moved in the visible world. Then the old man's unblemished right hand flashed from within the folds of the cloak, and rose to thrust back the hood. 'And was this,' asked Guimar, 'the face that made his sisters glad?'

He plucked away the face-cloth, and uncovered the awful visage left to him, almost lipless, one cheek shrunken away, the nostrils eaten into great, discoloured holes, a face in which only the live and brilliant eyes recalled the paladin of Jerusalem and Ascalon. And Cadfael was silenced.

Lazarus again covered the ruin from sight behind the veil. The quietness and serenity came back, almost stealthily. 'Never seek to roll that stone away,' said the deep, patient voice gently. 'I am content beneath it. Let me lie.'

'I must tell you, then,' said Cadfael after a long silence, 'that the boy has been sounding your praises to her, and she is begging him to bring her to you, since you cannot go to her, that she may thank you in person for your goodness to her lover. And since he can refuse her nothing, I think in the morning they will be here.'

'They will understand,' said Lazarus calmly, 'that there's no relying on us wandering lepers, the pilgrim kind. We have minds incorrigibly *vagus*. The fit comes on us, and the wind blows us away like dust. Relics, we make our way where there are relics to console us. Tell them that all is well with me.'

He put down his feet from the bench, carefully and slowly because of their condition, and courteously shook the skirts of his gown down over them, to hide the deformities. 'For with the dead,' he said, 'all is very well.' He rose, and Cadfael with him.

'Pray for me, brother, if you will.'

He was gone, turning away and withdrawing without another word or look. The heel of the special shoe he wore tapped sharply on the flags of the floor, and changed its note hollowly on the boards within. Brother Cadfael went out from the porch, under the slow-moving clouds that were not drifting, but proceeding with purpose and deliberation on some predestined course of their own, unhurried and unimpeded, like death.

Yes, with the dead, he thought, making his way back to the abbey in the dark, all is surely well. The child will have to find them work for their gratitude, instead. Their dead has accomplished his own burial, now let them turn rather to the living. Who knows? Who knows but the beggar-woman's scrofulous waif, fed and tended and taught, may indeed end as page and squire to Sir Joscelin Lucy, some day? Stranger things have happened in this strangest, most harrowing and most wonderful of worlds!

The next morning, after Mass, Iveta and Joscelin came to Saint Giles, with the abbot's sanction, and hearts full of goodwill to all those within, but seeking two in particular. The child was easily found. But the old leper called Lazarus had gone forth silently in the night, leaving no word where he was bound, and saying no farewells. They sought for him by all the roads from Shrewsbury, and sent to ask at every place of pilgrimage within three counties, but even on crippled feet he outran pursuit, by what secret ways no one ever discovered. Certain it is he came no more to Shrewsbury.

ABOUT THE AUTHOR

ELLIS PETERS is a pseudonym for Edith Pargeter, author of many books under her own name. The recipient of the C.W.A. Silver Dagger Award, she is also well known as a translator of poetry and prose from the Czech. Miss Pargeter makes her home in Shropshire, England.

Medieval Murder Mysteries
from...
ELLIS PETERS

Available at your bookstore or use this coupon.

_____ **THE SANCTUARY SPARROW**   20613   2.95
Brother Cadfael attempts to solve a man's murder while giving sanctuary to the man
who has been accused of the crime.

_____ **ST. PETER'S FAIR**   20540   2.95
Brother Cadfael must protect the niece of a merchant found murdered on the eve of
the great St. Peter's Fair.

_____ **THE VIRGIN IN THE ICE**   21121   2.95
A chilling story of murder as a young girl is found dead in thin ice and Brother Cadfael
puts himself in danger to solve the crime.

_____ **MONK'S HOOD**   20699   2.95
Can love wend its way through a monastery, and help solve a mystery with that
incomparable sleuth, Brother Cadfael?

_____ **DEAD MAN'S RANSOM**   20819   2.95
Brother Cadfael cleverly solves a murder mystery in such a way as to protect two
young lovers.

FAWCETT MAIL SALES
Dept. TAF, 201 E. 50th St., New York, N.Y. 10022

Please send me the FAWCETT BOOKS I have checked above. I am enclosing $....................(add 50¢ per copy to cover postage and handling).
Send check or money order—no cash or C.O.D.'s please. Prices and
numbers are subject to change without notice. Valid in U.S. only. All orders
are subject to availability of books.

Name_____

Address_____

City_____State_____Zip Code_____

Allow at least 4 weeks for delivery.   TAF-37

12